WIND RAVEN

Book 3 in the Agents of the Crown Trilogy

Regan Walker

"A salty, sweeping, evocative tale of romance on the high seas—and a good old-fashioned love story that will keep you up far, far past your bedtime. So, reach for the coffee. Brava for Regan Walker!"

—Danelle Harmon, *New York Times* & *USA Today* Bestselling Author

"*Wind Raven* is grand romance of the sea with much insight into piracy in the early 19th century and the tropical lifestyle of the island of Bermuda under British rule. The scenes of both everyday life and storms on a ship at sea were well done, very real."

—Jennifer Blake, *New York Times* Bestselling Author

HER LOVE WAS A TIDE
SHE COULDN'T HOLD BACK

"A fine fix we're in," Tara said, looking first at the captain and then at the night sky. The stars began to show themselves in the darkening canvas above, giving her the sense she stood on a precipice at an auspicious moment in time. It had only been a short while ago she had gained the insight she had now about the two of them. She should have realized the truth long ago.

"What do you mean?" he asked, coming up behind her, so close she could feel the heat of his chest. His warmth had always drawn her, and it was pulling her to him now like a strong undertow.

"Each of us withheld from the other the one thing we wanted," she remarked, staring into the night sky.

"And what would that be?" He put his hands on her arms, drawing her back against his chest. She shivered with his touch but allowed it, while fighting the urge to turn and fall into his arms.

"You wanted my body and, fool that I am, I wanted your heart."

He spun her around so fast her vision blurred. "My heart? You wanted my heart?"

"Yes, but I cannot seem to touch it." His eyes carried a look of astonishment. "Well, you can keep it," she said emphatically. "I don't want it anymore. And you shall never have me!"

He stared at her for only a moment. "Oh, yes, I will." As if she had defied one of his many orders and he was having none of it, he brought his mouth down on hers in a kiss that was claiming. One of his hands closed on her nape and his other arm wrapped tightly around her waist, holding her to him, trapping her with his powerful strength.

WIND RAVEN

Book 3 in the Agents of the Crown Trilogy

Regan Walker

www.BOROUGHSPUBLISHINGGROUP.com

WIND RAVEN
Copyright © 2014 Regan Walker

Digital edition created by Maureen Cutajar
www.gopublished.com

ISBN 978-1-941260-02-9

To my technical advisor and friend, Dr. Chari Wessel, who patiently answered all my questions and provided wonderfully detailed advice. A veterinarian by profession, on her off hours she is a gunner on the crew of the historic Californian, a reproduction of a topsail schooner of the period still in active service today— and a woman after Tara's heart.

ACKNOWLEDGMENTS

In addition to the invaluable assistance of Dr. Chari Wessel, I must also thank one of my readers. When Patricia Barraclough learned that *Wind Raven* would feature scenes in the waters off Puerto Rico (or "Porto Rico" as it was known then due to a mistake in the Treaty of Paris), she suggested I include a scene set at night in one of the bioluminescent bays. And so I did. As a result, Patricia will be getting a courtesy copy of the book! I love that readers suggest ideas...'tis wonderful!

As always, my critique group and beta readers have helped this story become a tale that I hope will bring you many hours of reading pleasure. Also taking time from their very busy schedules, authors Jennifer Blake, Virginia Henley and Kaki Warner read the manuscript and provided helpful comments. Danelle Harmon, *New York Times* bestselling author of high seas romances, read the final, and it thrilled me to hear her say I'd hit the mark. These authors are my inspiration and their gracious mentoring means much.

CONTENTS

WIND RAVEN

Book 3 in the Agents of the Crown Trilogy

Regan Walker

Prologue

St. Thomas, the West Indies, July 1815

Captain Jean Nicholas Powell stepped from the oppressive Caribbean sun into the dim light of the familiar dockside tavern, pausing for his eyes to adjust to the darkened room. Sweat dripped from his forehead, and he wiped it away with the back of his hand. Swallowing, his throat felt as dry as the dock he'd left baking in the sun.

Tobacco smoke hung in the hot, still air, so thick it obscured the tankards on the shelf behind the bar and the faded painting of a nude woman hanging above it. Casting a glance at the men who leaned against the counter nursing their drinks, he noted the man he searched for was not among them.

Striding from the bar, Nick weaved his way through the tables crowding the long, smoke-filled room. The sharp smell of tobacco, though familiar, made him regret there were so few windows. Some of the other captains looked up as he passed, their eyes acknowledging him as one of their own.

"'Lo, Nick," said Latimer, an English merchantman. "'Bout time you were joining us."

His eyes still searching the room, Nick said, "Had an appointment at the dock. I've been desperate for a drink for nigh on an hour. Seen Russ?"

"Think he came in earlier. Might be in the back."

A buxom redhead approached Nick with beckoning eyes. He recognized Molly, one of several wenches employed by Amos for the pleasure of those who patronized Esmit's Tavern.

"What would you like, Cap'n?" The invitation in her smile and the shoulder bared by her low bodice suggested she was offering more than drink.

"Just rum for now, lass. Thanks."

A familiar shout of "Captain!" from the rear of the tavern drew Nick's attention to the blond head of his first mate, Russell Ainsworth.

He resumed his path through the tables of drinking men and serving wenches, their conversations a dull roar, the stink of sweat and rum blending with the tobacco to assail his nostrils. Reaching the table where Russ sat alone with a tankard, Nick slid into the unoccupied chair as Molly delivered his rum and another smile. Lifting the tankard, Nick took a long draw on the lukewarm liquid. At least it was wet.

He wiped his brow on his sleeve and inquired, "Is all in order on the *Raven*?"

"It is. Wasn't pleasant, though. Last night's revelries are taking their toll. There were a few dropped crates and the netting for one load tore free, leaving one of the crew tangled in the ropes." At Nick's raised brow, Russ added, "But she'll be ready to sail on the tide. Did you have any success finding a bos'n?"

Nick threw back another swallow of the sweet liquor and let out a sigh. "I did. A big Swede named Johansson. You might remember him from a fight last time we were in port. The men said he fought like a gentleman but with fists of iron. When we lost the bosun last run, they suggested his name to me and said he might be in port today. I thought it would be good to have him on our side given the waters we sail. And it seems he's anxious for a change."

"Sounds like a good acquisition," Russ said.

Nick looked around, taking in those men he didn't recognize. At the next table two tawny-haired Americans argued with three hardened seamen. The older American's clothing and his air of command suggested he was a captain of an age with Nick. The conversation of the five men, who were clearly in their cups, grew boisterous, their disagreement apparent to any near enough to hear above the din of the crowded tavern.

Out of the corner of his eye, Nick watched the American captain raise his tankard in toast. "A drink to our sister, one of the finest crewmembers ever to sail aboard my ship!"

The other American, nearly identical in appearance and with the same tawny hair, clinked his mug against his brother's, the rum sloshing onto the table. "That she is, George!"

The old salts looked doubtful but nevertheless joined in what was obviously one of many toasts. "If'n ye say so, Cap'n George, but I've never been easy with such meself. Don't like sailin' with women," he said with a sneer. "Them's trouble. The captain I sail for would have none of 'em on his ship." His compatriots mumbled their agreement but took up the toast and, with dazed expressions, cheerfully quaffed their rum.

Nick shuddered as he tried to imagine what a woman would look like who crewed with men. One of those damned Yankee women, no doubt. Like most captains, he'd have no females among his crew. Passengers only occasionally and even those presented a risk. On rare occasions, he might invite an English girl with creamy white skin or a tanned island beauty with dark gypsy eyes aboard the *Raven*. But neither served as crew and neither sailed with them long.

With one pint of rum in his belly, he greeted Molly's return to their table with a smile and pulled her onto his lap. "There'll be no hag in the rigging on the *Raven*. I prefer only beautiful women and those in my bunk, not swabbing the deck." He glanced at the smiling Molly, whose bountiful breasts were pressing against his chest. "Seems the right place for a pretty lass, don't you agree?"

"You can take me on yer ship anytime, Cap'n Nick," purred the redhead.

Russ gave out a chuckle, and the American captain threw Nick a fierce gaze. With narrowed eyes and slightly slurred words, the tawny-haired captain pushed back his chair and stood to glare at Nick.

"You don't know our sister, English, so you can keep your views to yourself."

Nick set Molly aside and slowly rose from his chair. "I have no opinion of your sister, my good man, but if it's a fight you're looking for, I'll not turn aside a challenge."

The younger American tugged at his brother's shirt. "George, leave off. It's too hot to fight."

Ignoring the caution, the tall American captain leaped across the small distance, and with speed that belied his condition, slung his fist into Nick's jaw, nearly knocking him off his feet. Nick shook off the pain, shoved aside the table and threw a hard punch into the American's ribs.

The American fell backward, knocking over another table with a loud thud. Tankards of rum flew in all directions, splashing the liquor on those sitting nearby. Curses rose in a loud crescendo as the observers, doused with rum, stepped aside.

"Get Molly out of here, Russ," Nick ordered his first mate, who hastened to usher the barmaid out of the way. Nick and the American circled each other. The men in the tavern cleared a space around them and, shouting encouragement to their favorite, placed bets in what was quickly becoming the afternoon's entertainment.

"Two quid on the American!" shouted one.

"Five on Cap'n Nick! I've seen him fight."

Fists flew, and feeling the pain from another gut punch, Nick realized it might be some time before he could defeat this man, who, even foxed, was very much his match. Resolved, he slammed his right fist into the American's jaw, sending him to the floor.

Nick braced himself for the next round as the American picked himself off the floor, but the bartender stepped between them.

"Ye can take yer fight outside, captains," said Amos, with his fists on his broad hips and a scowl on his round face. "I'll not have me tables broken."

Nick dropped his arms to his side. "Sorry, Amos. Was just a misunderstanding between…ah…friends."

The American captain's blue-green eyes glared hatred, but his brother whispered into his ear and pulled him back to his seat. The men who had gathered around, seeing the fight had come to an end, ambled back to their chairs, mumbling words of disappointment as their bets were returned.

"Nick," whispered Russ, 'the last thing we need is a fight with an American. The war is over, remember? And England had declared St. Thomas a free port."

Russ was right. As a merchant captain, Nick looked forward to the lucrative trade peace would bring. Holding his hand over his heart, Nick dipped his head in grand gesture to the Americans. "My apologies, good fellows. Never meant to insult your sister. I like women just fine, though I prefer them in my bed and not cluttering up the deck of my ship."

The older American's thunderous expression told Nick that, notwithstanding his apology, he'd made an enemy. He hoped he would not see the American again soon. Dropping some coins on the table Russ had righted, Nick and his first mate left the tavern, a question rumbling in his mind.

What kind of a woman would crew with men?

"They change their skies, but not their souls who run across the sea."

—Roman poet

Chapter 1

London, May 1817

Tara pulled the offending pins from her hair as she paced across the parlour rug in front of her aunt, sending long tawny ringlets cascading down her back. Her eyes were drawn to the stern face of her Irish grandfather staring down from the painting over the fireplace in the elegant townhouse. She was certain he would not approve. But then he would not be the first male in her family who took a dim view of her seafaring ways.

"All these petticoats, corsets and pins, Auntie! How do women bear it? I've been in London nearly a year and still it feels like I've been lashed to a main mast and suffered a storm each time I don the frippery. My head and back ache. I cannot breathe." She paced another length of the drawing room and turned. "I will be glad when this Season is done and I can go home! How I long for salt air and a moving deck beneath my feet."

"Tara Marie McConnell!" her dignified aunt chided. "A young lady does not talk so. Where are your manners for heaven's sake?"

Tara sighed and slumped onto the sofa next to the older woman. "I'm sorry, Auntie. You have been so kind to host me in London. I must seem ungrateful."

"Really, Tara. How could I not respect your mother's dying wish? Your father vowed to her before the last war that you would come to me when the time was right. I could do no less than to see her wish fulfilled and my niece become a lady."

Tara felt guilty at the reminder it had been her mother's desire to see her schooled in the ways of a debutante by her aunt, a baroness. How could she complain? "Forgive me. It seems my manners have fled with the pain of the finery we women must wear. Do you *never* wish to be free of it?"

Her aunt smiled. "No, I rather look forward to dressing the lady, and the finery, as you call it, is a joy to me. A trip to the modiste for a new gown is one of my favorite pastimes."

"Perhaps I'm just different. Or it may be what I'm accustomed to. Being raised on my father's ship, I had no need for a corset." Seeing her aunt's countenance fall, Tara hastened to add, "I appreciate all you've done for me, Auntie; I do. And I have worn the gowns as you and Father wished. But you must remember, London's not my home—and never will be!"

"London may not be your home but it was where your mother wanted you to become a lady. And so you have. Why, the smiling faces of those handsome young men at the ball last night told me as much. Surely their admiration was worth the pain of dressing the part. Your Season has been a great success."

Tara's heart warmed at the kind words of the silver-haired woman, her American aunt who had married an English baron many years ago. Now a widow, she was respected for her charity work with the families of British seamen killed in the wars that had consumed the country in the past years.

"My brother Sean would be proud, Tara."

"Oh, to be sure, my father would be happy for the gowns I wear and all I have learned of dancing and dining and such. But despite their smiles, I rather doubt those young men you think so enamored of me are seeking an American wife. Why, only a few years ago our countries were at war! And besides, I'm not ready to marry. Even if I was, it wouldn't be to an Englishman."

"The war with America was not so important in England, Tara. It was stories of that horrid Frenchman Napoleon that filled our newspapers."

"Well, it was important to *us*. How can I forget about it when I lost a brother in one of those battles at sea? Do you know, every time one of those dandies smiled at me, I saw Ben's face? I felt like a traitor smiling back." Tara grew melancholy thinking of her youngest brother. Ben would have been twenty-four this year, five years her senior. Growing up, they were the closest of the five siblings and she missed him with a deep ache that never seemed to go away. When he was killed, it had been like losing a part of herself. She always regretted that she'd not been there to try and save him

"I have not forgotten, Tara. But you cannot dwell on the war, or the tragedy it brought the McConnells. So like my brother you are, both staunch Americans." Her aunt picked up her dainty teacup and took a sip.

"Father is not just an American, Auntie. He is a patriot. Why else would he name his four sons after our commander in chief and men who signed the Declaration of Independence?"

"Yes, and your mother always supported him, God rest her soul. I realize your father wants you to wed an American, but I know of Englishmen with whom you might have much in common who would make worthy suitors."

Tara felt torn in two. Her father expected her to return home to Baltimore a lady, worthy of a refined American statesman. And her aunt wanted her to wed an Englishman, likely one with a title, as she herself had married a baron. Did no one care what *she* wanted?

"No matter whom I would marry, I cannot help but wonder what my fate would be as a wife. You know well that sitting in drawing rooms, doing embroidery and serving up tea are not to my liking. I would feel a prisoner should I be confined to that life."

"There is much more to being a wife than that, my dear. I shouldn't wonder with the right man you would be quite content." Her aunt gazed off into the distance, appearing to ponder. "Yes, the right man could make all the difference."

"Father's greatest hope, I am sure. Perhaps he should have given me the name he first had in mind. It might have produced a more docile child."

"What name was that?"

"*Martha*, after George Washington's wife. Think if he had."

"Oh, my. That name doesn't suit you at all. Though I did think *Tara* an unusual choice," her aunt said thoughtfully.

"My mother apparently didn't hold by the name *Martha* either, at least not for her daughter. By the time I was born, they'd agreed on *Tara*, the name my father brought back from his last voyage. But it's not a name your *ton* would recognize."

"Perhaps not, but I think you should give the men of London a chance to win your affections, my dear."

"Auntie, I've danced with all those Englishmen and I haven't felt even a speck of the longing that I've read about in novels. I agree the right man could make a difference, but I want a man who appreciates me as I am, and is strong enough to confess his love for me. Not these refined English fops!"

"Not all Englishmen are fops, as you call them, Tara."

Tara rose to resume her pacing in front of the fireplace. "I cannot imagine any of them liking an American enough to wed one, Auntie. Besides, as I said, I have no desire to marry an Englishman. In that, I agree with Father. And I don't believe they want to marry an American."

"Well, I dare say they like American money, and that you have. And I disagree with you when you say they do not consider you a marriage prize, though it would not please your father to know it. What I observed last night were young men hovering about you like hummingbirds around a flower, hoping for some of your sweetness, a dance or even a smile. You have only to encourage them and you'd have suitors by the dozens!"

Tara took a drink of her tea, wondering if the young men hadn't responded to her easy manner and lighthearted banter—she was comfortable in the world of men, more so than the world of women. Raised among her father's crew, she'd been adopted by them and accepted into their banter at an early age. She had treated the men of London no differently.

But she could never see them as suitors.

"They are dandies, every one, Auntie. Nice enough if you want a ribbon untied or a carriage door opened, but my brothers would eat them for breakfast."

"Really, child. The way you speak. Anyone would think you'd been raised among wolves or—"

A knock sounded at the parlour door.

Upon her aunt's "enter," the butler moved fluidly into the room. Attired in gray trousers and a dark morning coat, the slight man with the morose expression and thinning gray hair balanced a small silver tray on his upturned hand.

"My lady," the butler addressed her aunt, "a messenger has delivered a letter for the young miss."

Tara set down her teacup. "A note for me? May I see it please?"

At her aunt's nod, the butler approached Tara with a veiled look of indignation, extending the tray to her as she reached for the envelope. Higgins didn't like Americans, owing to the fact his brother had died fighting in the Battle of New Orleans two years earlier, though he made an exception for her aunt because of her kindness to wounded British seamen and soldiers. While Tara sympathized with his loss, and had her own deep wound from the war, she would never apologize for the country she loved.

Tearing open the envelope, she acknowledged briefly the McConnell family seal, dark green wax impressed with a circle enclosing a leaping stag. Her eyes quickly scanned the note. The words caused her hand to fly to her throat as fear gripped her like a cold vise. "It's from George. Father…is ill."

"Oh dear. I hope it's not serious."

"Surely it must be, for my brother summons me home." Staring straight ahead, Tara's thoughts were an ocean away. Her father was ill. Perhaps even dying. She had planned to leave for home in the next month; this would have her leaving sooner still.

Looking again at the note, she read it a second time, seeing something she had missed before. She leaped to her feet. "Oh God…this was dated the first week in March. It has taken nearly two months to reach me! I must leave immediately."

* * *

Tara gazed out the carriage window, anxious to board the ship that would see her to Baltimore. Despite her urgent need to leave London, Tara had spent several anxious days before her aunt finally declared she'd found a vessel that was acceptable.

Tara's eyes drifted across the carriage seat to her plump maid, whose face, ordinarily flushed with health, had turned a gray pallor as the carriage bumped along toward London's waterfront.

"Ohhh," Rebecca groaned, "me stomach don't feel so good, miss."

Alarmed at what she was observing, Tara asked, "What is it, Becca? Are you unwell?"

"I woke this morning feeling poorly, miss. Must be something I ate last night. The thought of a rolling deck makes me want to lose me breakfast. I've always hated boats, ye know. Even this swaying carriage is making me stomach feel like it's pinned up with the laundry and flappin' in the wind. *Ohhh...*" The maid groaned again and wrapped her arms around her waist.

Tara's concern grew. "You do look rather pale, Becca. We are almost to the dock." Making a decision, she said, "Once we arrive, I am sending you home with the carriage. You'd best lie down for a spell."

"But, miss, ye cannot travel alone. It would nay be right. Yer aunt took me off my other duties to make me yer chaperone."

"Becca, I grew up on ships. And the son of my aunt's good friend, Mrs. Powell, captains this one. It will be fine. I've never had a chaperone on my brothers' ships. I expect this will be much the same."

"Can ye not wait for another ship?" Becca gripped her stomach and slumped down onto the carriage seat, writhing in agony.

Tara extended her hand to her maid, trying to keep her from rolling on the seat with each dip in the road. She hoped she could ease the woman's discomfort until the carriage stopped.

"No, Becca. It must be this one. The *Wind Raven* sails for Baltimore and Aunt Cornelia made clear it was the only ship I was to take. If I go back with you, my aunt would make me wait for another—and that could take months. My father lies ill, maybe even dying." Though she could not dismiss the possibility, Tara shrank from the thought. She only hoped she would not be too late. "No, it must be this one and it must be today. And I'll not hazard your health to join me on a ship that may face rough seas and storms."

At Tara's words, the maid squeezed her eyes shut and let out another moan.

"I worry such a voyage would not be in your best interest, Becca, nor that of the ship's crew if they have to take time from their duties to tend a sick woman or are worried about becoming ill themselves. So do not give my travel another thought. You must return home and recover." Then with a smile, she added, "Perhaps you might even rest a spell before the carriage resumes the trip home. It might calm your stomach…and I wouldn't want my aunt to know I'm without a chaperon until the ship sails."

Chapter 2

Nick strode onto the quarterdeck as Peter Greene, his cabin boy, handed him a mug of steaming coffee, the welcome smell of the hot brew rising to his nose. Though there was a chill in the brisk morning air, the sun was shining and only a few white clouds dotted the sky. His gaze traveled past the rail toward the other ships lined up at anchor in the Thames. He was proud of his schooner and the thirty crew who sailed her. A merchant ship, yes, but so much more. And that was one reason he detested this new assignment from the Prince Regent.

A moment later, his first mate, Russell Ainsworth, approached, the morning breeze blowing his sun-bleached blond hair across his forehead. They had sailed together for many years, making Russ a friend as well as a member of his crew. Nick took a draw on his coffee, comfortable sharing his thoughts. "I have begun to think Prinny sees my family as his own private stock of spies and henchmen, one he can draw upon for his misadventures any time the fancy takes him. First my father's privateering in the last wars, then my brother's...*activities* in France, and now *this*." He threw Russ a questioning glance. "How did I let him talk me into this...this Caribbean diversion?"

"He is our monarch, Nick. As I see it, you had no choice. Also, I expect he knows of our last successful run through those waters and is aware of the guns we carry from our days as a privateer. Few merchantmen have them. Even fewer are prepared to fight."

Nick pursed his lips and nodded. "Now that I think of it, his words did seem more a command than a request. Still, I don't relish spying on that rascal Cofresí, who's been harassing England's merchant ships. And he's not the only one. It seems there are more privateers turned pirate in the last years since the war with France. Too many seamen without employment." Frowning, he added, "It's a sea of scoundrels we're sailing the *Raven* into."

"We've survived worse," encouraged Russ. "Consider, too, along with the wine, silk and wool we carry, our stop in the West Indies will reap a harvest of sugar, spices and rum in great demand in America. The profits will be rich."

"True, and I take heart from that possibility, but this precarious detour will make us late into Baltimore. And I've never intentionally dangled the *Raven* before pirates who would consider her a great prize."

"I'd not choose to sail that course either," said Russ, shaking his head.

"What I am anxious to do is deliver my cargo and claim my new schooner. Since I first heard how those sisters of the wind called Baltimore clippers allowed the American captains to slip through the English wartime blockades, I've been hungry for one of my own. The one I've ordered from the London agent will be unique—a three-masted tigress." Nick took a drink of his coffee and stared longingly into the distance, seeing a sleek schooner with a narrow hull, a deep draft, not two but three raked masts and more sail. The vivid picture lingered in his mind. "She'll be faster than the *Raven*—twelve knots and more."

"You still want me to sail the *Raven* back to London?"

"Yes, yes I do." Nick turned from his daydream as the sounds of the traffic on the Thames rose to the fore. "We can divide the crew and pick up the extra men we'll need in Baltimore. It's time you had your own ship, Russ. You've earned it."

One of the crew approached, diverting Nick's attention. "Cap'n, there's a woman on the dock asking for passage to Baltimore. Are we taking passengers this trip?" He sounded doubtful.

"No, Mr. Smith," he said to the short seaman with the pudgy face, who he well knew frowned upon women on ships. "Definitely not. Certainly not a woman. Tell her to try another ship."

"I thought ye might say as much, Cap'n. But when I told her I expected you'd be thinking that way, she handed me this here note and insisted ye see it. She said she'd have this ship and no other." He sneered. "Something about her aunt telling her to take only the *Raven*."

Nick handed his coffee to Russ and accepted the envelope, on which was penned, in a decidedly feminine script, *Captain Nicholas Powell*. With a rising dread of what was coming, he hastily opened it. Inside was a note and money for passage.

"Damn." He looked into Russ's questioning face. "It seems the chit is the niece of a dowager baroness, Lady Danvers, who claims she's my mother's good friend."

"Didn't your mother just sail on the *Claire* with your father?" A puzzled look crossed his first mate's face.

Nick could feel his scowl building. "Unfortunately, yes. Since the mater is away, I cannot even verify this friendship I am forced to observe. She is always doing favors for her friends. Likely this woman is one of them. The social onus makes it near impossible to deny the woman passage—or else I face my mother's wrath. You know her, Russ. A French whirlwind when she's angry, she makes the Prince Regent look like a puff of hot air."

Russ guffawed. "I rather enjoy seeing you cowed by your mother. A formidable lady to be sure."

Nick scowled more deeply. Few could tease him about his mother's influence and walk away without a scar. Russ was one of them.

Shielding his eyes, Nick gazed toward the dock. "Where is the woman?"

"Just there," Smitty said. "Standing next to her sea chest and the crates our lads have yet to load." He pointed to a tall, slim figure clothed in a gray gown with a darker gray cloak, the hood drawn over her head.

Nick could feel his mood grow dour.

"Looks like a governess to me," Russ chuckled. "Stands straight as a board and drab as a London fog."

This was *not* the trip to be carrying passengers, much less a woman. The last thing he needed was a priggish governess whining about conditions on board or ordering his crew about. "God knows what mayhem we'll encounter before we reach Baltimore. Now this unwanted baggage!" Shooting a glance at Russ, he said as an aside, "Prinny has tied my hands, demanding I say nothing about his assignment until we leave port. We cannot even tell her we do not sail directly to Baltimore."

"Well, then, she'll just have to endure the consequences of seeking passage with us," offered his first mate.

"So she shall," Nick said, pressing his lips tightly together. "Damned chit."

Then thinking of another concern, he turned to Smitty, "Where is her chaperone? Has she no traveling companion?" What kind of an Englishwoman traveled without one?

"I asked her that, Cap'n. She said her maid took sick. The woman travels alone."

Perhaps it was best. One was bad enough. Two would be impossible. Still, he'd have to keep the men from her or account to his mother. Unhappy but resigned to the added nuisance, Nick could see his arguments were at an end.

"Tell the governess we will take her; then deliver her and her trunk to first mate's cabin and see that she stays there. Tell her she's fortunate I cannot send her away. Peter can fix her a tray. I'll not be having the woman wandering about my decks as we sail."

"Aye-aye, Cap'n." The sailor tugged his forelock, and with a grimace for the unwanted job, headed down the gangplank. "I'll tell her exactly what you said."

Nick turned his eyes to the Thames and to the distant horizon. Russ handed him his coffee. Without thinking, he took a swallow and scowled. *Cold.* Tossing the dark liquid over the side, he handed the mug back to his first mate.

"Sorry, Russ, but she'll have your cabin."

"I've no problem bunking with Mr. Baker. Nate and I have shared a cabin before." Then adding with a grin, "The thought of sailing the *Raven* home under my own command will help me survive the small inconvenience."

A seaman approached, smiling. "Cargo's loaded, Cap'n. And the tide be with us."

"Then cast off the moorings and make ready to sail," said Nick with a satisfied feeling. This was his favorite time on a voyage: pulling away from the dock with only blue water and sky before him.

Russ shouted the orders and Nick's spirits took wing as he shoved all thoughts of the governess aside and allowed his heart to respond to the call of the open sea.

Chapter 3

Tara paced within the confines of her small cabin, furious at being treated like some unwanted cargo. The short crewmember with brown hair, who had introduced himself as Mr. Smith and deposited her and her trunk in the small cabin with an ungracious huff, had been most direct in conveying the captain's views. She was not wanted.

Tara could still see the dark figure of the captain, clothed in black breeches and boots, his white shirt a beacon drawing her attention as he glared at her from the quarterdeck. His resentment at having to take her as a passenger was patently clear, no matter her aunt's letter of introduction. He might have no choice given the note, but then neither did she. Perhaps he was loath to take on a "missish English debutante," but she was no delicate flower. And she was not English. Far from it, thank God.

Still considering her next move, Tara was distracted when a familiar movement of the ship told her they were underway.

The crossing to Baltimore could take more than a month. She must have something to do with all that time. Surely he could not deny her an active role if she proved herself. She wondered if it would make any difference to the insolent captain. She smiled as an idea came to her. The sea was her playfield and she intended to have some fun.

A knock on the door of her cabin interrupted Tara's silent rumination. Swiftly she opened it, hoping it was the captain. She would have a word.

A boy of perhaps ten or eleven, with curly brown hair and sparkling brown eyes, greeted her, a tray in his hands.

"Hullo, miss. I'm Peter, cabin boy to the cap'n. He asked me to bring you some supper. Are you hungry?"

She smiled, instantly taking a liking to the handsome youth with a dimple that suddenly appeared in his cheek when he smiled. A refreshing change from the captain he served. "I am Tara McConnell, Peter. A pleasure to meet you. And yes, I'm always hungry at sea. Do come in."

The boy took two steps inside, set the tray on the chest at the end of her narrow shelf bed and set out a napkin for her. Tara joined him and lifted the cover off the bowl, inhaling the rich scent of lamb stew with vegetables. Her stomach rumbled its approval. "It smells wonderful."

"Our cook, old McGinnis, does well enough in the galley," the boy offered, "especially with stews, though it'll be pork or beef after today. But his rolls, as you'll see, are a bit wantin'. He's a right nice fellow, 'cept'n when he burns his fingers." The boy's eyes suddenly brightened as he encouraged, "You'll like him. He tells wonderful stories of the fairies in Ireland."

Tara could feel her mouth curving into a smile. "I see where your mind is roaming, young Peter. You think if I'm looking for something to occupy my time, I can help McGinnis in the galley with his baking. No doubt your captain thinks a woman's place is in the parlour or perhaps the kitchen. He's not fond of having a woman on board his ship. Do I have that right?"

"Well, miss," the boy drawled, his eyes suddenly taking an interest in his shoes, "the cap'n is awfully strict about some things. There's only been a few women on the *Raven*." He lifted his head and hastened to add, "But they were not like you!"

Tara wondered just what kind of women the captain entertained on his ship.

"He is a good captain, he is," urged the lad. "If it weren't for him, I'd still be eating out of London's gutters. He taught me to speak properly, too."

"I see. Well perhaps I'll meet your McGinnis and see what I can do. I have been known to bake tolerable rolls for my father and brothers." *But that is not where I intend to serve.*

The boy wished her well and departed, obviously pleased to think he'd solved a problem for the captain he so admired.

Tara closed the door and wasted no time sampling the stew. It *was* good, as good as that made by Maggie O'Flaherty, her family's Irish housekeeper in Baltimore. But Peter had been right about the rolls. They were hard as rocks, formidable weapons if one had the mind to use them as such. Still, the galley was not her priority. She had work to do on deck. The captain needed a lesson and she was just the one to give it to him.

Hearing a noise at her door and thinking Peter must have forgotten something, Tara pulled the door wide. She looked both ways but there was no one in the passageway and the captain's door, adjacent to hers, was closed. A sound drew her attention to the deck at her feet, where a large gray cat with two huge white front paws sat looking up at her with intelligent green eyes.

"Well, who might you be?"

The cat sauntered into her cabin as if merely tolerating Tara's presence.

"Do come in," Tara said sarcastically. The cat leaped onto the small bed. "Won't you make yourself at home and join me for dinner?"

As if in response, the cat curled up on the bed and began to lick one of its large white paws. Apparently the animal had already dined, no doubt on some fat rodent, as it showed no interest in her stew. Tara had known ship's cats before but this one seemed unique. It was not just the overlarge white paws, which made it appear the cat wore gloves, but the spark of intelligence gleaming from its green eyes. Tara sat on her bed eating her stew, watching the cat. With her free hand, she reached out to scratch one of its gray ears.

"You're a handsome one, I must say. And 'tis obvious you do not lack for food." Moving her hand to the cat's back, she stroked the soft fur. "Why you're as plump as a Christmas pudding!" When the cat purred and rolled onto its back, Tara forgot her stew and scratched its belly, noticing that for all its size the cat was a female.

"I wonder whose you are?"

* * *

The next morning, Nick stepped onto the quarterdeck and took a deep breath of the brisk, salt-laden air, an elixir to his London-weary mind. God he loved the sea and the roll of the deck beneath his feet. The *Raven* was home, the first ship he owned himself. He was deeply proud of the sleek, black-hulled schooner and the full partnership in Powell and Sons that came with it. In the eight years he'd been sailing her, he'd learned her every sound, every subtle nuance of the way she responded to the sea—like a woman responding to her man.

He walked to the helm to join his first mate in talking to old Nate Baker at the wheel.

Russ handed Nick a mug. "Morning, Captain. Peter just brought up the coffee. It's hot."

"Thanks," he said, and acknowledged Nate with a nod. Taking a swallow of the dark fragrant liquid, Nick quickly surveyed the sails and his crew then turned his attention to Russ. "What's our course this morning?"

"Sailing southwest, close-hauled for the most part."

"Holdin' steady at seven knots, Cap'n," added Nate.

"Let 'er have all the sail her belly can take. I am anxious to have done with this task in the Caribbean."

Russ gave the command to set the last sail. A few minutes later, a man's cry was heard above them. Nick followed the sound to the main topsail rigging, where a seaman dangled upside down by one leg. He had only escaped a fall to his death because his foot had caught in the sheet, where he now hung suspended far above the deck. His position was precarious, made worse by the sail luffing against him.

"Well, I'll be—'tis that same lad who got caught once before," Nate exclaimed.

"Young Billy Uppington," Russ supplied the name. "The one who hired on last voyage."

Nick swore under his breath, handed his mug to Russ and strode toward the shrouds nearest the mainmast, intending to climb to the young seaman's rescue. It wouldn't be the first time he'd scaled the rigging to pluck one of his men from disaster. Setting his foot on the first ratline, he looked up. A figure was moving swiftly to the footrope for the yard. Realizing he was not needed, Nick stepped back and joined Russ.

"Who is that monkey in the rigging?" he asked. "A new member of our crew I missed? He has the surest foot of any I've seen."

"If my eyes do not deceive me, Captain, *that* is your passenger," said Russ.

"What?" Nick's eyes narrowed in concentration as he watched the movements of the slim figure in dark gray breeches, white shirt and green vest edging along the footrope toward the stranded sailor. It was then he saw the long tawny braid swinging back and forth as the figure danced from one set of rigging to another.

"I was just about to tell you, Nick," Russ said, shoving a strand of hair out of his eyes as he handed Nick back his coffee. A grin spread across the first mate's face. "She was on deck early this morning dressed like that, and has been helping the men with their chores ever since. Smitty wasn't pleased, of course, but she's won a few of the others to her cause. It seems she knows something about schooners. I'd swear she has crewed one before. She can tie a bowline knot better than most of the men and, as you see, she is at home in the rigging."

"A woman? With my men? All morning doing...*chores*?" Nick was incredulous.

"She works hard, odd though it may seem."

Nick cursed. "I'm surprised they didn't have her on her back serving *them*."

"Not likely. Our bos'n, Mr. Johansson, has appointed himself her protector. Seems he has sisters and treats her as one of them. The men won't touch her, leastways not while Jake's around."

"No self-respecting Englishwoman would dare wear such garb or attempt such a reckless act," Nick said under his breath, letting go a few choice oaths about governesses in breeches. He looked into the rigging, continuing to watch the drama unfolding above him.

"Well then, there's no problem," said Russ.

Puzzled, Nick turned his head to see his first mate grinning.

"She's not English."

Nick eyes returned to the figure high above them, reaching for the stranded sailor. "Not English? What the hell is she?"

"Oh, did I forget to say?" Russ smirked. "She's American."

Without thinking, and still pondering what an English baroness was doing with an American niece, Nick took a sip of his coffee and immediately spit it out. *Cold.* Damn chit robbed him of his morning coffee—again. Stepping to the rail, he tossed the contents over the side and returned his attention to the girl in the rigging. He watched, amazed, as she moved like a circus performer at home on the high wire. Deftly maneuvering sideways, she held on with one arm. The men watching on deck held their breath. Adroitly, she freed the sailor's trapped leg and helped him to reach the topsail yard. When the rescued sailor began to climb down, a loud cheer went up from the crew.

The girl looked down at the men gathered far below. Standing on the yard while holding onto the mast with one arm, she bowed deeply and smiled, apparently delighted to have entertained them. Her long tawny plait fell over her shoulder, a saucy addition to her bow.

Even from the long distance, Nick could see the clothing she wore hid none of her curves. She didn't look like any governess he'd ever seen. And she certainly did not act like one.

Nick let out the breath he'd been holding. "Good God." Turning to Russ, he said, "Send her to my cabin. I want a few words with our...*passenger*!"

* * *

Tara's foot touched the deck, and the tall, blond first mate handed her the wide-brimmed hat she'd discarded when she'd climbed aloft.

"Mr. Ainsworth. Good-day to you."

"That was quite an impressive accomplishment, miss."

Tara couldn't help the smile that spread across her face as she plopped the hat back on her head. She had been quite pleased at how the morning had gone, especially her effort to rescue the young seaman. "All in a day's work aboard ship, right, sir?"

"Ah, yes, well," the first mate stifled a grin, "the captain would like to speak with you, if you don't mind. *In his cabin.*"

"All right. I expect it's time I met your scowling leader. Captain Powell, isn't it?"

"Yes, miss. And he'll not be in a good mood to be sure. Try not to rile him. The Raven can be hot tempered at times."

"The Raven?"

"A nickname his father's crew gave him as a young lad when he sat on the crosstrees. All they could see was his long black hair blowing in the wind. The ship's actually named for him, you see. But we rarely speak the name to his face, unless in jest."

"It fits. Dark and brooding, he is, and looks about to take flight." Tara remembered the ship's unusual figurehead she'd seen while standing on the dock—a raven in flight. She had thought it merely reflected the name of the ship; obviously it was also a reflection of her captain, the one who charted her course.

The first mate chuckled. "You have the right of it, miss. Though the men would follow him anywhere."

Knowing schooners as she did, Tara knew well the location of the captain's cabin. She quickly descended to the lower deck and walked determinedly down the passageway. Removing her hat, she paused at the captain's door. She experienced a flicker of trepidation remembering that this man was not one of her brothers. For a brief moment she warred with herself as to what to say, then decided not to be cowed. She had done nothing wrong.

Her resolution firm, she knocked.

"Come!" a deep voice commanded.

He was sitting at his desk, his dark head bent over a chart. A quick glance told her it was a map of the Spanish colonies of Santo Domingo and Porto Rico. The cat Tara had already encountered lay asleep in a shaft of sunlight on one corner of the desk. The captain's shirtsleeves were rolled up, revealing bronze, muscled forearms and long-fingered hands. On the little finger of his left hand he wore a ring with an oval blue stone that appeared to shimmer. It was set in a band of gold with carvings on the sides.

She wondered at so delicate a piece of jewelry worn by a hardened man of the sea.

Her gaze moved slowly about the cabin, unsurprised by all she saw. Her brothers' ships also had well-appointed captain's cabins with paneled walls of dark wood. The *Wind Raven* was a larger schooner than those her brothers sailed, allowing this cabin a raised overhead so that there were windows on the sides. Light streamed through the panes of glass framed by azure blue curtains. Against the rear bulkhead, a large mahogany shelf bed with a cover of the same blue as the stone in his ring spoke of comfort. A small Turkey rug in tones of blue and dark rust lay beneath a pedestal table that held a fenced tray, on which sat two glasses and a flat-bottomed decanter of what she assumed was brandy. A small black stove had been centrally placed to warm the cabin.

In addition to his desk and two chairs, there was a bookcase built into the side of the cabin to the left of the cabin door. It was filled with books secured by wooden strips. Everything had been designed for efficiency and bespoke a man who insisted upon order and discipline. Well, except for the cat, perhaps. Somehow the cat with the huge white paws lazing on his desk seemed an anomaly to Tara.

Without looking up, the captain spoke. "That was some fancy footwork on the rigging this morning, Miss—"

"McConnell, Captain Powell. Tara McConnell." At Tara's words, the cat raised her head and appeared to study her. Tara forced herself not to twist her hat in her hands. It was not like her to be nervous around men.

"Oh, yes. I remember the name from the note. Well, Miss McConnell," he finally looked up, "much as I appreciate your saving young Billy, I'll not have a passenger in the shrouds or climbing my rig, especially not a woman."

The captain's voice brooked no dissent, but the arrogant look on his face triggered Tara's temper. *He should be grateful!* Reminding herself this was not one of her brothers, she tamped down her anger and studied the man glaring at her from behind his desk.

It was the first time she'd seen him this close. She had noticed his handsome appearance from where she had stood on the dock, and she already knew he was tall, at least six feet, from comparing him to his crew when he first came on deck. But now she took time to study his face. It was the tan face of a ship's captain in his mid thirties, rugged from years at sea, with strong features and lines at the edges of his eyes. Her father and brothers had the same lines on their faces from squinting into the horizon.

The captain's thick ebony locks, as black as the bird whose name he bore, curled about his collar. His lips were well shaped and she wondered if he had kissed many women. Likely the arrogant man had kissed many.

His eyes held her gaze. Framed by dark lashes, their golden amber color was mesmerizing. His brows rose in impatient manner. Tara realized he was waiting for her to speak.

"Captain, I am most comfortable working in the rigging. I've sailed on my father's ships since I was a child. And, as you have seen," she couldn't help smiling, "I can be helpful."

His amber eyes flashed flecks of gold and his jaw tightened in what was obviously an exercise in restraint. "The answer is *no*," he said vehemently. Tara almost took a step back at the force with which he'd delivered the words. "You've paid for passage and I'll not have your safety in question. You will stay out of the rigging, Miss McConnell, and that is final."

The man was a tyrant! This would be a very long trip if she were to be confined to her cabin with only a brief evening stroll about the deck. But she could see there would be no persuading him. Since he was the captain, she defied him at her peril. "You are not, I assume, banishing me from the decks, are you, sir?" The challenge in her voice was clear. Let him try.

"I could, and the thought occurs perhaps I should," he said in a low voice as his eyes slowly raked her body in frank male assessment. "You look like trouble, Miss McConnell, if you don't mind my saying so. But no, I will allow you free run of the deck...for now."

"Thank you for the *favor*," she said, unable to control the sarcasm in her voice. Anger rose in her chest at the arrogant liberties his eyes were taking with her person. "I can assure you there will be *no* trouble." Before her Irish temper could be further unleashed, Tara turned on her heels and departed.

As she passed through the cabin door, she heard his soft laughter behind her and his words.

"Trouble's already here."

Chapter 4

Nick tried to return to his charts, but his mind refused to focus. Giving up, he reached out his hand to idly stroke the lounging cat. Then, resting his elbows on his desk, his chin on his entwined fingers, he stared at the saber hanging on the far bulkhead. He'd been displeased with this trip from its inception, and now he had to deal with—what? A hoyden with the face of an angel and blue-green eyes that reminded him of a tropical lagoon. Wearing breeches, no less!

Tara McConnell had entered his well-ordered world like a fast-moving storm and he didn't like it—not one bit. She didn't fit into any category he had for the female sex: not exactly a lady, not a whore, and not a shop worker or a servant. Disturbing, that's what she was. But then, the few Americans he'd known had been a different lot. Perhaps their women were all like this. There was something familiar about the girl, too, though he couldn't fathom it. He'd never met her before, certainly not in England. He would have remembered that face and that body.

He was still pondering the arousing picture of his passenger in breeches when three sharp raps at the door sounded the familiar knock of his first mate.

"Come!"

Russ peeked his head around the door. "Am I disturbing anything?"

"No, just some pondering. Where is our passenger now?"

"Coiling line on the bow with Jake Johansson and Nate. How did your talk with her go?" Russ opened the door wider to enter.

"I don't suppose the impudent chit will act the lady, but I've made clear she's to stay out of the rigging."

"How did she take it?"

"Not well, I think." In his mind's eye, Nick could still see the indignant look she'd given him at his order. "She has a bit of a temper that one."

Russ shut the door behind him, chuckling. "Well that should make for an interesting crossing since you've a small temper yourself."

Nick frowned. Russ was a good friend and entitled, when they were alone, to take liberties, but Nick needed no reminder he was short on patience just now. "I wonder if she'll tire of playing the part of the crew."

"I doubt it. I heard her tell Nate she was glad to be at sea again working on a schooner."

"She mentioned something about having crewed on her father's ships. I suspect he indulged the chit, allowing her too free a rein. You don't suppose she sailed with the American privateers in that last disagreement between our two countries, do you?"

"I can't think her father would have exposed her to such danger," said Russ, "but one never knows. She'd have been young. Hell, she can't be more than eighteen or nineteen now."

"I doubt she sailed during the war. The privateers were the only navy America had." Nick thought about how young she had seemed as she stood before him in his cabin a few minutes earlier. Young and vulnerable, despite her brave front. "I suppose I should have a word with the crew to assure no harm comes to her."

"I've already seen to it. At the risk of your ire, to a man I believe they will comply. Smitty's none too pleased, of course. You know he abhors women aboard ship. But he will not give us trouble. As for the rest of them, any who might be inclined to take advantage will be quickly dissuaded from such a path with Jake her watchful protector."

"Good. I've no wish to be defending the virtue of a woman roaming the decks." Changing the subject, he asked, "How is the crew faring?"

"A few are still recovering from their last night in London and their last wenching for a while. I had to send Jake after a few of them. The new crew, Billy Uppington, is going to be a challenge, as you have seen, but the men seem up for it. Young John Trent said he would help the lad and you know old Nate will see he completes his chores. Oh, and I had the extra stores of food loaded that McGinnes requested."

"You should have heard McGinnes talking in the galley this morning, rambling on about some sign of his Irish fairies and impending disaster. I swear he actually believes those myths."

"The men love his tales, Nick. Staves off their boredom at sea. Much like the singing on deck in the evenings. Not all of them read like you and I do."

"I suppose you've the right of it. There are few pleasures we can give the men while at sea, save their rum and their songs."

Russ leaned over the top of the desk to pet the cat, but the feline jumped down and strolled toward the stove. "I see your cat still prefers only your company."

"It's not my cat."

"Tell that to the animal." The first mate gave the cat a parting look, then turned his gaze to the charts scattered in front of Nick. "Ah, the West Indies."

"Yes, it's time I told the crew where we're bound and the task we're about." Nick leaned back to give Russ a better view. "I've been going over Cofresí's territory and the list of prizes he's seized. It seems the *Retribución* preys on ships caught anywhere near Porto Rico not flying the Spanish flag—and with great success, as Prinny noted."

"Are we to engage?"

"The prince asked only that I make inquiries regarding the pirate's operations and his hiding places, I suspect for later engagement by the Royal Navy. But I'm certain our monarch would be pleased if we disarmed the pirate ship or captured it as a prize. He hinted as much, though I have no desire to risk the *Raven* or the crew. Nor do I want to drag a damaged *Retribución* into Baltimore. If we wish to avoid a direct engagement, there is always stealth. A significant theft of gear and spiking their guns when they are in port, perhaps."

"The crew would enjoy that. And I made sure the Spanish flag and other markers of a Spanish merchantman were loaded. We've only to change the name to *Viento del Cuervo* when the time comes and raise the flag of Spain."

"I suspect such a disguise will be needed," said Nick, wondering what it would feel like to sail his ship under the Spanish flag. But like his brother Martin, a spy for the Crown, Nick was not above donning a disguise for his country.

"What about the Laffite brothers? Any word?"

"They are caught up in squabbles with their associates just now."

"Perhaps they will stay farther north?" Russ suggested.

"We can only hope." Finding the chart that showed North America, Nick shoved it toward his first mate. "The gulf is their usual playground. But there are others around. It seems that many privateers have turned to piracy since the end of the wars with America and France."

A loud thud sounded from the deck above. Exchanging a questioning glance with Russ, Nick rose from his chair. "I'd best see what that's about."

"I'll join you," echoed Russ.

Once on deck, Nick searched for the source of the sound. The ship was holding steady and all was in order—save for their passenger on her knees before a seaman lying on the deck. Nate Baker stood over them, a concerned look on his wizened face. Jake Johansson rested a hand on the rail nearby, shaking his head.

"Looks like young Trent," Russ offered.

"What happened?" Nick asked, striding toward the small group.

"It were the batten on the shrouds, Captain," said Jake, walking toward him. "Just snapped in the middle, *ja*? Took a slice out of the lad's leg as he fell. Miss Tara is tendin' him."

"'Tis a nasty gash," added Nate, "but the lad will live."

Knowing Nate as he did, Nick was surprised by the look of admiration on the old tar's face as he watched the girl carefully checking the wound. Nate was treated more like an officer than a member of the crew and had many jobs of his own choosing. One was tending wounds, and he'd saved many a life over the years. As he watched the older seaman, Nick realized he'd seen that look on the Nate's face before, usually when he was talking to Nick's mother. Odd that.

His passenger looked up. "He'll be fine, Captain, as long as the wound is kept clean and allowed to heal. I've some ointment in my cabin that works wonders. And thread. The cut will need stitching."

John Trent smiled up at his nurse with a look of awe. "Whatever ye think is best, Miss Tara."

Oh for Christ's sake. His crew was turning to mush in the girl's hands, though he thought he saw resentment in the eyes of a few who remained on the sidelines watching.

"I'll get the salve and bandages," his passenger said as she rose and hurried toward the hatchway, casually acknowledging him as she passed.

"Mr. Greene!" Nick yelled, realizing it came out more harshly than he'd intended. His cabin boy miraculously appeared, as he often did.

"Yes, sir?" The lad stood at attention, a few brown curls blowing in wild abandon across his forehead.

"Fetch some whiskey from Mr. McGinnis, Peter, and see that Mr. Trent here gets a good dose. As for the rest of you," Nick looked around at the gathering crowd, "back to work!" The crew, who had left off their morning chores to watch the girl tending the downed seaman, scurried like rats before the ship's cat to quickly resume their tasks. The bos'n, Jake, followed, advancing to the rigging.

Nick tilted his head to the sky and gazed far into the distance, gratified to see there were no clouds gathering on the horizon. For a while, at least, they would have fair weather. By his side, Russ said, "I'll stay on deck, Captain."

"Fine." Nick headed toward the aft hatchway that would return him to his cabin. There was still the ship's log to see to.

He had just descended the ladder when Tara McConnell, racing to the companionway with her hands full and looking down at her feet, plowed into him, losing her balance. He reached to steady her, bringing her body flush with his chest. When she looked up, her lips were mere inches from his.

"Oh, sorry, sir," she said, flustered. For a moment their gazes locked. Her cheeks were reddening as she quickly stepped out of his arms. "I…I was hurrying to see to John."

She might be young, but she had all the feminine parts he favored. Tall, slim and with breasts sufficient in size so he noticed. Somewhere she'd left her ridiculous hat behind, and wisps of honey-colored hair had pulled free from her plait and were blowing about her oval face. Light from the hatchway caught the golden strands framing her aquamarine eyes. For a moment, her beauty robbed him of breath.

Clamping down on the impulse to pull her into his arms, Nick spoke gruffly, "Miss McConnell, please take it more slowly in future."

"You may call me *Miss Tara*, sir; everyone on my brother's ship does." She gave him an impish smile and looked aside as if remembering something. "Well, almost everyone." With that she scooted sideways in the tight space, obviously trying to avoid touching him. The top of her head passed under his nose as she reached for the ladder. The unmistakable scent of jasmine wafted to his nostrils. He'd had too many well-tended women in his bed not to recognize the alluring smell. Now why would an American tomboy smell of jasmine?

The flowery scent and the memory of her warm breasts pressed against him produced an unwanted ripple of desire. Surprised at his reaction to what was no more than a sprout of a woman, and needing the distance her formal name would provide, he said, "Miss McConnell, while I appreciate your concern for my crew, do take care not to become a casualty yourself, hmm?"

"Of course, Captain," she said over her shoulder as she deftly climbed the ladder. "I shall endeavor not to be a burden to you!"

"Oh, Miss McConnell, I should tell you, as I will the crew shortly, we will be making a stop in Bermuda for supplies, and another in the Caribbean. I am sorry but it will, of necessity, delay your arrival into Baltimore."

She stepped down to the deck to stand next to him. "What? But I must get to Baltimore as soon as possible. My father—"

"There is nothing I can do, Miss McConnell. I was not free to inform you before we sailed. When you insisted on taking passage on my ship, you accepted the risk of the itinerary changing."

She grimaced but said nothing. He could feel her displeasure as her blue-green eyes glared at him before she turned again toward the ladder and abruptly began to climb.

Nick shrugged as he glimpsed her long legs in dark stockings and rounded buttocks covered in breeches ascending the ladder— and ordered his body to relax.

Yes, definitely trouble.

* * *

Scrambling up to the deck as fast as she could, Tara let a curse escape under her breath, one she'd learned from her father's crew at an early age. The captain was insufferable! And now there would be a further delay in her trip home. Weeks more, likely. And he'd seemed not at all apologetic for adding those weeks to her travel. Nor did he care that she was desperate to reach her father, who was ill and perhaps getting worse.

She remembered the captain's penetrating gaze. Though he was as tall as her oldest brother, he had none of George's mirth. She recognized that look when she saw it. It was that of a domineering male regarding with disdain what he obviously considered a lesser creature—a woman. She'd seen the look before on the faces of her brother's new crew before they were given strict orders to respect her as one of them, the same look she'd seen on some of the *Wind Raven*'s crew.

But Tara would not dwell on the captain's biases, nor the feel of his muscled chest as she'd careened into him, nor his fresh masculine scent mixed with sea air, which oddly made her want to linger in his presence. Nor could she do more for her father at this point.

Instead she hurried toward the place where she'd left the downed seaman, and dropped to his side. He was a young man, John Trent was, and attractive, with his mussed brown hair and eager blue eyes. She thought he'd probably been only a few years on the ship, though already his face was weathered from the sun and the salt.

The bleeding from John's wound had worsened, not unexpectedly, as she'd removed the pieces of wood. Jake had returned to his bos'n duties, but old Nate crouched next to her, trying to humor John as she assessed the wound more carefully.

"I cut away a bit of his pant leg for ye," Nate said.

"Thank you, Mr. Baker." Tara examined the wound. Lodged in the gash in his leg were pieces of wood that must be removed. "This may hurt a bit as I pick out the splinters," she told John.

The young seaman looked at her, a bit dazed. "I don't mind, Miss Tara, not if you're doing it."

"Can I help ye?" ventured Mr. Baker.

"Some water from the scuttlebutt would be welcome. I'll need to clean the wound." She thought that given his years at sea, Mr. Baker had likely treated many wounds and was being kind to let her take the lead. She was grateful to offer what skills she had and happy to feel useful.

The cabin boy, Peter, stood nearby holding a bottle of whiskey. "Is that for John?" she asked.

The boy nodded.

"He could use some, I wager," she said, smiling at John.

"The captain told me to fetch it," said Peter. "Mr. Trent's had one swallow already, but 'tis certain he'd like another." Handing the bottle to John, the cabin boy took a seat on the deck, sitting cross-legged as he watched her working to remove the splinters.

So the captain was considerate of his crew. He had that to his good, at least. "Save some for the wound," she told John, seeing him take a healthy swig. "Best not to drink more. We don't want you falling down on deck, do we?"

"Whatever you say, miss," said John, wiping his mouth on his sleeve and handing the bottle back to Peter.

Nate returned with a bucket of water and set it next to Tara. Wetting the cloth she'd brought up from her cabin, she began to clean the wound. The coppery smell of blood rose to her nostrils and the cabin boy turned pale and winced as she carefully removed the pieces of wood lodged in the wound. Before John could anticipate the sting, she doused the wound with whiskey. He let out a screech.

"Sorry," she said in sympathy, watching him try to brave through the pain.

"'Tis no matter," he said in a voice too high.

Her hands trembled as she quickly stitched the gash. When it was done, John let out the breath he had been holding, and she secured the wound with a bandage.

"There," she said, glad the ordeal was over, "you're all patched up. And you've been very brave."

The lad beamed.

Gathering up her supplies, Tara rose from the deck. Peter and Nate helped the young seaman to stand. Stuffing the whiskey in his pocket, Peter provided support for John, who slowly limped off, saying he'd better find the ship's carpenter to repair the batten. Tara was left alone with Nate, watching the pair make their way to the hatch.

"Ye've done this before, lass," Nate observed.

Yes, she had, and each time it saddened her to see the wounds, some scarring the sailors for life. "Many times on my oldest brother's ship in the year before I went to London. After the war I was allowed to sail with him again." Her work done, Tara plopped her hat on her head and went to get a drink of water. She sat back against the scuttlebutt, content she had been of some help.

Nate joined her, pulling his pipe from his pocket as he took a seat on the deck. He had the face of a man who'd spent his life at sea, wrinkled and browned like leather left in the sun. It was one reason her father had insisted she wear a hat. But she liked Nate's face. It was kind and spoke of wisdom, not unlike that of her father. She thought old Nate's wiry gray hair might have come early. He might be younger than he appeared. His brown eyes often held an excitement that belied his apparent age, and she'd seen him move agilely across the deck. He might be only in his forties.

"Tell me about yer family, lass."

She took a deep breath and slowly let it out. "It's just my father, my brothers and me. My mother died when I was young. It's hard to remember her now." A feeling of wistfulness came over Tara as it always did when she thought about the mother she'd lost when she was only six. "I was raised by my father with my four older brothers. Our housekeeper, Maggie O'Flaherty, took care of us when we were at home."

"Yer brothers all sail, do they?" he asked, leisurely puffing on his pipe.

"Yes, though we lost Ben, the youngest, in the last war."

"I'm sorry for yer loss. War is never a good thing. I've lost many friends to it, family, too. 'Tis hard."

She gave him a sympathetic look before saying, "Ben and I were close." Shrugging off the memories that still haunted her, she resumed her story. "Since the war, my father has been more engaged in the shipbuilding side of the business. By the time I left for London, George was sailing less, too, leaving John and Thomas as the two ship's captains in the family."

"They made it through the last skirmish between England and America, I take it?"

"All but Ben, though the three who survived have wounds to show for it." The fact that at least three of her brothers had returned safely from the war gave Tara a great sense of relief. She had begged them to take her with them, if only to tend the wounded, but they had refused, leaving her at home for those few years. She'd had much time to worry.

"Ye must be spoiled being the only girl among so many men."

"Does it show?" At his grin, she added, "I suppose they have spoiled me. They are much older than me. George and John are in their thirties, and Tom right behind them in his late twenties." She looked at the older, wiser seaman and knew he'd understand when she said, "I arrived a bit late, or so Father tells me." Curious about the man she found so irritating, she asked, "Is your captain from a sailing family?"

"Like yers, there were four sons. All were raised for the sea, though one does not sail now. Only the Raven had the fire to follow his father as a privateer, plundering the French with letters of marque from the Crown."

"And the Americans? Did the captain and his crew sail against us?" She couldn't help wondering if the arrogant English captain had preyed on her family's ships—though to be fair, her brothers had gone after the English. As privateers, they'd captured or sunk more than a dozen ships before returning home to Baltimore two years ago. It was when she'd resumed sailing with them that her father, watching her in the rigging one day, had decided to send her to London.

"Not often. The Raven mostly went after the French, which always surprised me since Nick's mother is French. But o' course, he was raised in England." The older man chuckled to himself, apparently finding humor in his statement.

So the captain and his father had, at least at some point, plundered the Americans. Well, what did she expect? He was English. "An interesting family."

"That they be, lass."

"Have you sailed with the captain long?"

"Since his first ship. And before that with his father." The older seaman relit his pipe and puffed for a moment. "What brings ye to the *Wind Raven*, lass?"

"I was in London, where I've been living for the last year with my Aunt Cornelia, when my oldest brother sent for me. My father is ill, you see, and George wanted me home. I sought the first ship sailing to Baltimore that was acceptable to my aunt. Since she is a friend of Captain Powell's mother, I was told to take this ship."

"Fate sometimes has unusual ways," he said in a low voice as he looked into the distance.

Tara wondered at his statement but decided not to ask. It was the kind of thing their housekeeper, Mrs. O'Flaherty, would say. Maggie was the closest thing Tara had to a mother since her own mother had died.

Finished with her water, and hearing the eight bells that announced it was noon, Tara decided to take a look at the galley. "Is this a good time to meet your cook?"

"As good as any, lass. The man's a curmudgeon, though I 'spect ye can charm him."

* * *

As ships' galleys went, the *Wind Raven*'s was fairly average. It was not large, but Tara thought it sufficient in size to produce the simple meals served to the more than thirty officers and crew. A rack holding carving knives, kettles and pans was set into the bulkhead, the tools of the cook's trade swaying with the motion of the ship.

Crates and barrels containing salted meat, flour and rice stood in a neat row nearby. Canvas bags holding a supply of coffee, dried peas and oatmeal leaned against them. Above her head, small squares of heavy glass were set into the weather deck, acting as miniature skylights providing dim light during the day. These were aided by the glow from the large black stove radiating orange light from the open firebox, and from a lantern hanging above. Tara could see quite clearly the stout middle-aged man laboring over a chopping block. His graying red hair was in disarray, sprinkled with the same flour that coated his hands, as he kneaded a large mound of dough.

Sitting on a small stool watching him with wide eyes was the captain's cabin boy. Behind him Charlie Wilson, the gunner, leaned against a stack of crates in one corner with his arms crossed over his chest. Charlie was a seasoned member of the crew, his deeply tanned skin and sun-bleached brown hair a testimony to his life at sea.

"'Tis not my favorite of the stories Cook tells, that one about the banshee," said Mr. Wilson, scratching his stubbled chin. "All that screeching as a herald of death would send me screaming over the rails. I like the one about the *leanan sídhe*. Tell us that one, McGinnes."

"Oh, yes!" joined in Peter enthusiastically, his dimple in full display.

McGinnes looked up while still kneading the big lump of dough, his green eyes fixed on Tara as he began to speak, a faint hint of an Irish brogue in his voice. "The *leanan sídhe* be a tall one, fair-haired and beautiful, a fairy mistress of dreadful power." Tara avoided the cook's pointed gaze and smiled at Peter as she accepted the stool he offered and continued listening to the fascinating tale the cook was weaving for them.

Never taking his eyes off Tara, McGinnes spoke. "She often bestows a gift like the power to create art or music or she might give her protection and healing. In doing this, ye'd best be aware," he said, passing a look of warning to the gunner and the cabin boy, "the *leanan sídhe* seeks the love of mortal men. If a man can refuse her, she will be his slave, but if he loves her, he will forever be hers."

"Sounds wonderful," said Peter with a wistful sigh.

"Nay, 'tis not so wonderful, lad," he said, diverting his gaze to the boy. "The *sídhe* can be quite fierce if angered, and the price of her dark gifts is often sorrow and a broken heart. The more suffering she inflicts, the dearer she becomes to the one she desires. 'Tis said she will only meet her mortal lover in *Tir-na-n-Og*, the land of eternal youth. Sure an' a man who would be hers must first pass through death."

Silence hung in the small space as the seaman and the boy, held in rapt attention, appeared to contemplate the high price for love of an ethereal being.

The cook's fingers resumed working through the dough and his sudden slap of the raw pastry sent up a cloud of flour dust, startling the two men out of their daydreaming.

Tara let out a sigh and rose, disrupting the silence. She thought it time she offered her greeting. "Mr. McGinnes, we've not been introduced. I am Tara McConnell."

The cook gave her a skeptical look, his eyes falling to her breeches. "I've heard much about our passenger. Sure an' not all of the crew welcome a woman aboard. Mr. Greene here tells me you'll be offering your cookin' skills to my galley."

Tara cast Peter a sidelong glance, knowing the offer to help would not be well received by the ship's cook who, she was certain, viewed the galley as his domain. "Oh, no, Mr. McGinnes. I would never presume to suggest I have skills such as yours, but since I've been limited to the deck for any help I can offer the crew, I'd be pleased to do what I can to assist you." She smiled broadly. "Besides, the galley on my brothers' ships is usually the best place to find not just food, but good conversation."

"'Tis the same here," said Charlie. "Better still, McGinnes is the keeper of fairy lore."

At her wide smile, the cook's gaze sharpened and he looked at Tara with sudden interest. "Are ye Irish then?"

"Half," said Tara, hoping it would make a difference.

"Well, then." His mouth turned up in a grin and he slapped his dough again. "Sure an' I'll be directing meself to that half, Miss Tara. Ye can help in the galley if you've a mind to."

"Why, thank you, Mr. McGinnes." Tara sensed he'd bestowed upon her a great honor, though she wasn't sure it was much of an honor to serve in what was the ship's kitchen when she much preferred serving as crew. Still, she liked this Irish cook and wanted the man who made her meals on her side.

"McGinnes will do."

"I'd better see if the captain needs anything," said Peter, nervously looking toward the cabin door. "I've been gone a while."

"Take the skipper his coffee, lad," admonished McGinnes, handing the boy a mug of the steaming brew he had just poured.

"But I took him coffee this morning," protested the cabin boy.

"I'll have none o' yer arguments now. The skipper does better with the drink close at hand. Oh, and take this tidbit for Sam." The cook handed the boy a piece of what appeared to be cooked pork.

"Sam?" Tara asked. She couldn't recall hearing of a seaman named Sam and wondered why the cabin boy would be delivering bits of meat to him.

"The captain's cat," said the red-haired McGinnes. "Followed the skipper onto the ship one day in St. Thomas a year ago. The crew accepted her as one of 'em. Named her after the fighter Dutch

Sam. They had a fondness, ye see, for the boxer called 'the man with the iron hand.' Sure an' it seems fittin' for a cat with too many toes and paws as big as a fighter's fist, don't it now?"

"Samantha might be a better choice," she teased, "since the cat's a female."

McGinnes just shook his head and went back to pounding his floured dough. "Females!"

Chapter 5

A few evenings later, Tara received an invitation to dine with the captain in his cabin. The idea had obviously pleased his cabin boy, because Peter was wearing a broad grin when he delivered the message. Though it wasn't unusual for a captain to ask a passenger to join him for the evening meal, she could not help but wonder what had precipitated this change in the captain's otherwise distant demeanor. Was it to lecture her on something she'd done? Perhaps one of the crew who mumbled their discontent at having a woman aboard had been urging the captain to keep her in her cabin.

"The cap'n asks you to join him and Mr. Ainsworth for dinner at four bells in the evening watch. That is six of the clock, Miss Tara," he said, his dimple evident in his smile.

"I know what four bells is, Peter, but thank you for making the time clear." It was easy to like the cabin boy. "You can tell your captain that I accept his invitation." No matter what lay behind the invitation, she was already tired of dining in her cabin alone, and she knew the captain would not be pleased if she joined the crew when they took their meals, as she often did on her brothers' ships. When the cabin boy lingered, looking down at his toes, she asked, "Is there something else, Peter?"

He raised his head. "Yes, Miss Tara. Cap'n asks that you dress like a lady." He must have seen her frown because he blushed and added, "He always dresses for dinner when he has company."

"I see. All right, Peter. I will do as your captain requests in this as well."

So he wanted her to dress like a lady, did he? Well, she supposed she could accommodate the oh-so-English captain. But she would do it her way. Digging into her trunk she found the gowns Aunt Cornelia had meticulously selected for her first Season, the ones Tara had packed knowing it would cheer her father to see her wear them. Feeling a twinge at the thought of her father, she sent up a prayer for his well-being and dug deeper into her trunk to find the gowns that had been modified per Tara's own requirements, one of which would do quite nicely for tonight.

The bodice of the cerulean blue silk gown she chose to wear was separately made from the high-waisted skirt and only loosely attached to it with buttons under the wide green sash. She was slim enough she didn't need a corset, only a firm bodice lining, which allowed her much greater freedom of movement. The most marvelous part was that the skirt could be torn away to reveal the breeches she wore underneath. Anyone looking at her would see only the gown. While the dress appeared like one of those she'd worn to events of the London Season, in fact, it was two pieces with breeches beneath.

It made her feel secure knowing she could tear away the frippery, if need be, and still be decently clothed and able to scale the rigging. It had been a source of amusement for her brothers, who were aware of what their sister hid beneath her feminine attire as she acted the hostess for visitors aboard their ships. Her father had never known of the ruse.

Tonight her hair had been a bit of a struggle, but she'd finally managed to gather it into some semblance of order at her crown. Checking her appearance in the small mirror, she draped the blue and green shawl over her shoulders, and fortified herself against what she thought might be a difficult evening.

At her knock, the captain's cabin door opened and young Peter bid her enter, going out as she came in. On the right side of the cabin next to the windows stood the captain and his first mate, each holding a glass of brandy. Used to the ship's gentle roll, it was easy enough to walk to them while still acting the lady.

"Ah, Miss McConnell," said the captain, raising his glass in toast while sliding his gaze from her eyes to her silk slippers and back again, settling on her breasts where the mounds rose above her bodice. A gleam flickered in his golden eyes for a moment. She was used to the approving glances of men in her life, but she had never before encountered such a brazen inspection of her body. The intensity of his perusal made her want to squirm.

"Your appearance presents quite the transformation, Miss McConnell," he said with a wry smile. "Why, you almost make me think you are on your way to a London ball."

Tara did not appreciate his sarcasm. After all, she was dressed this way at his insistence. As young Peter had assured her, the captain was elegantly attired and damnably handsome in a black superfine coat, ivory silk waistcoat and buff-colored pantaloons that descended into shiny black Wellington boots. His skin, bronzed from the sun, was a stark contrast to his white shirt and simply tied cravat. Even his mane of black hair, usually in wild disarray from the wind on deck, was tamed this evening to fall in soft waves at his nape. She'd never seen any man in a London ballroom as virile and handsome as Nicholas Powell. And she'd never felt the stirrings of attraction for any man as she did for the *Raven*'s captain.

"I've had my fill of London's ballrooms, Captain."

The first mate glided to her side. With his well-groomed blond hair, dark blue coat and gray breeches, he looked the part of a gentleman. Bowing over her hand, he acted the part as well, rising to bestow upon her a look of approval.

"Do not allow Captain Powell's teasing to bother you, Miss McConnell," he said with a warm smile. "You are lovely."

"Thank you, Mr. Ainsworth. I can assure you it was quite an effort to accommodate the captain's request without my maid. I am pleased you think I've succeeded."

"As there are none aboard ship to assist a lady's dressing," said the captain, reaching for a liquor decanter sitting on his desk, "we salute your efforts. The gown is a welcome change from the breeches you seem to prefer." Then holding up a glass, he ventured, "May I pour you something to drink? Sherry, perhaps?"

"I'd prefer what you and Mr. Ainsworth are having." Brandy was the drink her brothers favored, and she was used to the powerful liquor, though she typically sipped it, aware of the fierce burn it would bring to her throat if she swallowed too much at one time.

The captain raised a brow at her words before shrugging and pouring her the drink she'd requested. "Certainly."

Her fingers grazed his as she accepted the glass from his outstretched hand, sending a shock through her arm and a sudden realization of how vulnerable she was to his masculine presence. He seemed amused, as if aware of how he affected her. *Arrogant Englishman.* He was the kind who attracted women, likely by the droves.

Tara brought the brandy to her lips and took a healthy swallow. Letting the liquor burn away thoughts of the handsome captain, she glanced at the table set with gilded china as fine as any she'd seen in London. A lantern in the center provided subdued lighting.

"Do you often dine in such a manner while underway?" Her brothers never put on such a show while at sea. Perhaps it was a British characteristic to formally dine aboard ship.

"No. But then it isn't often we have *guests*," said the captain, emphasizing the last word as he followed her gaze to the table, "or the calm seas to entertain them."

Additional lanterns were set about the cabin, and together with the light from the stove, they cast a warm glow over the features of the two men. "Mr. McGinnes, with the able assistance of Mr. Greene, has outdone himself, in your honor I suspect," said the first mate with a grin.

Tara's thoughts warmed at the memory of the dimple-cheeked boy. "Where has the lad gone?"

"He'll be along shortly with our food," said Mr. Ainsworth. "He went to see if McGinnes is ready, and to enlist Billy Uppington's help in carrying the dishes."

She'd been helping the young seaman Billy with his knots and had been glad he and the cabin boy were friends for she knew Billy was lonely. "And how is John? I've not seen him today. Is he healing well from his fall?"

"A little slower on the deck, perhaps, but he'll be fine," said the first mate.

The captain smiled lazily at her over his glass, his face taking on a curious expression. "*Tara*—the name sounds Irish. Is it?"

She took another sip of her brandy. *At least now he's looking at my eyes instead of my breasts.* She didn't know whether she should politely smile in return—the last thing she wanted was to encourage him—but since he was being nice, she said, "Well, yes, it is Celtic. Tara is the place where the Irish high kings dwelled, but my father was reminded of it in quite a different context, and that is how he came to give me the name."

"Really? And how is that?" said the captain.

"He'd always been interested in myths and stories. On a voyage to the South Seas the year before I was born, he learned of the Polynesian sea goddess, Tara."

"The goddess of the sea...hmm," the captain said, peering down at her from his great height. His golden eyes darkened in the soft light and suddenly it was as if there was no one in the cabin save the two of them. She could feel the heat from his penetrating gaze. What was it in his eyes she was seeing? A shiver raced up her spine. She took another swallow of brandy to quiet her nerves and looked away as Mr. Ainsworth spoke.

"It's a beautiful name, and it fits you somehow. It might be your eyes, the same blue-green of those tropical waters." The compliment from the first mate made the heat rise in her cheeks. It brought a frown to the captain's face.

"Thank you," Tara said. "I can assure you I vastly prefer it to the name he had been saving should he be blessed with a girl."

The captain raised a dark brow in question, suspending his glass of brandy in front of his lips.

"*Martha*," she said in answer to his unspoken question.

The first mate coughed, nearly choking on his brandy, then laughed. "Nay, you're no Martha."

"I would agree. The name *Tara* appealed to Father's romantic nature. A blustering sea captain at times," she said, looking directly at the captain, "he can be sweet, too." She let out a sigh. "A rare man." She turned to the captain. "Will we be long in the Caribbean? I am anxious to see for myself the condition of his health."

"Hopefully not long, but it is too soon to tell." The captain shot an enigmatic glance toward his first mate. She had a feeling the two shared some knowledge they were keeping to themselves.

A knock at the captain's door interrupted her thoughts as Peter and Billy entered, carrying trays laden with covered dishes. The smell of spices filled the cabin, making Tara's mouth water.

"Whatever McGinnes has in store for us tonight smells wonderful," said Mr. Ainsworth.

"'Tis a beef dish, sir," said Peter. "He's been preparin' it all afternoon. There are vegetables and roast potatoes, too. Oh, and he sent up your favorite French wine, Cap'n."

The captain pulled out a chair for Tara. She took her seat and the two men joined her as Peter and Billy began serving the food.

"Here are the rolls." Peter placed a basket on the table and winked conspiratorially at Tara—she'd spent much of the afternoon helping McGinnes with his baking. "I've set the cinnamon and raisin tarts on your desk, Cap'n, when you're ready for dessert. Billy and I will return later to collect the dishes." With that, the two young men departed.

As they ate the wonderfully tender beef dish, they slipped into easy conversation, made even easier by the Bordeaux wine. Tara sensed a kind of truce emerging between her and the captain. There was still tension between them, but somehow the mood had changed. Perhaps it was Mr. Ainsworth's witticisms, which acted much like grease on the skids, making it easy for Captain Powell to be gracious. Cautiously, she determined to accept the captain's apparent offering of peace between them. She had to admit that the English captain could be charming when he wanted to be. And when he laughed, the sound was a deep, rich baritone. Perhaps donning a lady's frippery had been worth the effort after all.

"These rolls McGinnes cooked up tonight are a far cry from his usual fare," remarked the captain as he took another bite.

Tara kept her eyes fixed on her plate.

"Has he suddenly gained a knowledge of baking?" he asked Mr. Ainsworth. "Or are some of his fairies working in the galley?"

"You might say so," the first mate said, grinning at Tara as she looked up. "Miss McConnell has been sharing her knowledge with our cook."

"*You?*" The captain shifted his attention to her. His golden eyes were full of wonderment. "You had something to do with these?"

"I have been spending part of my day helping Mr. McGinnes, yes."

"Hmm," he murmured as he took another bite, "very good. My compliments. Seems your talents are not limited to scrubbing the deck."

He was deliberately baiting her, but she would not allow his teasing to have its normal effect. Any compliment from the captain was a coup, even if he did add that annoying bit about scrubbing the deck, which he well knew she did not do. She just wished the compliment he'd chosen to convey hadn't been for her cooking. She would prefer he recognize her skills at helping to sail the ship.

"Miss McConnell, I've been curious," said the captain, "how is it your father allows you to dress like a man?"

"I didn't seek permission, if that's what you mean." Seeing she had the two men's interest, she elaborated, "One day a few years after my mother died, when he and my brothers were in port, I borrowed some clothes from my youngest brother, Ben, and went aboard my father's ship, asking to be taken along. They were my family and I wanted to be with them. Perhaps my father felt sorry for me. Anyway, he relented."

"What about your education? Did you have no governess?" Mr. Ainsworth asked.

"Eventually Father may have come to that, but he already had a tutor for my brothers, who traveled with them when they went to sea, so it was rather convenient to include me in their lessons. I suppose for my father it was like gaining another son. As for me, I would have done anything not to be left behind. Dressing like a lad was part of being one of the family. Then, too, once I was on the ship, I found I loved the life at sea. Those were some of the happiest days for my brothers and me. We had lost our mother but we had our father and we had each other. We were all together." Tara knew she sounded nostalgic as she spoke of those days. She had truly loved all things about her father's ship, and tagging after her brothers had been a great adventure.

The captain rose and went to fetch the tarts, offering them to Tara and his first mate. "How long did you do this?" he asked, resuming his seat.

Tara bit into the raisin and cinnamon tart, a recipe she had given the cook. The wonderful aroma of the cinnamon blended with the pastry and the plump raisins to win a moan from her as she licked a drop of juice from her bottom lip. Reluctantly, she set down her fork. "I sailed with my father for seven years, until I was fourteen. By then the war had began. My oldest brothers had their own ships and Father insisted I stay home."

"Is that where you were when you left for London?" Mr. Ainsworth inquired.

"No. Two years ago when the war was over, I took up sailing with my brother George, mostly on his runs to the Caribbean. I'd just turned seventeen when, one day, Father came onto the ship. When he sighted me in the rigging, he suddenly became furious and informed me he was sending me to my Aunt Cornelia in London."

Mr. Ainsworth chuckled behind his napkin. "No wonder you are so comfortable acting as one of the ship's crew. You have been doing it most of your life."

"Seems to me, Miss McConnell, that your days as a seaman are over," pronounced the captain. "Surely you must see your father has the right of it?"

Tara bristled inwardly. He of all people should understand how she felt. "No, Captain, I do not. It's difficult to give up something you love. The sea and ships have been my home, more than any parlour in London or America. I will sail as long as I can, perhaps if I am fortunate, for the rest of my life. It may be possible my brothers will allow me to sail with them, for they haven't always agreed with Father."

Tara had not really thought about what she would do when she returned home, but she knew in her heart that, while she would miss Aunt Cornelia, she had no desire to return to the social whirl of London society. Perhaps she might become a part of her family's growing shipbuilding enterprise—even if she could no longer sail as one of the crew.

"Time will tell, Miss McConnell," said the captain, shaking his head. He did not look happy. Why he should care how she spent her life was something she did not bother to ponder.

When the lads came to clear away the empty plates, Tara rose and the men followed suit. "Dinner was wonderful. Thank you. If you don't mind, I think I'll take a turn about the deck since there is light still."

"I'll accompany you," said the captain. Tara didn't resist, aware it was probably better if she was escorted—dressed as she was. The watch would notice her feminine attire and not all of the captain's men were like Mr. Johansson. The bos'n had become her guardian angel, but he might not be on deck at this hour. The captain's presence might discourage an unwanted leer.

Once they were topside, she walked beside the captain toward the bow. The ship was gliding through the waves and the sun was just setting. She drew her shawl around her shoulders. Keeping apace beside them was the gray cat.

"Oh, there's your cat," said Tara, admiring Samantha's graceful movements despite her unwieldy front paws.

"Sam isn't my cat. She comes and goes as she wills."

"The crew thinks she's yours. And cats have a way of selecting their owners."

They had reached the rail on the starboard bow, where Tara stood in silent admiration of the grand display of color splashed across the horizon. Brilliant swaths of violet, crimson and orange held her attention. It was more beautiful than any painting she'd ever seen. Permeated by golden light from the dying sun, the surface of the ocean reflected the sky's colors of red, pink and gold. The schooner sliced through the water, making a soft hissing sound, as if the ship were whispering soft words on the evening air and the ocean was answering back.

She let out a sigh. The grandeur of God's work in the evening sky always reminded Tara of her mother. Tara had very few memories of the woman, but she did remember that her mother wore bright colors like those in the sunset. On the night Lucy McConnell died, Tara had carried her mother's crimson cloak to bed with her, wrapped herself in its warm folds, and cried herself to sleep while breathing in the jasmine scent that clung to the fabric. She had slept with the cloak for days until she'd discovered her mother's bottle of jasmine perfume. When she grew older she began to wear the scent as a tribute to the mother she loved.

A tear slipped down her cheek as she recalled those days from her childhood.

* * *

Nick had stared at the girl across the table at dinner as she'd made light conversation. She might not favor the drawing rooms of London but she would have done well there. With her aquamarine eyes and tawny hair reflecting the candlelight, she had been desire itself—a vision shimmering in blue, green and gold. Now, here on the deck, with the colors of the sunset glimmering on her face, she was even more alluring. Tawny curls gathered at the crown of her head reflected the light, making her hair appear like burnished gold.

As she watched the sunset, he watched her. Tonight she was the alluring lady, not a young woman playing at being a lad. The swells of her breasts were like ripe fruit rising above the bodice of her gown. He didn't know which he preferred, her enticing bottom encased in breeches or the pale mounds of her full breasts begging to be touched. Her seductive innocence called to him like a siren. She was a woman any man would desire, but to him she was more, a woman who loved ships and the sea. It was a dangerous combination. And tonight there'd been no sharp tongue, no hoyden antics to draw his ire. He had an irresistible urge to reach out and touch her, and idly wondered if the siren could sing.

As she stared into the distance, a tear rolled down her cheek and she brushed it away with the back of her hand.

"What is it that makes you sad while gazing at so glorious a sight, Miss McConnell?"

She faced him with a watery smile. "A memory of my mother. I was young when she died."

"If you don't mind my saying so, you are still quite young." A temptress, yes, but a young one still, he thought. If he had it figured right, he was fourteen years her senior.

"I was *very* young then," she said, her smile brightening. "Just six. But I remember her."

"That would be a tragic loss at any age, but six is very young to lose a mother. How did she die, if I may ask?"

"In childbirth, trying to bring into the world a sister I'll never know."

"I'm sorry. I understand it happens all too often, even to women who have successfully birthed other children."

"Yes, that is what the doctor told my father. Her death shattered him; he never thought he could lose her. None of us did."

She looked up at him with sad eyes, deep blue-green pools of unshed tears. He could lose himself in those eyes.

What made him take her into his arms he could not say, but it felt right to hold her, to comfort her, to run his hands up and down her back trying to sooth her. She rested her cheek against his shoulder. For a moment the world seemed to still. The heat from her body burned into his soul and they swayed with the movement of the ship, bathed in the colors of the brilliant sunset. His reaction to her was unlike his feelings for any other woman. He wanted to protect her—even from himself.

He lifted her chin with his finger. Her lips parted as she gazed up at him. The siren called and Nick was powerless to deny her. Bending his head, he touched her lips with his. They were soft and sweet. Though a voice told him to leave off, he could not stop. Driven by a powerful desire to merge with her, he kissed her deeply and she responded, only slightly hesitant in her innocence. He was suddenly overwhelmed by all that was Tara McConnell—the feel of her in his arms, her jasmine scent, her sweetness. Time slowed while he savored her. He may have been her anchor in the memory of a storm, but to him she was a wild fury, tamed perhaps for only a moment, but he would take that moment.

Reluctantly, he broke the kiss. She did not move but opened her eyes and looked at him as if seeing him for the first time. "Oh…" she breathed, coming out of her daze. The passion in her eyes faded. Stiffening as if she just realized where she was and who was holding her, she quickly glanced to where the watch would be. "Your crew—"

"—will have the good judgment to be looking elsewhere just now."

She stepped away from him, and he let her go. Turning, she fled to the hatch leading to the deck below and to her cabin. He watched her go and his eye caught the movement of a figure a score of feet above him in the rigging, the bos'n, Jake Johansson, who had the watch. The eyes of the large blond seaman narrowed on his captain in unspoken warning. Nick shrugged. By the time he looked again toward the hatch, the girl had disappeared.

Nick turned back to the sunset, curling his fingers around the smooth brightwork of the rail as he stared into the darkening sky.

The brilliant colors of a short while ago had faded into a palette of purple, gray and rose, as his passion faded into a memory of a siren who he feared would drive him mad with desire before they reached Baltimore.

He cursed under his breath for allowing himself the kiss. He had wanted to kiss her since he'd seen her impudent smile the morning she'd danced in the rigging, but she was no tavern wench. She was a passenger entrusted to his care by his mother's good friend. Even if Tara McConnell were willing, he would not take her to his bed. Since Caroline, he'd avoided virgins. And he was certain the blushing American who wore breeches was a virgin. His love for Caroline had been a young man's folly—not something ever to be repeated.

He recalled the day he had proudly taken Caroline to the docks to see his new ship. It had been a rare summer's day and he'd thought it the perfect setting to show the woman he loved the ship that held his heart. But with a perfume-suffused handkerchief held to her nose and a sneer cast at his crew, she had shown her disdain for the men he cared for and the ship he loved. No matter the *Wind Raven* and the other ships in the family business would make him a fine living. Foolishly, he'd still made love to her, thinking to make her his wife, excusing her behavior as that of a young woman unused to the sea.

With the retrospect the years allowed him, he wondered if she had only feigned love until the better offer had come along. And it had come along soon thereafter in the form of a title he could never give her. The way she had told him she was leaving him, abrupt and cold, had been ugly. And it had made him wonder if she would always be free with her favors.

No matter how accomplished a sea captain he might become, no matter how much worth he might obtain as a leader, a man or a merchant—he would never have been a proper suitor in her eyes, certainly never a peer. She had played him for a fool.

Caroline's rejection eight years ago had torn him apart. But he survived, firmly closing the door to his heart. He was not about to open it again.

* * *

Tara slammed the door of her cabin and leaned against the wood planks, her heart racing from her flight from the captain. She had let him kiss her. Her first real kiss.

She took a deep breath and slowly let it out, trying to calm her pounding heart. Bringing her fingers to her still-sensitive lips, she marveled at her own vulnerability to the hardened English captain. He had caught her at a weak moment; that was all there was to it. Warmed by the brandy and the wine, and drawn to the comfort he offered in response to her sadness, she had not thought to resist. Indeed, embarrassing though it was to recall, she had willingly responded.

Her brothers had warned her about such men; she should have been prepared. He was a rake if ever there was one, and he had outmaneuvered her. She had never had to face such a situation before. On her brothers' ships, no man would touch her for risk of losing their position. But this captain was different. Instinctively, she knew she would have to be cautious if she were to avoid being seduced by the handsome Englishman, because innocent though she was, she was suddenly aware she wanted more of his kisses.

As her heart slowed to its normal pace, she stepped to her bunk, where the gray cat sat licking one of her white paws. The animal had raced into her cabin when she'd opened the door. Sitting on the edge of the bed, Tara stroked the soft gray fur and the cat's purring calmed her.

"The captain has no appreciation for a female's wits, Samantha," she told the cat, calling her by the name *she* preferred for the beautiful animal. The cat's green eyes seem to consider her words. "He probably thinks of you as a mere decoration to grace his desk, not a member of his crew, though indeed you work as hard as any, ridding his ship of vermin as you do." Tara realized then she was talking to herself as well as the cat. No matter how much she desired to be respected as one of them, the captain saw her as only a woman. He had admired her gown and complimented her baking, but when it came to sailing his ship, his only reference to her skills was to acknowledge her "fancy footwork" the day she'd rescued Billy. The insufferable captain would never recognize her sailing prowess, as her brothers did. Why did it matter? And why was she attracted to such a man?

"It's so unfair!" she said to the cat. "Why did it have to be him? He's English! I cannot care for an Englishman."

The cat didn't answer but the green eyes seemed to convey understanding.

"Samantha, you probably want to be about your night's hunting, don't you? It's when you do your best work for the captain."

She was having a conversation with a damn cat! The cat jumped down from the bed and padded the short distance to the cabin door, rubbing her body back and forth against the wooden panel.

"All right, then. Be off with you," she said, opening the cabin door. "I shall work on exorcizing my attraction to your arrogant master."

Chapter 6

Tara's life aboard ship over the next several weeks fell into a familiar routine. She rose early, just before dawn, and after a brief stop to visit with McGinnes and eat a bowl of oatmeal, she was up on deck helping the crew with their chores. Jake was always there, scowling at the seamen whose interested gazes lingered too long upon her. He reminded her of her oldest brother, George, who was ever protective. She knew the crew whispered about her and the captain, and she vowed to provide no further scenes for their speculation.

This morning Tara sat back on her heels on the weather deck watching Billy Uppington concentrate on trying to tie a bowline knot. The seas were calm and the ship steady, but he struggled as if on a rolling deck, trying to bring the resisting threads of line together. His dark curls falling around his face, he reminded her of her brother Ben. The ache that never went away settled in her heart once again. Ben had sought to please their older brothers as Billy sought to please the crew. Even though she had been younger than Ben by five years, she had helped him. The knots that came so easily to her had been as difficult for Ben as they were for Billy.

The deck rolled with a swell, making only more difficult the young seaman's efforts to create a knot that looked like the one Tara had shown him.

"Me fingers are all thumbs!" Billy threw down the half-tied knot, frustration clear on his face. Tara sympathized. The intricate work she had learned as a young girl was only made more difficult by the young seaman's large, work-roughened hands.

Tara picked up the entangled knot, turning it over as she studied how best to complete it. "You must give it time, Billy. Just be patient with yourself. Before long you'll be able to tie it upside down, backwards, even facing the opposite way. See," she held out the tangle of threads, "this thread fits in here," indicating the one he'd missed.

Billy scarcely gave the knot a glance. "In truth, Miss Tara, I've been wonderin' if I really want a life at sea. I'm ever clumsy scalin' the rigging, and I'm always trippin' over my feet on deck."

She held out the knot for Billy to observe as she showed him how to twist the rope to the desired end. "There, see, it can be managed!"

"I see how *you* managed it, Miss Tara."

"You can do it too, Billy," she urged. She wanted the young seaman to succeed. It was like helping Ben. When their older brothers teased him unmercifully, she had been his champion.

"All right. I'll keep trying," he said grudgingly, accepting the knot from her hand. She knew he would, if only to please her. He was a sweet lad. But Billy might be right about not making an able seaman if his heart wasn't in it. She hoped he would continue trying.

"It just takes time," she said. "I was terrible when I first began and my oldest brother was quite rude in his tormenting me." Seeing discouragement in his brown eyes and not wanting to leave him that way, she asked, "Where is home for you, Billy?"

"Derbyshire," he said wistfully. Then shaking his head, he added, "But the times are not good there now. The crops have been in trouble since last year and the new machines are replacing many men in the weavin' trade. The people are unhappy. Some families are starvin'. My own family has struggled. My father has been out of work since the war ended. And the iron works doesn't have the orders it once did. I thought if I tried something different than farming or the iron works, I could make a better life for meself and help the family."

"And you will." Tara urged. She felt keenly the responsibility the young man had assumed and hoped she could help him. "Did you leave a girl behind?"

"No...or well there *was* a girl I liked," he said, blushing, "but we'd only started to talk some when I left."

Tara rose and shook out her legs, cramped from sitting so long. "Perhaps she is waiting for you. But if not, there will be many girls for you to choose from, Billy."

At those words a big smile broke out on his face. "Do you think so?"

"I'm certain of it," said Tara, seeing his cheeks redden in another blush.

Mr. Smith, hurrying by, scolded, "Don't waste that seaman's time, Miss McConnell. He has chores that need doing."

She wouldn't explain herself to Mr. Smith, or Smitty, as the crew called him. That he resented her presence was evident by his sullen demeanor whenever he encountered her. "We are finished, Mr. Smith." Then, smiling at Billy, she said, "I think I'll visit with Mr. Baker," and she headed aft.

Before she reached the helm, she saw Nate and Jake bent over a coil of rope, their backs to her. Hearing her name mentioned, she slowed as she approached.

"*Ja*, I can see that, Mr. Baker, but do you think the lass will be safe with the captain? I don't like the way he looks at her, like a starvin' man lookin' at a beefsteak."

"The question is, Jake, will the cap'n be safe with Tara McConnell? That I rather doubt." The older seaman chuckled, and Jake turned to stare at Nate in wonder.

Tara did an about-face and quietly padded to amidships, wondering at Nate's words. Why did he think the captain was not safe with her? Wasn't it the other way around? When the captain was on deck, Tara often felt his eyes upon her. Like mysterious fingers reaching out to touch her, his stare could send shivers up her spine. Worse, his presence drew her gaze despite her resolve to avoid him. At those times, she would turn to see his broad shoulders draped in a white shirt billowing in the wind, his powerful muscled legs in black breeches and boots, and his ebony hair flying around his face. She was afraid to get too close, afraid he would see what she tried so desperately to hide. Despite her initial reaction to him, she had come to respect the way he handled his crew. But remembering his kiss and his rakish smile, Tara admitted to herself she had other feelings where he was concerned, and those she would disclose to no one.

Tara spent her afternoons with McGinnes and the men who chose to take their break in the galley to hear the cook spin stories of fairies and to gain a few scraps of food as the cook prepared the evening meal. She and McGinnes were now friends since his new rolls had drawn many accolades from the crew. Once done with the galley, she would head for her cabin, the gray cat following to curl up on her bed for a nap.

Some nights she dined with the captain and the first mate, but for the rest she ate in her cabin and read by the light of a lantern. The seas were not always calm, but when they were, once in a while, at Nate's suggestion, Tara joined the men on deck as they entertained themselves with seafaring songs until the sun sank into the sea. It was a pleasant way to pass the time. They sang of the sea and the loves they left behind. Several of the men had musical instruments—a guitar, a fiddle and a flute among them. Together they made a rousing good sound.

Tonight there was a large group gathered on deck, among them Mr. Adams, the thin sailmaker with the reddish-brown hair whom she'd helped to mend the foresail that morning; the gunner, Charlie

Wilson, who cared for the guns like they were his children; John Trent, the young seaman whose leg had been injured in the incident with the broken batten; and even the ill-tempered Mr. Smith. Watching in the background, as always, was Jake.

"Miss Tara," said John Trent, "do you sing any songs by yourself?" She had watched him walk on the deck that evening. Even with the roll of the ship, he seemed to be moving with only a slight limp.

"Sometimes I do. My brothers like the ballad of 'Barbara Allen.'"

"Would you sing it for us?" asked the sailmaker, who had set down his fiddle to ask.

"If you wish it." She glanced at Augie, Charlie and Mr. Smith, the ones playing instruments. "Do you know the tune?"

"*Ja,*" said Jake, "they know it."

Mr. Adams lifted his fiddle to his chin. The others with instruments joined him and the men began to play the opening chords of the sad song her brothers loved.

> *'Twas in the merry month of May*
> *When the green buds were a swellin'*
> *Sweet William came from the West Country*
> *And fell in love with Barbara Allen.*
> *He courted her for seven long years*
> *'Til his heart in him was failing*
> *And asked his love to marry him*
> *But "No," said Barbara Allen.*

A few verses into the ballad, out of the corner of her eye, Tara saw the captain striding toward them, his face an indiscernible mask. He paused when he neared Tara and the group of seated men, and crossed his arms over his chest as he leaned against the rail. He appeared to listen with interest as her voice lifted in clear tones, the ballad descending to a sad note.

> *On a somber rotten day*
> *When all the leaves were fallin'*
> *Sweet William on his deathbed lay*
> *For the love of Barbara Allen.*

Tara sang on, the story taking a turn as the lovesick lad's servant summoned Barbara Allen to his master's bedside, only to have the girl turn him away. The crew gave her their rapt attention when she sang of the young man's death and Barbara Allen's subsequent remorse.

> *As she was walking o'er the fields*
> *She heard the deathbell knellin'*
> *And every stroke it seemed to say*
> *"Hardhearted Barbara Allen."*

The looks on the faces of the men turned serious as they listened to her sing of the girl who spurned true love's call, only to realize too late she'd lost the only man she would ever love, and so died of sorrow.

> *They buried her in the old churchyard*
> *And William they buried nigh her*
> *Out of William's heart there grew a rose*
> *Out of Barbara Allen's there grew a briar*
> *They grew and grew to the steepletop*
> *'Til they could grow no higher*
> *And there they twined in a true love's knot*
> *The rose wrapped round the briar.*

When Tara finished the ballad, there was silence for a long moment. Even some of the hardened seamen seemed moved. Mr. Smith looked away as if fighting a memory, and it made her feel sympathy for the often-disgruntled seaman. Then young John Trent said, "'Tis beautiful, Miss Tara."

"Reminds me of home," said Mr. Adams, setting down his fiddle.

"Ye've the voice of an angel," said Billy. "Me mum used to sing that song and it was beautiful to hear ye sing it."

The men murmured their agreement with Billy's sentiment, though Tara noticed the captain remained silent in the shadows. Was he pondering what love he might have passed by? The somber expressions on the faces of the crew told Tara it was time to lighten their mood. She suggested they next sing one of her brothers' favorites, "The Maid of Amsterdam." The men seemed happy to take up the old drinking song.

As they began to sing, Tara joined in, and the ship's cat curled up at her side, the overlarge white paws for all to admire.

> *In Amsterdam there dwells a maid,*
> *Mark well what I do say;*
> *In Amsterdam there dwells a maid,*
> *And she is mistress of her trade.*
> *I'll go no more a-roving with you, fair maid,*
> *A-roving, a-roving, since roving's been my ruin,*
> *I'll go no more a-roving with you, fair maid!*

Tara's mood rose along with that of the crew as she sang the song favored by her brothers, clapping her hands in time with the rousing music, old Nate by her side. When they got to the next verse, she caught the captain leaning forward.

I took the maiden for a walk
And sweet and loving was her talk.
I put my arm around her waist,
Says she, "Young man, you're in some haste."

It was then the captain moved out of the shadows, raised a brow and fixed his gaze on Tara, a scowl spreading across his face, but she and the crew continued singing.

I took that girl upon my knee,
Says she, "Young man, you're rather free."
I put my hand upon her thigh—

At this last line, the captain dropped his hands to his side and stalked toward her, a thunderous expression on his face.

Tara stopped singing, as did the men.

"I think it's time I escort the young *lady* to her cabin," the captain said, casting a dark scowl at his crew. None of the men uttered a word and the music trailed off. She rose and left with the captain, not wishing to challenge his authority in front of his men, though it was none of his business if she sang the salty songs.

"You may continue," the captain said over his shoulder to the seated men. His hand took hold of her elbow and he escorted her to the hatch leading to their cabins. She felt chided and embarrassed in front of the men. Yet his touch, which was none too tender, sent shivers coursing through her. No man's touch had ever excited and frightened her the way his did. Whatever one might say about Nicholas Powell, he was a formidable man. And the heat of his chest touching her shoulder deeply affected her. Though she was dressed in a lad's breeches and shirt, he made her feel like a woman grown, so attuned was she to this English sea captain.

"I don't understand you, Miss McConnell," he whispered in her ear in a stern tone, as he motioned for her to descend the ladder. "Why are you not satisfied with being a woman? And why must you interfere with the duties of my men?"

She grabbed the side of the ladder and descended to the deck below. "It's clear you know little of what motivates me, Captain. I do not interfere with the work of your crew. And ordering me about will not render me compliant."

He followed her down the ladder. "I daresay it has not. You must see how unseemly it is for you, a young woman, to be singing bawdy songs with my crew."

They walked down the companionway. "Really, Captain, on my brothers' ships I have frequently participated in the crew's entertainment."

"Are you certain *you* were not the entertainment?"

"Do you mean to say the song I sang about Barbara Allen?" she asked as they arrived at her cabin door. She paused, turning to face him, indignant at his question and awaiting his answer.

"No, Miss McConnell, I do not refer to your song. I confess I enjoyed it. It is what drew me to the deck."

"Then to what do you refer, sir?" She was tiring of this game he played.

"To you, Miss McConnell," he said, letting his eyes drift down to her breasts, then back to her eyes, "to what the men must be thinking. To this—"

He pulled her into his arms and his lips crushed hers before Tara could speak a word. It was not the tender kiss he'd given her the night they'd watched the sunset. It was a kiss of fierce possession, his tongue invading her mouth to stroke hers sensually as he held her captive between her cabin door and the wall of his chest. She struggled against him but to no avail. As he continued to kiss her, he gentled. Though she was angry at the liberties he was taking, soon she was lulled into submission within the confines of his strong arms. When he pressed his body against hers, she melted like hot wax, feeling every inch of him. It was like drowning. She was sinking beneath the rising passion so new to her, helpless to break free of the magic he was spinning as his hand dropped to her hip and he pulled her tightly into his body. Tara raised her hands to his shoulders and held on as she rode the wave that washed away her objections and her good sense.

He lifted his head and in a gruff voice said, "Do you see what I mean, Miss McConnell?"

Still dazed from his kiss, Tara looked into his golden eyes, now dark in the dim passageway. He was breathing heavily, as was she. He seemed to be fighting for control.

When he loosened his hold, she pulled away from him as much as she could given the cabin door at her back. "I see only a man who thinks he can take what he wants without asking."

"My point exactly, and you'd do well to observe it. There are men in my crew who would take more. Half the crew drools over you each time you're on deck. Not all would honor your virtue."

"I don't believe the men would harm me. Nate invited me to join them in song and Mr. Johansson watches over me whenever he and I are on deck. Besides, I'm not wearing a gown nor seeking to tempt any of them."

"You would tempt a man with those lips, that hair and that body no matter if you wore a grain sack, Miss McConnell."

She glared at him, not knowing whether he'd just paid her a compliment or insulted her. She wondered how tempted the captain had been that he should force his kiss upon her. She was certain he had enjoyed that kiss, that he was as attracted to her as she was to him. Still, it bothered her that she seemed helpless to deny him.

Taking one last look at his golden eyes in the dim light of the corridor, she muttered "Good night, Captain," and turning in his loosened hold, she hastily entered her cabin.

***

Nick cursed under his breath and slammed his cabin door. His only intention had been to frighten the girl into being sensible. This was a ship full of men and she was a woman who, even in breeches, would never appear the lad to his seasoned crew. Tara McConnell was too desirable for her own good. It wasn't safe for her to join in the men's entertainments. The bawdy songs would only give them ideas. The young men might worship her, but what he'd seen in the eyes of some of the older crew gave him pause. Not all were half in love with her as were John and young Billy. But the ones who were not knew him well enough not to go after a woman under his protection—whether Jake guarded her or not.

It had not been Nick's intention to fall under her spell again. It had all started with that song she sang. Her voice had, indeed, been that of an angel. He would not soon forget the lilting sound. And the old tale of love realized too late caused him to brood about what regrets he might have one day if he let the right woman slip through his fingers. It certainly hadn't been Caroline. He could see now he'd been blind to her real character. She had flirted, teased and acted the simpering miss, declaring her love while planning a future with another man. No, he was well rid of that flighty piece. She'd made love to him one day and accepted the invitation to become a peer's wife the next. Perhaps it was precisely because he so valued honesty that he found his pleasure in the arms of women with experience. Better an honest whore than a lady who lies.

Tara McConnell was another matter, a rebellious young innocent he very much wanted. And she was ever before him, pitching in to help his crew with their work, stitching up the wounded and showing poor Billy how to do something. He had to admit she didn't treat any man as beneath her. Unlike Caroline, her nose wasn't in the air or covered with a perfume-soaked handkerchief. Only yesterday, he had come up on deck to see her blacking the guns.

Striding toward the prow, he had stumbled upon her and his gunner.

"Miss McConnell, just what are you doing?"

She looked up from the deck where she sat blacking one side of the gun while Charlie rubbed the metal polish on the other side. Made of soot and oil, the mixture stunk up the deck, but it assured the guns would not reflect the sun and give away their position. With the possibility of encountering the pirate, he was taking no chances.

Her long tawny plait had fallen over her shoulder and she tossed it back, smearing the side of her face with the black grimy substance as she did. It only made her more winsome.

"I should think that is obvious. I'm helping Mr. Wilson."

"Yes, I can see that. But it's unseemly."

"Not to me. It's a task like any other. I may not be able to lift a gun but I can black one." She grinned at Charlie, telling Nick they'd already had such an argument and the gunner had lost. Nick didn't like it, not one bit, but short of confining the hoyden to her cabin, he supposed he'd have to tolerate it. If she wanted to blacken her face along with his gunner, so be it.

"Do not linger long here, Miss McConnell. You're distracting my men." He had seen the older members of his crew pausing in their work to watch the girl. And Smitty was scowling from where he polished the brightwork. She seemed oblivious to their intrusive stares. He was not.

"As you wish, Captain," she said, going back to her work. "I'm almost finished anyway."

It had riled him the chit could be so troublesome—though even smeared with soot she was a beauty.

He had returned to his cabin, where he shuffled through the charts until he found the one he sought. Checking their course, he had been pleased to realize they were only a few days out of Bermuda, where he'd planned to stop for provisions.

"There will be a new crop of rats for you, Sam," he had said to the cat lounging on his desk.

The men would be happy, too, with a night in port and the pleasures that awaited them there.

Now, after tasting Tara McConnell's lips once again, he had to ask himself, what of his own pleasure? There were women in St. George and Hamilton who would greet him with welcoming arms, but the prospect suddenly had little appeal. Instead, his mind conjured the image of a long tawny plait moving against a well-shaped backside.

He knew he would not sleep well that night.

* * *

Tara walked along the deck looking for a place she could offer her help. As she passed by Mr. Wilson, he looked up from where he was cleaning one of the guns, his sun-bleached hair blowing about his tanned face.

"Morning, Miss McConnell."

"Morning, Mr. Wilson. The guns are looking fine."

Mr. Wilson cast her a smile, obviously pleased someone had noticed his workmanship. "Thanks to your help with the blacking polish." The day before when she'd helped him at blacking the guns, Tara had thought it odd that the gunner was preparing for trouble. It caused her to wonder why a merchant ship would be carrying such guns. Did the captain expect to need them?

"Is there a reason you spend so much time with the guns lately?"

His smile faltered and his gaze slid away. "One never knows."

His answer was evasive even if true. Her brothers had often remarked on the increasing numbers of pirates plying the waters of the Caribbean since the war. Could it be the crew was worried?

Tara continued down the deck, heading aft. Nearing amidships she spotted Jake walking toward her.

"Good morn to you, Miss Tara," he stopped to say. She didn't miss his wary glance toward one of the crew who had been surreptitiously watching her from the rigging where he worked a repair.

"It is," Tara said, tipping her wide-brimmed hat back to observe the clear blue sky. She had grown used to the presence of the tall, muscled bos'n and his nearly white blond hair. Her guardian angel. "I thought I might visit Nate at the helm. Do you have time to join us?"

Eyes the same color as the sky looked back at her with regret. "No. I must check on the lads. They're roustin' the anchor hawser and seein' it's clean and dry for Bermuda. Can't have rot settlin' in, *ja*?" She nodded and he left her to stride toward the fo'castle, where Tara had observed a small cluster of younger crew bent over the anchor cable.

Old Nate Baker and the first mate were at the helm when she arrived, Nate at the wheel and Mr. Ainsworth asking, "How does she bear?"

"She's been makin' good, still holdin' true at south by southwest, sir," answered Nate.

"Hullo," Tara said as she joined the men.

"Good morning, Miss McConnell," said Mr. Ainsworth.

"Mornin'," Nate echoed.

"Mind if I look at the log, sir?" she asked the first mate. She had been checking the ship's log when she first came on deck. It was a habit she'd picked up on her father's ship in the early days.

"Not at all." His mouth hitched up in a grin. "I see you do it often. Is it something you do on your brother's ship?"

"Yes, but it began even before I sailed with George." Tara leaned toward the binnacle and took the pegboard into her hands, noting the ship's speed and heading from the last watch change.

As she studied the log, she felt more than saw the captain step on deck. The sound of his boots on the planks as he neared sent a wave of heat flowing through her. Daring a glance at him, she saw black hair whipping around his face as he stood, legs spread, his back to the wind. He raised the mug he'd brought with him to his lips and set his piercing gaze upon her. "Miss McConnell, what brings you to the helm?"

Was he smirking at her? Surely he knew she was interested in all the workings of the ship. "I often join Nate at the helm early in the day. It might be you've slept through my visits."

Mr. Ainsworth chuckled and Nate rolled his eyes, discretely looking out toward the sea, but the captain's back stiffened at her inference.

"I have no need to explain my schedule to you, Miss McConnell," he said with a frown.

"Of course not, Captain." She had made her point and he had made his. She bid the men good-day and left for the galley.

Chapter 7

Nick watched his passenger disappear down the hatch, fascinated by her agility on a moving deck. Most women would struggle for balance. Not Tara McConnell. But then, the honey-haired hoyden was not like most women. Indeed, she insisted on appearing more a man than a woman, in her breeches and hat. Then another image appeared in his mind: Tara McConnell wearing a fetching blue gown nearly the color of her aquamarine eyes. It had revealed what her vest normally hid, reminding him she could be entirely feminine. She'd worn other gowns in the nights since she'd first joined him and Russ for dinner, each one bewitching. The kiss he'd stolen was never far from his mind. The taste of her lips and the feel of her curves pressed against his body haunted him.

As if he'd heard Nick's thoughts, Nate said over his shoulder, "She's not like the others, and ye'd best be rememberin' it, lad. This one's not there for yer pleasure."

Nick darted a glance in Russ's direction, but the first mate's attention was focused on whatever he was seeing through his spyglass.

"What makes you think I want her, old man?" asked Nick with good humor. He was enjoying his banter with the old salt, as usual, but somehow this was different, more personal.

"I see the way ye look at her—the whole crew's talking about the two of ye staring at each other. 'Tis like a keg of powder about to flame whenever you and the girl are on deck. A few of the older crew have been grumblin' about a woman aboard ship."

"Miss McConnell is an attractive young woman, Nate. And if you haven't noticed, there are few of those about until we reach Bermuda. The whole crew stares at her."

"It ain't the crew I be worryin' about; 'tis you, lad."

Nick passed Nate an amused look but he could see his old friend's warning was given in earnest.

* * *

The next morning, Nick was roused from a deep sleep while his cabin was still cloaked in darkness. The ship was rolling like a drunken sailor, flinging his body to and fro upon his bed. A mug left on his table crashed to the deck and a book left unsecured on his shelf joined it with a loud thud. He came instantly awake, his years at sea telling him what such omens portended. A storm was on its way. A big one.

Rubbing the sleep from his eyes, he rose quickly and dressed in the dim light of just before dawn. Anxious to be up on deck, he yanked opened his cabin door. A small shadowy figure swept past his boots and darted into his cabin. The huge white paws stood out like dismembered appendages as Dutch Sam let out a protesting yowl. Given the animal's usual habits, the cat was a bit early, but perhaps she was anxious at the coming storm. Animals sensed those things.

"The cabin's yours, Sam. Best stay below. It will be a rough one, I expect."

With a loud meow, the cat leaped onto the unmade bed, settled herself against a pillow and trained her probing green eyes on him. Why he felt scolded he couldn't fathom.

Nick skipped his usual stop in the galley for breakfast and hastened up the ladder. There was almost no wind, though the ship was rolling and pitching over huge swells.

Russ approached, his gait unsteady and a concerned look on his face. "I've called up the sleeping watch, Nick, so you'll have all hands at the ready."

"Thanks, Russ."

When the additional crew began scrambling onto the deck, Nick shouted, "Stow the loose gear and supplies. All guns into the hold!" The men acknowledged the order and hastened to the tasks. He was glad they'd have time to take the guns below. The task would take time, but they were equipped to do it and he wanted no unnecessary weight above decks.

Nick spotted his passenger working with Jake, Nate, John and Billy to rig manropes from fore to aft. If the coming storm, as his instincts told him, proved to be formidable, the long lines would be needed to keep the men from washing overboard. He was sure Nate had anticipated the need and begun the task before either Russ or he could make it an order. The girl, bent in concentration over her work, looked up, as if sensing his gaze. His gut tightened at the sight of her. Nate had been right. He couldn't help but stare at the picture she presented, her rounded backside in breeches and the long tawny plait reminding him she was a woman, a very attractive and vulnerable young woman. He hoped the hoyden didn't give him too much trouble when he ordered her to her cabin. The thought of her on deck when the storm hit was more than a little unsettling.

John Trent struggled to remain standing as the ship rolled, his injured leg obviously still paining him. He would be among the first Nick would send below decks.

An oddly colored light grew brighter around him, causing Nick to turn and witness the sun rising in a reddening sky. But in the west, clouds were just beginning to form on the distant horizon. "Russ, see that any who have yet to eat do so shortly. There will be only cold biscuits and dried beef after that. It may be a long while before the galley is reopened and McGinnes can put hot food in their bellies."

"Aye, Nick I will. You ought to take your own advice. I've already had breakfast."

Ignoring for the moment his first mate's counsel, and bracing himself against the rising swells, Nick spoke his thought aloud, "Since we are not far out of Bermuda, I'm thinking this could be a hurricane."

"Bit early in the year for that, isn't it?" asked Russ.

"True. But you know as well as I that there are always exceptions with storms, and if it isn't a hurricane, it's going to be one hell of a black squall, or perhaps a series of them." Nick studied the rising wind and the waves and consulted the barometer, which was dropping fast. The wind speed and direction and his experience told him there might be sufficient time to sail around the storm. He had to try.

"Set our course south, Russ, and see the lads put on more sail. I am going to try and circle around the storm, keeping it over our starboard quarter."

"Aye, will do. You going below?"

"Just for a short while. I want to check one of the charts and get some food. Can you see that all the hatches, save the centerline, are battened down?"

"I'll take care of it, Nick. Mr. Adams has already made sure the extra sails and storm-sails are ready." The *Raven*'s sailmaker, Augie Adams was conscientious so Nick was unsurprised the seaman had anticipated the need for extra canvas should the storm take some of their sheets and sails, a possibility Nick dreaded.

He made his way to where his passenger was working alongside Nate, straining to pull the manrope tight. She raised her head in question when he paused next to her.

"Miss McConnell, have you had breakfast yet?"

"Not yet, Captain," she said, returning her concentration to the rope. "I wanted to help Nate and Jake with this first."

"Mr. Johansson," he said, addressing the bos'n working nearby to secure the long rope, "I'm taking Miss McConnell below. You and the men finish this and then check the rigging. The lady may return but not for long. I want her below when the storm finally hits. Is that clear?"

"*Ja*, Captain. I see to it." Protective as Jake was of the girl, Nick suspected he welcomed the order. Nick was taking no chances with her safety. He intended to assure his peace of mind by locking her in her cabin.

Hearing the bos'n's words, his passenger stiffened, looking to rebel. "I can wait for breakfast, Captain. I want to help secure this line."

"And *I* want to speak with you, Miss McConnell. Moreover, as you may have heard, I've ordered all the crew to eat, and since you seem to feel you are one of them, I'll be treating you no differently. You'll be coming below with me."

Turning the rope over to Nate, who nodded his encouragement for her to comply, the girl sighed and silently followed Nick as he made his way toward the hatch leading to the galley. Crossing the deck was a challenge even for Nick as the growing ocean swells kept the ship lurching up and down. He looked over his shoulder to see the girl doing well keeping up, surefooted thing that she was. She had forgone her hat this morning, apparently anticipating the rising wind, and wisps of her tawny hair flew about her face. All Nick could think of was the need to keep her safe.

* * *

Tara sensed the captain was worried. She'd observed his serious demeanor when he'd first come on deck, his black brows forming a discernible frown on his tanned face as he gazed into the horizon, his ebony locks blowing about his head. It would take great skill to balance the need to add sail to try and beat a path around the storm against the mandate to bring down the sail before too much wind made it impossible. She marveled that he had chosen to try. She'd lived through storms with her brothers, the ones that tore up the seaboard and the ones unique to the northeast, and knew the close calls that would have to be made. It was she who had anticipated the need for the manrope, and Nate and the others had joined her in the task. What little there was of her gear was already stowed.

She followed the captain into the galley, the smell of recently fried bacon and freshly made coffee making her stomach rumble. McGinnes was bent under the worktable, securing supplies, sending up a great noise of clanging pots and pans with each pitch of the ship. Heat still emanated from the large black stove, but as Tara expected, the fire had been extinguished in anticipation of the storm. The stack of wood that usually lay beside the stove was gone.

Rising from his work, McGinnes greeted her. "Good-morn to ye, Miss Tara." And, tipping his head to the captain: "Skipper." Placing his large hands on the chopping board, he asked, "Is it food the two of ye be wantin'?"

"Whatever you can serve up, McGinnes," said the captain, "and you'll likely see a few more stragglers who have yet to be fed. I should think a half hour would be sufficient before you close the galley and switch to whatever cold food you have at the ready."

"Sure an' I was expectin' that, Skipper."

Tara placed one hand on the cook's worktable to steady herself against the pitching ship as McGinnes produced bread and butter and thick rashers of bacon he'd obviously cooked up in anticipation of a quick meal. Hungry from her morning work, Tara eagerly began eating. The bacon was still warm and tasty.

"Has Peter been here yet?" the captain asked as he snatched a slice of bacon off the plate.

"Aye, just left for your cabin. Here's yer coffee," the stout cook said, handing Tara and the captain mugs of the hot liquid. Tara wrapped her hands around the mug and lifted it to take a swallow.

"She's gonna be a big one, ain't she, Skipper?" McGinnes asked with a penetrating gaze.

"I suspect so," said the captain, stuffing another piece of bacon in his mouth and downing it with a swig of coffee.

"Aye, me bones tell me 'twill be a severe one." Then running his hand through his graying red hair, he said, "I could've sworn I sighted a mermaid in the wake last eve. A bad omen, to be sure, always a sign of coming storms and rough seas."

"We've weathered many a storm, old friend," said the captain. "We'll weather this one, mermaids or no."

He may be stern at times, Tara thought, but it was clear the captain cared for his crew. McGinnes had mentioned he'd known the captain's family for a long while, and she could see there was trust between them.

They soon finished eating, and the captain directed her down the passageway. When they arrived at her door, he gestured her on to his cabin.

"Miss McConnell, a word if I might?" Seeing his stern countenance, she did not refuse.

Peter was just finishing the captain's bed when they stepped through the doorway. The gray cat jumped up and settled herself onto the freshly made linens, her tail twitching.

"Hullo, Miss McConnell," Peter said. Then to the captain, "Is there anything more you require, sir?"

"No, Peter, thank you. But see that you stay below when the storm descends. I'll not have you slipping overboard."

"But, sir, I should be bringing you food to keep up yer strength and your rain cloak when it gets wet on deck!"

"If I want for food, I'll send word, and you can ask Mr. Ainsworth for a good place to stow my greatcoat topside."

"Aye, Cap'n, and if'n ye need me after that, I'll be with McGinnes or helping with the pump crew."

She was glad Peter would be one of those below decks. Many cabin boys would wait upon their captains during a storm, bringing them dry clothes and coffee. She admired the captain for letting the slim youth remain below. Smiling at Tara, his dimple on full display, Peter departed, leaving them alone.

"You wished to speak to me, Captain?" Tara tried to remain calm, but being alone with the man who had kissed her twice was, to say the least, disconcerting. She tried not to look at his bed. He leaned against his desk, crossing one booted foot over the other. The sight of his black hair tousled by the wind and his golden eyes framed by his dark eyebrows scattered her thoughts.

"I want you below decks and in your cabin when the storm hits, Miss McConnell. You might even want to tie yourself to the bed so you're not tossed to the deck. It's going to be rough."

"This isn't my first storm, Captain." Surely the man must know by now that she could pull her own weight with the crew.

"Perhaps not, but it's your first storm aboard my ship, and I'll not be taking any chances with your safety. Is that clear?"

"Perfectly." He was staring at her as if he wanted to say something more but then shrugged and pushed away from his desk. A sudden lurch of the ship brought her careening into his chest. He steadied her with his hands on her upper arms and, for a moment, stared into her eyes, then at her lips.

Instead of letting her go, he drew her more tightly against his chest, his golden eyes boring into hers. "I don't seem to be able to resist you this close, Miss McConnell."

She felt the heat between them as he bent his head and kissed her, a kiss as fierce as the storm she knew was fast approaching. Her body seemed to come alive as his arms held her. His lips lifted from hers.

"I wish I had time to show you more, but right now my ship requires my attention." He set her away from him and, reaching for a chart from his desk, swept up the rolled document and strode from the cabin as if the ship wasn't rolling beneath his feet.

Tara gripped the edge of his desk to steady herself, and not just because of the swells that had the ship constantly dipping and lunging. *Damn the unmitigated gall of the man!* What made him think he could kiss her whenever he wanted? More troublesome still, why had she let him?

Holding her hand to her still-racing heart, she could feel the scrape of his unshaven face on her chin, could still taste his kiss and smell the scent of salt air and man. She scolded herself ten times over for allowing the man such liberties, for not fighting harder to convince him she was not his toy for the taking. The fact she had not fought him disturbed her, and left her slightly amazed as she realized, to her dismay, that she was beginning to like the arrogant captain.

* * *

They were making good progress, now sailing south, when several hours later Nick searched the darkening sky to see a great mantle of billowing gray clouds, stirred by fierce winds, encompass the ship. Though he had made good time in his effort to circle the storm to the south, he grew sullen at the realization that they would experience at least the edge of nature's fury. Nick gave the order to begin reefing sail, furling from the top down.

"Douse the t'gallant!" Russ shouted, his voice thin above the wind. The crew scrambled to comply, and Nick was satisfied they were dropping sail before it was too late. Just as they finished, the clouds opened up, pelting them with a cold, hard rain.

"Reef the topsail, fore and main!" Russ shouted to be heard over the descending storm.

When the wind rose, Nick braced himself and said to Russ, "We'll fly only the storm trysail, the headsails and the one jib, and hope that will suffice." Those sails would provide balance, allowing the *Raven* to run before the wind, or at least he hoped it would be so.

To the seamen working amidships, Nick shouted the order, "Set a sea anchor!" And leaning closer to Russ, he said, "I fear we're going to need it." He hoped the spare sail rigged as a drag-chute would hold the ship's bow into the oncoming waves and stabilize her so when the full fury of the storm struck, the ship would resist turning sideways into the large waves.

His eye caught Tara McConnell helping his bos'n and two seamen secure the topgallant along the bulwark, and knew it was past time she should go below. "Miss McConnell, go to your cabin!" He had to yell to be heard above the wind blowing the rain sideways. When she didn't move, he added, "Now!"

She looked up at his shouted words. "But, Captain!" Her tawny hair hung wet against her head, darkened by the rain running down her face. A water sprite come aboard his ship to taunt him. There was no way he'd allow the fetching creature to stay above decks, where the raging storm and pitching deck could toss her into the sea.

Ignoring her protest, he called to the blond bos'n, who stood as tall as Nick but with much greater bulk, "Jake, escort our passenger to her cabin." Making his way to the bos'n, he pressed into Jake's hand the key he'd kept against this moment. "Lock her in."

The blond giant latched onto the girl's elbow, and with an eager "*Ja*, sir, I see to it," took her below. Nick didn't allow himself to look at her face; the anger he was certain he'd see in her aquamarine eyes would be one more unneeded distraction.

Though it was only midday as told by the sounding of eight bells, a foreboding darkness settled around them. On the distant horizon, which he and Russ had been carefully watching, a bolt of white lightning streaked from the black clouds through the sky to the ocean, a silver finger of the gods pointing to the depths below. Thunder, like an exploding cannon, rent the air. As the rain continued to fall, Nick donned his greatcoat and Russ did the same. The rain, now coming in torrents, joined the huge waves crashing onto the deck, causing the ship to reel. Nick braced himself on the quarterdeck, preparing for what he knew lay ahead.

"Mr. Trent, go below," he ordered, "and see if our sailmaker needs help checking the water in the well. I don't want you up here again. Mr. Adams can send me reports. Join the pump crew on your watch."

"Aye, aye, sir," said John as he carefully made his way to the centerline hatch, the only one left open because it was sheltered by a protective housing.

Nick turned to Russ. "Find out if Smitty or Nate needs help at the helm and whether they've secured the wheel."

"I saw to the wheel earlier, but I'll check on the men," Russ said as he wiped water from his eyes with the back of his hand.

"Good man," acknowledged Nick, watching his first mate reach for the manrope and make his way to the helm. The rain, coming down in sheets, blurred Nick's vision, making it impossible to see clearly, but he thought he saw Russ join the two experienced seamen, who were manning the wheel despite the waves crashing over them.

Nick studied the ship as it rode the large waves, pleased the topsail, fore and main had been reefed and that the sea anchor was holding them steady.

Suddenly lightning filled the sky, streaking down on all sides and rendering the deck nearly as bright as day. The waves breaking onto the ship appeared to be on fire with blue flames dancing on the white crests. He tilted his head back, unsurprised to see blue flames atop the two mastheads, making them appear like two huge candles.

"'Tis St. Elmo's fire!" yelled Smitty.

"My God," said Russ, rushing to Nick's side, "I've never seen the like of it."

"I've seen it once before, in the Mediterranean on my father's ship. One of his Portuguese sailors called it *corpo santo*, holy body. Some seamen say it's an omen."

A puzzled look appeared on Russ's face. "For good or for ill?"

"Depends on who you ask," Nick shouted to be heard as a wave crashed over them. He wasn't worried about the appearance of the blue flames, but he knew many on his crew would not see the phenomenon as benign. Sailors were a superstitious lot.

The crew stopped their work to stare in wonder at the blue flames. Some were startled. Others were clearly frightened. "Don't be concerned, men," Nick shouted, trying to be heard above the violent storm. "The blue fire won't harm the ship—or you."

Smitty encouraged the others. "Aye, the cap'n is right. I've seen it before."

A gigantic wave—fifteen feet high—rose up and crashed over the deck. Nick turned to Russ and yelled, "Get all those below we can spare!"

Chapter 8

Locked in!

Tara's mind screamed the words.

Furious, she paced five steps, turned and paced five steps back. Still angry, she took a deep breath and threw herself on the bunk, forcing her mind to think logically. Her brothers would never have imprisoned her in a cabin. Not even her father on his most ill-tempered days would have done such. She should be considered a valued member of the crew, not a passenger who had to be restrained! Why couldn't Captain Powell realize that simple truth?

Tara flipped to her back, bracing her arms against the outer edge of the bunk to keep from being tossed with every pitch of the ship. She took another deep breath, thinking of all that had happened that morning. Grudgingly, she admitted Nicholas Powell was a careful captain. She could see him in her mind's eye, standing firm on the deck, his hands on his hips as if defying Neptune to do his worst. The captain had wisely guided the crew in the steps necessary to ready the ship for the storm. She respected his knowledge of when to set more sail and when to start strapping things down for the blow that had finally come. He'd carefully watched the signs of the developing storm as the wind carried them south, setting a course that gave them every bit of wind he could squeeze from the sails until the gale rose and the rigging could take no more.

Though she knew he was desperately trying to outrun the storm, he had not overset the masts and rigging. At just the right moment, he'd sent the crew aloft to douse and furl sails. She had watched her father making the same careful, astute decisions on many occasions.

The comparison between the *Raven*'s captain and the man she all but worshipped was a startling revelation.

Tara tried to imagine what was occurring on deck as the ship pitched and rolled. The wood creaked and the waves roared as they crashed onto the deck above. She could only hope they'd come through it. After a few hours she was exhausted, and during a lull in the storm, she began to doze in and out of sleep.

Sometime later, she awoke to a loud boom, followed by the sound of splintering wood and a resounding thud on the weather deck, which sent shudders throughout the ship. The *Wind Raven* suddenly pulled hard to port. In the dark it was frightening. But Tara knew those sounds. A mast had broken. She could help! And she needed to ensure that if the ship were to go down, she would not be trapped like a rat in the hold. But how could she get out?

Her thoughts scattered, frantically seeking an answer. And then she remembered the time she'd lost the key to her jewel box and had to use a hairpin to pick the lock. With a lurch, she rose from the bunk and felt for her trunk. Finding it, she pulled one of the pins from the case where they were stored. Quickly, she braced herself against the door and, feeling in the dark, found the lock and applied the pin, all the while trying to keep her hands steady.

The ship lurched, spilling her onto the deck. Frantic, she clawed her way back to the cabin door, the pin still clutched in her fingers. It took another try and another pin to finally conquer the lock, but at last the door swung open. She lurched toward the centerline hatch, her body slamming against the bulkhead every time the ship pitched with the storm. Clinging to the ladder, she climbed and made it through the hatch.

On deck, everything was in chaos. Despite the rain, the smell of spent lightning and wood smoke hung in the air. There were shouts of men trapped beneath downed rigging. Waves a dozen feet high broke over the rails, flinging men into the broken rigging of the foremast, its top half missing. The sails and rigging had fallen over the rail leeward, dragging the ship in that direction like a great sea anchor. It was then she saw Billy, trapped in the fallen rigging swept over the side. He was struggling to climb over the downed rigging back to the rail.

"Man overboard!" a seaman shouted as the men battled to get to the young sailor, but a huge wave crashed over the deck, driving them back.

Tara was closest to the young seaman and, she realized, Billy's only hope. Careful not to slip on the wet deck, she reached for the rigging, using it to make her way to the rail. The wind buffeted her and the rain soaked her shirt but she pressed on. Once there, she extended her arm toward Billy, whose face was frozen in terror. Waves washed over her making it difficult to see.

"Take my hand!" she yelled in the direction she'd last seen his panicked face. She reached her arm as far as she could, leaning over the rail while still holding on with one hand. Relief washed over her when she felt Billy's fingers tighten around hers.

The ship slewed around and the sails and rigging slipped farther into the water as the rough seas sought to claim them. Her one hand would not be enough to hold him. She had to get Billy up to the deck before the crew cut the lines and broken spars to save the ship. "Billy, hold on!"

She could feel his hand slipping. Desperate to get a better grip, she let go of the rail to reach with both hands. It was a chance she'd have to take that to save him she, too, might be swept overboard. Bracing herself against the rail, she screamed, "Take my other hand!" Suddenly Billy's hand was ripped from hers as she was grabbed from behind. Strong arms lifted her, hauling her away from the rail. The crew rushed in to cut the lines and Billy floated away. "Billy!" she screamed.

Locked in the arms that held her, the rain pouring down, she watched another huge wave crash over Billy. He fell away with the rigging and torn sails, his head bobbing in the choppy waters. Lost to the sea. "No!" she cried.

Tara felt herself carried down the hatch but was hardly aware of who held her until she was thrust into the captain's cabin and tossed onto his bed. The gray cat that had been sleeping there rose with a hiss and jumped to the deck.

"Why didn't you stay below?" the captain bellowed, his black hair wet around his face, his expression as thunderous as the raging storm.

"You let Billy go! You let him die!" she cried, tears streaming down her face.

"We could not save Billy, and in your valiant efforts, I almost lost you! I shouldn't even be down here now; I should be with my crew!"

Tara had never seen him so angry—but she didn't care. Billy, her friend, the boy from the Midlands who reminded her of the brother she'd lost, who tried so hard to tie a bowline knot, was gone forever. Shivering, she wrapped her arms around her middle and let the sobs come.

The captain reached into a chest, withdrew a blanket and tossed it to the bed. "Get out of those wet clothes. I'll not have you dying of lung fever." He spun around and strode to the door, then looked back over his shoulder. "This time you'll not find it so easy to gain your freedom, Miss McConnell."

He stalked from the cabin, slamming the cabin door behind him. She heard a key turn in the lock and a block of wood slide into a slot as he barred the door.

Tara slumped onto the bed.

Gone. Billy was gone. All who sailed accepted the risk such a thing could happen and she'd seen men lose their lives before at sea, but never one so tender of years, so hopeful in his desire to be more than his beginnings would have made him. Tara cried until her tears ran dry. She cried for Billy and she cried for her brother Ben. Both were gone from this life.

Shivering with cold, weariness and grief, Tara was too numb to move. Her clothes were indeed soaked through with both rain and salt water, for she'd worn no cloak when she'd hastened above decks. The captain had demanded she shed her sodden garments, and though she knew he was right, she had no dry clothes of her own to put on. It seemed she had little choice but to see what she might find in his sea chests. Remembering where they stood against the bulkhead, in the dim light the flashes of lightning provided, she slowly worked her way toward them.

The ship was still tossing in the waves like a child's toy thrown into a raging river.

Feeling one chest before her, she raised its lid. She could see and feel only books. In the second chest, she found the shirts and breeches that had been her goal. The captain was tall and well muscled. It was hopeless to think they would fit, but perhaps she could wear one of his shirts. He might leave her here all night. And if they did not survive the storm, what mattered the garment she wore? Peeling her wet shirt, vest, breeches and chemise from her, she used one of his shirts to dry herself off. Then sitting on the wooden planks of the deck, the ship creaking and moaning with the storm, she donned one of the captain's shirts, rolling the sleeves to her wrists. She stood, feeling the fabric fall to just above her knees.

Weary and emotionally spent, Tara crawled into the captain's bed. Her body ached and her eyes burned from the salt and the tears. After hours of agony remembering Billy's face as she'd last seen it, weariness claimed her and she succumbed to sleep.

* * *

Nick stepped onto the deck and back into the weather that was tearing apart his ship. God, he'd almost lost the girl. The thought terrified him, his anger at her the proof. Another moment and she would have joined Billy in the sea.

The loss of the young seaman had been a tragedy, one Nick deeply regretted. It was a somber few men who remained on deck to do what they could to keep the ship afloat. He'd told the boy his efforts to adjust the rigging could wait till the storm subsided. But Billy, eager to do his part, ventured into the rigging while the storm spewed its vengeance. Nick had seen the look of terror on the lad's face as the lightning struck with a bright flash. Even in the rain, Nick could smell the singed wood from the severed mast as the lad and the rigging went over the side.

The storm was not over. Nick and his crew had fought it for most of the day and now would come the night, not that there would be much difference since the dark clouds pouring down rain left them mostly in darkness, save for the lightning and the white foam of the crashing waves. Wet and bedraggled, he encouraged himself with the thought they had come this far. His instincts told him the storm was lessening.

"Get some rest, Russ. You can relieve me at the next watch."

"Probably wise or neither of us will be any good tomorrow. Are you sure you don't want Nate to take command of the ship for a while? He just came up for his watch."

"No, but you can send up some food. I'll stay to fight the storm with the crew until you return. I'll want to see Mr. Adams for the sails we'll need, and you can tell our carpenter we'll be getting a new mast and spars in Bermuda, but until then he'll have to make do."

In the hours that followed, the storm gradually ebbed and, as best they could, Nick and his weary crew cleaned up the mess left on deck by the broken fore topmast and torn rigging. The storm's persistence meant much of the crew's work would be left for the next day.

It was midnight, the end of the first watch, when Nick gratefully heard eight bells sound. The storm had dwindled to wind and light rain as Russ relieved him.

"You look terrible, Nick. I'll take over. Get some sleep."

"I'm overdue, I know, but I wanted to make sure we'd survived the storm and the ship was not taking on more water than Mr. Adams and the lads could handle."

"I checked as I came up. They are doing well. The crew is relieved the worst is over, but they're dispirited at losing young Uppington. Many have expressed their appreciation of your skills in seeing them through this one."

Nick thanked God they'd weathered the edge of the hurricane, for he was convinced that's what it was. "We were fortunate, indeed, though we'll be limping into Bermuda. By my rough calculations, we should arrive late tomorrow."

Exhausted, Nick descended the ladder to his cabin, the aft hatch now open again. He wondered what he'd find. Peter met him at his door, wanting to resume his duties, but Nick sent him to bed.

He lifted the bar, unlocked the door and stepped into darkness. He'd allowed no lanterns before, but since the storm was waning, he felt it safe enough to light one now. He shed his great coat and found the lantern on his desk. As the flame flickered to life, he looked for his passenger—and found her curled up in his bed, the cat nestled against her. Golden tendrils of hair spread across the pillow, having fallen out of her plait. Dutch Sam raised her head to briefly gaze at him, then closed her eyes and settled back to sleep.

Weary to the bone, Nick shed his cloak and damp clothes and donned a fresh shirt, which fell to his thighs. He normally slept naked, but he didn't want to frighten Tara McConnell, though on second thought, he suspected little would frighten the girl. And he was not giving up his bed for what few hours of sleep would be his.

He slipped between the sheets and felt the softness of her warm body as he curled around her. Giving into a compulsion, he wrapped his arm around her waist and drew her into the curve of his body. As infuriating as she had been, it felt right to hold her. He had been frightened for her safety and he wanted her close. He wanted more. But his complete exhaustion allowed him only to join her and the cat in sleep.

* * *

Warmth behind Tara interrupted her dream as she slowly opened her eyes to sunlight. A hand stroked her belly then slid up to her breast, where it cupped the warm flesh and sent a shiver of pleasure coursing through her and a delicious ache to her woman's center. She had no memory of any such feelings before. It was disturbing and wonderful at the same time. Excitement flowed through her veins as her mind shed the dreamy state she'd been in.

With sudden awareness, she realized the hand moving over her was no dream.

She blinked against the sunlight streaming in through the windows—of the captain's cabin. *Him.* It was the captain behind her, the captain who had been stroking her belly, the captain whose hand touched her breast!

A sudden knock on the door caused the man caressing her to moan as if he, too, was shaking off sleep's stranglehold. *Why, he doesn't even realize it is me, the oaf!* What had been a new and tender experience for Tara, one that had her body thrumming, had been merely a dream to him.

Tara flung herself from the large shelf bed, relieved the ship's motion had returned to a gentle rocking. Her eyes darted around the cabin in search of her clothes. They were lying where she'd left them in a pile next to the captain's sea chests. Reaching for them, she discovered they were still wet. She dropped them to the deck and grabbed a pair of breeches from the captain's still-open chest.

"Cap'n?" said Peter's familiar voice from the other side of the cabin door. "You awake yet?"

Tara hastily donned the breeches and tucked in the captain's shirt she still wore, rolled the pants to her ankles and reached for a piece of rope she found lying next to the chest to secure the loose pants at her waist. She pulled on her boots, salt encrusted from the storm.

The captain's voice, husky from sleep, spoke from the bed. "Yes, what is it?"

"'Tis Peter, sir. Did you want me to bring you a breakfast tray?"

"No, Peter, I'll be up…shortly," the captain replied, his voice growing stronger. Tara heard the cabin boy walk away, the sound of his footfalls fading in the passageway.

She considered the man whose hands, a moment before, had been touching her. His eyes were at half-mast, his face bore dark stubble and his black hair was in disarray as he slowly rose to a sitting position and dropped his bare legs over the side of the bed. His long fingers skimmed through his hair, the blue stone in his ring flashing in the morning light. He was more handsome than a man rising from bed had a right to be.

"Excuse me, Captain, but I'll be leaving now," she said and walked in determined fashion toward the cabin door.

"Miss McConnell!" His deep voice, like steel, cut through the air, bringing her to a sudden halt.

"Yes?" She turned to face him, and their eyes met. Tara thought she saw a glimmer of guilt in the golden eyes.

"Have you just awakened?"

She wouldn't admit to being in his arms only moments before. "No, but it took me some time to find dry clothes and dress, given my choices. I hope you don't mind that I borrowed some of yours until I can change in my cabin."

His eyes surveyed the shirt and baggy pants she'd made use of. "No, I don't mind."

"My own clothes are still wet." Tara was anxious to be away from the man, his bed and his roving hands.

"All right," he said, his eyes devouring her from where he sat on the bed. "I will see you on deck."

* * *

Still a bit disoriented, Nick remained on the edge of his bed trying to remember. Wasn't he just holding a warm willing woman in his arms? Perhaps it *had* been a dream. But the scent of jasmine, though faint, was real enough. And the body of the woman he'd held through the hours of sleep was still vivid in his mind. Soft and warm with curves in all the places they should be. Tara McConnell and he had shared a bed—that much was certain. It was rare for him to spend even part of a night with a woman, but it felt right to have Tara McConnell lying next to him. And seeing her this morning in his clothes was temptation itself. He had to remind himself once again she was an innocent.

Bermuda could not come soon enough.

The gentle rocking of the ship told Nick the storm had indeed passed. Rising, he padded to the window and peered into a cloudless blue sky. *Thank God it's over.* The memory of young Billy's loss caused a tightening in his gut. He would have to deal with that this morning. Though the sea had claimed the lad's body, a memorial service was in order to remember him and offer prayers for his soul.

Nick washed and shaved, then donned fresh clothes and boots. He could smell coffee calling to him as he strode to the galley.

"Morning, McGinnes. Is the galley restored to order?" Nick gazed around the warm galley, comforted by the smell of sausage cooking and the coals glowing in the stove as the cook pounded a large pile of dough.

"Sure an' all is as she should be, Skipper. Here," he said, shoving a mug of coffee and a plate of sausages at him, "put this in yer belly."

"Looks most appealing after the cold fare of last eve." Nick reached for the plate. The dried beef he'd chewed during the storm was long gone. It was good to feel his ship returning to normal.

The cook kneaded the lump of dough, scattering flour over the chopping board as his green eyes peered up at Nick from beneath thick copper brows. "Miss Tara was just here for her morning porridge."

"Oh? Did our passenger weather the storm, do you think?"

"She's takin' young Billy's death hard, but that one is as at home on the sea as ye are, Skipper. Half fairy, if ye'd be askin' me. Sure an' she might even be a *leanan sídhe*. Ye'd best beware."

Nick had heard the cook's Irish tales so many times this mention of one of his fairy creatures was not surprising. That McGinnes would recognize another Irish soul in their passenger was also to be expected. Amused but distracted by the morning's tasks that lay ahead, Nick asked, "What do you mean, 'beware'?"

"Now don't be makin' light of it. Truth is if a man can refuse the *leanan sídhe*, she will be his slave, but if he loves her instead, he will forever be hers. But he must pass through death to have her," the cook said, plopping the lump of dough into a pan.

Nick barely recorded the words *must pass through death to have her*, still focused as he was on the tasks ahead.

Turning to go, he said, "We'll be having a service for young Billy soon if you'd like to join us." It wasn't an order but McGinnes would come. All the men would be there for the lad.

* * *

Six bells sounded in the early hours of the morning. Tara stood on deck with most of the thirty crewmembers gathered under the clear sky in solemn assembly. Captain Powell stood on the quarterdeck, all eyes upon him, and opened the Bible he had carried above decks. It seemed to her his face had gained a line or two since the voyage began, though he stood tall and straight on the gently rolling deck as he began to read.

"They that go down to the sea in ships, that do business in great waters; these see the works of the Lord, and His wonders in the deep. For He commandeth, and raiseth the stormy wind, which lifteth up the waves."

Tara recognized the passage from the book of Psalms and the familiar verse he read next from Genesis.

"In the sweat of thy face shalt thou eat bread, till thou return unto the ground; for out of it wast thou taken: for dust thou art, and unto dust shalt thou return."

He closed the book and his eyes. "Father, you have taken the lad Billy Uppington. We ask you to receive his soul." Opening his eyes, the captain searched the faces of his crew. "The storm reminds us that we are in the Creator's hands, and today we remember a young seaman who was with us for only a short while. He wanted to prove himself worthy and always tried to do his best."

The men murmured their agreement. "*Ja*, he was a good lad," said Jake.

"He often helped me oil the guns," echoed Charlie Wilson, looking out at the dark blue sea.

"Sure an' he loved the Oirish stories of the fairies," said McGinnes wistfully.

"He helped me with my chores for the cap'n," whispered Peter, his voice wobbling as he stood next to Tara. "He was my friend." She reached her arm around his shoulder in comfort.

"The lad could be counted upon to help mend a sail," Augie Adams said in an emotion-filled voice while twisting his hands. "Never turned away from my need for help." His reddish-brown hair blew around his face and Tara thought she saw a tear roll down his cheek. "He was a good lad, that one."

"Captain," Tara interjected, "can we take up a collection for his family in Derbyshire? I'd like to contribute. Billy was very concerned about them as the times there have been hard."

When the captain nodded, Nate offered, "I'll see to it, Cap'n."

"I'll add what is collected to his pay," said the captain, "along with my own help for his family." Then, looking to his first mate, "The *Raven* can carry it back along with his gear." To Tara, he said, "That was a fine idea, Miss McConnell."

Tara admired the way the English captain had handled the sad event. His dignified manner conveyed his respect for the lives of his men, and it was clear they appreciated it, knowing he would have done the same for any one of them.

For all of the morning, the crew remained in a serious mood. She thought perhaps they were thinking of their own short days upon the earth. She had seen it before, the death of one causing the many to consider their mortality.

About noon, the repairs began in earnest, at least the ones they could make before they docked in Bermuda, now less than a day's voyage away, according to what Mr. Ainsworth had told her. Tara watched as the ship's carpenter and a few of the crew cut away what was left of the broken spars and the dangling rigging. Working together, they created a temporary masthead for the broken foremast by tying a spar to the stump of the old mast. Mr. Adams, together with Jake and several other seamen, rigged temporary sails that would allow them to make port.

As she watched the men working, the first mate came to stand by her side. "There's fine cedar to be found in Bermuda. We'll get the new mast there," he encouraged. "They'll have the sheer hulk fitted with poles and pulleys to lift the new mast into position."

"My brothers told me Bermuda cedar is used for the sloops and schooners they build, which are supposed to be especially good for sailing upwind."

"They are right," said the first mate, his sun-bleached blond hair blowing across his forehead, "Bermuda's ships are famous for being swift; their privateers have taken many prizes. The captain has often admired them, though it is the American ships he covets most."

Tara was aware from the tales her brothers told around the fire when they'd returned from battle that the privateers of Bermuda, sailing their fast sloops, had captured more than two hundred American ships. She was glad the captain had not sought to have one.

* * *

In the afternoon when she went below to her cabin, Tara noticed the captain's door ajar. She knocked, and hearing him say, "Come," gingerly stepped over the threshold.

"I wanted to tell you how grateful I was for this morning's service for Billy, Captain."

He looked up from his charts and for a moment said nothing, his golden eyes fixing her with an intense stare that brought back the memory of his warm hands moving over her body only hours before. She wondered if he, too, was remembering. She was beginning to feel uncomfortable when he finally returned his gaze to his charts.

"It is the least we can do for a man lost at sea," he said. "He isn't the first who has gone down in a storm, and unfortunately, he will not be the last."

There was something comforting about his presence as he sat with his sleeves rolled up and the gray cat lounging on the corner of his desk. It all seemed so normal, as if the storm had never happened, as if Billy were still up on deck. But when the golden eyes once again looked her way, they were hard. She wondered if he'd forgotten how to smile. The cares of the ship and his men, she knew, weighed heavily. Behind those eyes she sensed roiling emotions and wondered at their source.

Reminding herself of her other reason for coming to his cabin, she asked, "Captain, might I borrow a book? I've exhausted my own supply."

"Certainly. There are some on the shelf," he said, gesturing to the bulkhead, "and more in the chest over there." He pointed to the other side of his cabin.

She went first to the shelf, feeling his eyes follow her. There she found some volumes she would expect to see in any captain's collection: almanacs and tables for figuring the ship's position, his Bible from the morning's service, *Pilgrim's Progress* and two medical books by Richard Reece, M.D., including a *Medical Guide for Tropical Climates Particularly the British Settlements*. At the end of the row of books was a small polished wooden box that she knew held a ship's chronometer. Her brother George had one just like it.

On a second shelf she found books that surprised her. Among them were works by the social philosophers Hume, Descartes and Adam Smith, and Joseph Priestley's *Experiments and Observations Relating to Various Branches of Natural*

Philosophie, as well as the writings of Lavoisier. Tara knew of Priestley because her tutor told her the philosopher and theologian had moved to America as a result of his support for the French Revolution. As for Descartes and Lavoisier, if, as Nate had told her, the captain's mother was French, perhaps he also read French. It seemed he was, like her father, a well-read man. For a moment her thoughts wandered to the man who had been the guiding light in her life, and she again felt fear for his health. Was he still living? She prayed she would find him well when she arrived in Baltimore.

Crossing the short distance to the chest where she'd fingered the volumes the night before, she found a wealth of novels, including Sir Walter Scott's *The Black Dwarf*. At the bottom of the chest lay six volumes of Gibbon's *Rise and Fall of the Roman Empire*. She took the first one and turned to face him.

"It appears your interests in reading are varied, Captain. I did not expect so grand a selection."

"As you must know, Miss McConnell, long voyages and smooth seas allow much time," he murmured, still bent over his desk.

His midnight hair had fallen onto his forehead, making her wonder what he'd been like as a boy, the one his father's crew had dubbed "the Raven." And for a moment she considered what it would be like to love the man he'd become. Startled by her own thoughts, she shook her head. What had she been thinking? Had she forgotten what the English did to her family? Had she forgotten about Ben?

"Yes, Captain. A long voyage certainly leaves time for reading and reflection."

Chapter 9

His hands steady on the ship's wheel, Roberto Cofresí gazed into the distant horizon, seeing the white dot he knew was a sail. Pulling the spyglass from his waist where he'd tucked it into his sash, he studied the ship coming closer. *Sí!* A merchant ship riding heavy in the water, weighed down by her cargo.

Quickly he shouted orders that would set the *Retribución* on a course to intersect the path of the other ship. When the ships came within sighting distance, as if unaware of the danger, the merchant captain unfurled the British Red Ensign. The action only amused Roberto, who gave his quartermaster, Portalatin, the wheel. Taking his hatchet from his waist, he began sharpening the blade as his schooner drew ever closer to its prey.

A few moments later, sheathing his axe at his waist, he shouted, "Raise the standard!" The black flag ascended the mast, the skull and crossbones making clear his intent. The ships were so close he could hear the shouted orders from the merchant captain to his crew, carried on the wind, ordering his men to their fire muskets at the *Retribución*. Roberto was astonished. To fire on a pirate ship was asking for a violent end—and all who sailed the sea knew it. It was also for naught. The muskets fired, sending white smoke into the air and shot toward them, but so bad was their aim that all the balls fell short of their target, landing in the water feet from his ship.

"Very foolish, *mi capitán*," Roberto uttered under his breath as his ship closed the distance to the merchant ship, now his for the taking. The English crew struggled to reload their muskets and Roberto yelled the next order.

"Run out the guns!" Familiar with the course of action that would follow the raising of his standard, his crew anticipated him, bringing the guns into place even as he'd issued the order. "Fire!" Roberto ordered. The air filled with white smoke as the balls shot across the small distance, ripping through the sails of the English merchantman and shattering the mast. Confusion reigned on the defenseless ship, its bell clanging loudly in alarm, as Roberto ordered the *Retribución* brought smoothly alongside the other vessel. Slinging grappling hooks over the rail, his crew locked the two ships together in a dance that would lead only to death.

Hatchet in hand and followed by his men, Roberto boarded the English ship in a single leap as her crew still fumbled with their muskets. Pieces of mast and spars, fractured by the *Retribución*'s guns, lay strewn about the deck along with wounded and dying men. The English captain stood amidships, covered with soot from the blast, bravely but ignorantly urging his crew to meet the pirates' concerted attack. They stood not a chance.

Letting loose the blood-curdling screams that sent most seamen over the side, his pirates raised their knives and machetes and cut a bloody swath through the English crew. Wielding his hatchet like an extension of his arm, Roberto sliced through the air, sending his sharpened blade into the neck of the English captain before the man could even fire his pistol, nearly severing his head. Blood splattered in all directions as the defeated captain fell to the deck of his ship. In a matter of minutes the deck was consigned to the dead English crew, Roberto's pirates standing over them with satisfied smiles.

"Take a few men below and search the hold for any who hide," Roberto called to Portalatin, whose dark head rose above the others. Not one man of the English crew would be allowed to remain alive, though Roberto need not tell his men any women or children would be spared. He had a code all his men knew they defied at their peril.

"Aye, Capitán," Portalatin acknowledged as he wiped the blood from his face. It was not his.

Roberto sent the rest of his crew below with orders to bring up the cargo and valuables. A few minutes later, his quartermaster stepped through the hatch with a boy in tow.

"Found this one in the captain's cabin," said Portalatin.

Roberto considered the cabin boy standing on the deck, his white blond hair blowing in the wind and his wide blue eyes full of fear as he looked at the bodies lying on the deck and then at Roberto. Surprise was reflected in the boy's eyes when he realized the pirate captain who stood before him was as fair in coloring as any of the English crew.

Speaking in English, Roberto said, "Have no fear, boy. You will live." And though he rarely explained his actions, he added, "Your captain was a foolish man or he and his crew would yet be alive." It should have been unnecessary for him to take the life of the English crew. Most merchantmen were not prepared to fight a pirate, nor so stupid, but if one was he would quickly learn El Pirata Cofresí was not to be thwarted.

The boy said not a word, his wide-eyed gaze turning again toward the carnage around him.

Once the search for treasure was completed, Roberto's crew began to transfer the captured goods to the hold of their ship. He watched the procession for a few moments, gratified to see the large wooden chests being carried aboard, then placed his hand on the shoulder of the frightened boy and gently guided him across the plank.

From the deck of the *Retribución*, Roberto gave the order for his crew to bore holes below the waterline in the hull of the

English ship to sink her. He would not take the damaged merchantman as a prize and had no intention of the hulk being found. The boy would be blindfolded until he reached his destination.

Roberto glanced again at his bloody hatchet and shrugged. He had little regret. It was enough he had spared the boy. With every ship he seized, he felt the satisfaction of having gained some measure of justice for the crime committed by the English against his family.

The rape his sister would never forget.

He could still see the tears streaking down Juana's beautiful face, the bruises on her tender flesh, the torn dress and the shame in her eyes. He had only been a boy, but a burning rage had taken hold of him that day. The vicious slap across his face and the hard abuse he had received from the English sailors when he'd ignorantly sought justice from their captain had only hardened his heart for the retribution he would one day seek.

A seething anger, unabated in the years since, still burned within him. A sardonic smile crossed his face as he watched the merchant ship sink. Aye, the *Retribución* was aptly named. The merchant captains who plied the waters of the Caribbean Sea, save for the Spanish, feared El Pirata Cofresí, while the people of Cabo Rojo called him *héroe*. Sharing their seized treasure with the poor families of Porto Rico, the crew of the *Retribución* put food in the bellies of the island's children, and for that they were revered and protected.

He set his hands on the wheel, turning it to the south as the sails above him billowed with wind, carrying his small, fast schooner into Mona Passage lying between Santo Domingo and Porto Rico. Today was a grand day, the sun beaming down from a clear blue sky, and in his hold a treasure of fine cloth, jewelry and silver. He was pleased.

Soon he and his crew would reach *Isla Mona* and the caves that were his *guarida*, his refuge carved deep into the high cliffs soaring hundreds of feet above the waves rushing to shore. The formidable sight always stirred him.

He smiled, thinking of the rich harvest of prize ships that the spring had brought. His people would fare well. But deep inside, Roberto felt a rising discontent. He had enough treasure. Now his desire was for a life with more meaning and a woman of his own.

"Capitán!" shouted Portalatin, rousing Roberto from his musings. "Do we stay the night?"

"No, we unload and sail to Cabo Rojo." Roberto intended to stow his spoils in the caves above the beach until he could arrange for their sale. It was his village that called to him. "I want to anchor in Boquerón. I have a taste for Juana's *empanadillas*." His mouth watered at the memory of the crescent-shaped turnovers filled with lobster and crab that were his sister's specialty. All of Cabo Rojo knew of his sister's cooking.

Casting a grin at his bos'n, Manuel, Roberto said to his crew, "Our newly wedded friend here must deliver the English boy to Father Antonio before he can hurry home to his bride."

The bos'n made no reply except to shyly gaze toward the approaching cliffs.

Portalatin laughed along with the rest of the crew. "Aye, he was little use to us today for his thoughts were only of the beautiful Maria."

"All will be well, Manuel," Roberto consoled. "I will send you to Father Antonio with silver enough for his coffers and the English boy's expenses, and afterward, Maria will be waiting for you."

His bos'n visibly relaxed and smiled.

Roberto gave the command to heave to as they slipped into the hidden cove, where they would lower the boat that would carry ashore the seized cargo. As he did, his eye caught the reflection from his boarding axe leaning against the base of the binnacle, its blade still dripping with the blood of the English captain.

**

Tara stood at the rail of the *Wind Raven* as the ship's bow parted the waters and glided toward Hamilton Harbor, the main port in Bermuda. Beside her, Mr. Ainsworth leaned against the brightwork and raised a spyglass toward the land in the distance. She liked the first mate with the easy smile and laughter-filled eyes. He was not so unsettling as his captain.

In the distance, Tara could see a swath of green rising from the azure blue waters. A glimmer from the spyglass the first mate held caught her eye and she turned to study it more closely. The first draw of the long brass device bore an inscription, though the script was too small to read from where she stood.

"That's a fine instrument you have, Mr. Ainsworth." Tara had seen many spyglasses—each of the men in her family had one—but this elegant polished brass, extending well over a foot, was exquisite.

"'Twas a gift from the captain," he said, handing the instrument to her.

She carefully accepted what was obviously a treasured piece and read the inscription: *To Russ, my right arm and friend. May you know only fair winds and following seas. Nick.* She took a quick look through the eyepiece and noted the clarity of the land she could now see coming closer. "A useful gift." Then handing it back, "Surely you earned it."

"The captain can be a generous man, Miss McConnell. I had only begun to sail with him on the *Wind Raven* when this showed up in my cabin, but we had long known each other, having both sailed with his father. We faced many battles against the French together, both for his father and then on Nick's ship when he got the *Raven*. And we are, indeed, friends. I hope it will always be so."

Tara had sensed the bond between the captain and his first mate and wondered about the captain's father. Was he dark and brooding, hardened by a life at sea like his son? Did he, too, create fierce loyalties in his men?

"What was it like sailing with the captain's father?"

The first mate seemed to think for a moment and then pursed his lips before answering. "It was never dull. Simon Powell is a skilled captain who was once a privateer. He is fair with his crew and devoted to his wife and his sons. It was a privilege to serve under him. I suppose to know the Raven is to know his father. The two are much alike, save the father has golden hair as well as eyes and his features are a bit more rugged. Of course, he has some gray now."

She had come to admire the captain's leadership so perhaps this was its origin. "A man not unlike my father," she said as her thoughts turned to the man who had raised her. Perhaps what attracted her to the captain were the qualities he shared with her father. She thought again. Though he did have a temper, Sean McConnell was not arrogant nor did he constantly frown and order her about.

Tara returned her gaze to the sea, hearing the sails above her filling with wind, the rigging straining, the masts creaking and the water rushing against the prow. She was so comfortable with the sounds of a ship underway they often faded into the background, but for some reason today her senses were keenly aware of the small noises that had always been a part of her life. And with them there was now a vague yearning for more, something that might wait just over the horizon. She was aware, even before her father had noted it, that her body was changing, taking on the form of a woman. Captain Powell and his kisses had only made her more acutely aware of this change. Not for the first time she wondered how long she could sail as one of the crew on her family's ships. Perhaps those days were coming to an end. She hoped not.

The day was sunny and over warm, causing her to be grateful for the wind that blew wisps of her hair across her face. She brushed them aside and settled one hand on the rail as her mind filled with memories of all that this island meant to her countrymen. She shuddered knowing she was entering the lion's den.

Less than three years before, the English Royal Navy had sailed from Bermuda to launch its attack on Washington. The American privateers, including her brothers, responded by seizing the unprotected cargo of Bermuda's merchant fleet. A few months after the English had burned the White House, they again left their base in Bermuda, this time to sail into Chesapeake Bay to attack Baltimore, Tara's home and the base of many American privateers.

Tara still remembered the night she'd stayed awake listening to the mortar shells exploding in the distance as the British attacked Fort McHenry. Rain fell in torrents and thunder rent the sky but she could still hear the bombs exploding in the night. All the lights were out in the city but the flare from the rockets lit up the sky. She and her family had not known until the next morning what a sweet victory was theirs. Mr. Key, a friend of her family, was so inspired by the sight of the American flag rising above the fort when dawn came, he wrote the poem "Defence of Fort McHenry" that had inspired them all. Pride welled in Tara's chest as she recalled how the Americans had rallied to repay the English for taking Washington.

"A beautiful harbor, is it not?" said Mr. Ainsworth, tossing her one of his many smiles.

Tara looked again at the sight before her. They had sailed closer to the island that was their destination. Scattered across the entrance to the picturesque harbor were many smaller islands with tree-covered hills. She could see mangroves, junipers and palm trees. Buildings rose up between the greenery, painted in pale shades of yellow, pink, coral and green. The white stepped roofs rendered the architecture unique, reminding her of her father's vivid descriptions from his early voyages to the island.

"Yes, I suppose it is beautiful, even if it is home to the English Navy in this part of the world."

"Surely, Miss McConnell, you must recognize the disagreement between our two countries is long over," he said with a teasing grin.

"My brother George would agree with you, Mr. Ainsworth, but then he is more pragmatic than I am. The memory of the war so close to home is still too vivid. I was just sixteen when the English attacked Baltimore and I shall never forget it." The words came with a shudder she was powerless to deny.

"Yes, I can well imagine that must have been frightening. But it is over now. There will be no more battles between our countries. The captain plans to introduce you to his friends in Paget, not far from the harbor. I met them last year. Some, though English, are quite fond of Americans and have been educated in your country. Oh, and you'll have a real bath and a comfortable room with windows. Now isn't that something to look forward to?"

Tara smiled. She would enjoy a real bath after weeks of being at sea, and a few days on land would not go amiss. "It certainly is, sir. For that, I will be truly grateful."

A few minutes later they entered the harbor, and Tara asked, "Will we be mooring close in?"

"That depends," said the first mate.

She turned to study the brown eyes of the enigmatic officer. "On what?"

The first mate looked toward the helm, where the captain had the wheel. "On whether the captain likes the wind he has enough to sail her straight to the dock with our makeshift foremast."

"He can do that?"

"He can. The only other captain I've seen do it as well is his father, who until his son surpassed him was the best merchant captain in England. There's no one like the Raven with a ship, Miss McConnell. 'Tis almost magical the way he handles the helm. Why, it's like watching a man with a—" He stopped abruptly and looked at her sheepishly. Tara could swear she saw him blush and realized what he'd been about to say.

"A woman? You were going to say like a man with a woman, weren't you, Mr. Ainsworth?" she teased.

He shrugged. "I was going to say like a man with a woman he loves."

* * *

Tara had watched in fascination as Nicholas Powell sailed the *Wind Raven* right into its berth alongside the dock, shouting orders to his crew to drop sails as they approached. Using the rudder and a few sails to gently guide the ship in, he'd ordered the last sails doused as the mooring lines were tossed to the dock. The maneuver had been so smooth he'd made it look easy, but she knew it was not. After the crew's loud cheer for their captain's mastery of his ship, and the praise for his expertise shouted from those standing on shore, the captain hied himself off to the dockside tavern with a group of his men. Tara supposed after what they'd all endured it was a gesture of good will for the captain to lift a tankard in toast to their deliverance from the storm.

Mr. Ainsworth had suggested she should be dressed in feminine attire when the captain returned in a few hours' time so that she would be ready to leave the ship. For the few days they'd be in Bermuda for repairs, fresh water and supplies, she and the captain would be staying at the home of a wealthy merchant, the Honourable Francis Albouy and his wife, Ann. The first mate had explained it was a high honor to be Mr. Albouy's guest as he was a member of His Majesty's Privy Council, the leadership of the colony's government. He was also the supervisor of the marine militia, having sailed during the war with France. When she'd predictably stiffened at his mention of an English naval man, the first mate had assured her Mr. Albouy was a jolly soul and heartily welcomed guests to his home even, he said in laconic manner, Americans.

In eager anticipation of seeing more of the island, albeit the den of the English lions, Tara had once again donned the frippery of a debutante that would have made Aunt Cornelia proud. She'd managed to pin her hair up in simple fashion, and the gown she wore was the traditional white muslin with a sash the same azure blue as the waters of Hamilton Harbor.

Once she had put her gown to rights, she went up on deck to stand at the rail, the ribbons from her bonnet blowing in the breeze. It was late afternoon, though the sun was still strong in the sky, when she looked toward Front Street just in time to see a few of the crew from the *Wind Raven* emerging from the tavern. Mr. Smith and Mr. Wilson were teasing young John Trent as they walked along together. She was happy to see that the young seaman no longer limped. Behind them was Captain Powell, with a rare smile on his face and his arm draped around the shoulder of a raven-haired woman in a crimson satin gown whose arms were wrapped around his waist. They obviously knew each other well, and why that disturbed Tara she didn't want to consider.

Tara turned her back on the pair ambling toward the ship. The captain was a man like any other man and had been confined to a ship for many weeks. Of course he'd have a woman in a port he frequented.

Old Nate sidled up to her as she strolled to the starboard side of the ship. The old salt must have been observing her because as he lit his pipe he said, "Chloe's been after the captain fer years, lass. Don't let it bother ye. He don't take 'er seriously. He's just being friendly."

"If you're referring to that woman draped over him like a sodden cloak, why should his being *friendly* with the likes of her bother me?" Tara silently chided herself for sounding like a harpy.

"I ain't saying it does, but if'n ye think he's involved with the girl, he's not, leastways not so it matters."

"I see." Tara felt embarrassed at the comfort Nate's words brought her. The old man saw too much, or perhaps, Tara conceded, she revealed too much. Besides, Nate's statement didn't mean the captain wasn't bedding the woman. She did not want to think the English captain had a woman stashed away somewhere. She would prefer to think he had no woman at all, however unrealistic that might be.

When she heard the captain's boots step onto the deck of the ship, she turned, relieved to see he was alone. "Ah, Miss McConnell," he said, striding toward her, "aren't you a sight! Why, I hardly recognize you without your breeches."

Tara couldn't tell if he was being flattering or insulting, sincere or sarcastic. "Thank you, Captain. I trust that is a compliment."

"It most certainly is." Something about the way his eyes followed the curve of her gown where it was pressed against her body by the breeze made her very aware of the feminine manner in which she was dressed. She looked away.

"I've just ordered the carriage that will take us to Bel Air."

"Bel Air?" She returned her gaze to the golden eyes still focused on her.

Nate explained, "It's called that on account of the view from the balconies of the harbor and the dockyard, and the fair air that is around the house. They just finished it when we were here last year. It reminded me of some I've seen in the West Indies."

"That's because Albouy designed it to look like a West Indian plantation," said the captain. "Give me a few moments to change, Miss McConnell, and then we can leave. Did you pack some clothes for the next few days?"

Tara pointed to her small valise sitting near the aft hatch. "Just there."

"Good. By the time I return, the carriage should have arrived."

The landau carriage that pulled up to the dock was uncovered, though Tara would have welcomed the shade the cover would have provided. She opened her parasol to shelter her skin from the hot tropical sun and allowed Captain Powell to assist her into the vehicle. He wore a tall gentlemen's hat and a gentleman's clothing, so unlike the sea captain's garb he wore on board ship. They might have been on their way to Hyde Park if it weren't for the tropical setting. Pulled by a pair of grays, the carriage provided a comfortable ride as they traveled to the estate of his merchant friend.

Tara stole a glance at the captain's elegant fawn-colored breeches stretched tight across his muscled thighs as he sat next to her. He was so close they were nearly touching. It sent a shiver of excitement through her. His tanned hand with its long fingers rested on his knee. Even at rest, he had the power to intimidate her, and to draw her to him, especially when she was dressed as she was. The frippery made her feel more vulnerable to his virile masculinity.

"I imagine we'll have some time before the evening meal to refresh ourselves," he offered. "They always expect me to arrive coated with salt and in need of a wash."

"I am so looking forward to a real bath," she remarked, for a moment forgetting it was not a topic she should have raised with a man. He laughed and the sound of it was so surprising she turned to him to see the unusual mirth in his eyes. "I don't think I've ever heard you laugh before, Captain."

"You'll hear more of it tonight, I expect," he said, flashing her a bright smile, his teeth white against the bronze skin of his face. "If Albouy is true to form, it will be a merry group at his table." Nicholas Powell was a different man off his ship, Tara decided, as if a heavy burden had been lifted from his shoulders. She wondered just how different the captain would be once they arrived at their destination.

A short while later, the carriage climbed a hill and circled around a wide drive to stop in front of a grand two-story home, a confection of pale pink graced with white shutters and a long gallery with white lattice railings that wrapped around on both floors. Like the other homes she'd seen since they sailed into the harbor, it was crowned with a white stepped roof. "Why do the roofs look like stairs?" she asked.

"The white limestone roofs are designed to catch water. Have you never seen them before?"

"No, not that I can recall."

"Well, here they are a necessity. There is no fresh supply of water on the island save for rain. The roofs collect rainwater that is then stored in cisterns."

"How clever."

He offered his hand to help her down from the carriage just as a servant in livery approached and pulled out a step for her foot. "Thank you, Tom," said the captain.

The servant returned his smile. "Yes, sir, Cap'n Powell."

The captain nodded and continued his explanation. "The islanders are forced to prepare for the weather they face. The roofs are often coated with turtle or whale oil to provide weather-proofing, and the walls are strengthened against the hurricanes that can arrive without warning."

A portly man dressed in fine clothing emerged from the door of the large house, and despite his size, he nearly flew down the stairs to arrive at their carriage. Along with his light-blue coat, white silk waistcoat and tan breeches, the well-dressed older man wore a jovial expression as he brushed back his graying brown hair.

"Welcome to the shores of the Bermudas," he said, "and to our lovely islands!"

"Good-day to you, Albouy," said the captain, reaching out to shake the man's hand. Then darting a glance at Tara, he said, "Allow me to present Miss Tara McConnell, my passenger traveling with us to Baltimore." And to her, "This is our host, Mr. Albouy."

The older man took her offered hand and bowed as his girth allowed. "Welcome to my home, Miss McConnell. My wife, Ann, will join me in a moment to greet you." As if summoned, a small woman with light-blonde hair dressed in pale blue silk glided down the stairs. When she reached them, Tara could see the woman had a dignified air about her despite her diminutive size, in part from the gray that laced her pale hair.

"Captain Powell! It is so good to see you," the woman said. "We were delighted when you sent word you'd be able to stay with us a few days." Then looking at Tara, "Is this lovely young woman the passenger your note spoke of?"

"She is." The captain said and introduced Tara to their hostess.

"Miss McConnell, we are delighted you shall be our guest," Mrs. Albouy said, a sincere smile on her face. "I expect you will want to freshen up after so many days on a ship; I know I would. But after you do, we've a lovely dinner planned." She took Tara's arm and guided her up the stairs, and the men followed. "Some of our guests tonight are very familiar with America. I think you will enjoy meeting them." Tara tensed as the vision of an English naval officer telling stories of the attack on Baltimore swirled in her mind. She was relieved when Mrs. Albouy added, "Justice Esten and his wife, Esther, will be here as well as some other friends. Justice Esten studied law in America."

The servant Captain Powell had called *Tom* opened the door and they stepped over the threshold. A butler, standing just inside, accepted the captain's hat and her parasol. As she removed her bonnet, Tara noticed circles of thick glass embedded in the polished cedar floor.

"How interesting," she observed, looking down.

"Many of our guests are fascinated with those," said Mr. Albouy. "The glass tiles allow light into the servants' quarters and the kitchens below."

"We have a similar lighting feature on the *Wind Raven*'s weather deck," said the captain.

"My brothers' ships all have deck prisms," offered Tara, "but I'd never considered such glass for the floor of a home."

"That is where my husband got the idea," said the older woman. "It is so practical. The servants working below have the light they need most of the time without having to resort to candles or lanterns, which would make their rooms too warm, especially in the summer months. And if they need more light they can resort to a lantern."

The Albouys escorted them into the parlour. It was a bright room with walls the color of goldenrod flowers. Tara was surprised to see the polished dark wood furniture and coral brocade sofas set on a cream-colored carpet edged with pink and green flowers.

Unlike the outside of the house, the interior resembled the finest homes in Baltimore. Perhaps, she thought, they had followed the American colonies in their furnishings, being closer to America than London.

A servant approached with a tray, offering orange-colored drinks in glasses, each containing a long stem from a plant. Gingerly, Tara sipped the drink she'd been handed by Mr. Albouy, not knowing what it might be. Finding it to her liking, she took a large swallow. "This is very refreshing! What is it?"

"It's our own version of the swizzle, my dear," said Ann Albouy, "a local drink and quite a delight in these warm summer months. It's made with a bit of rum and the juices of limes, pineapples and oranges. The rest is water and sugar. To 'swizzle' the drink there's a stem from the allspice bush."

"Swizzle?"

"Yes, here I'll show you how it's done." She walked to the nearest table and set down her drink. "Just rub the allspice stick between your palms so it spins back and forth. See how it churns the drink?"

Tara soon followed suit and enjoyed herself immensely swizzling the golden drink till it frothed. "What fun!"

Captain Powell looked amused. Tara ignored him and happily resumed drinking more of the wonderful concoction. Stepping close, the captain whispered, "Take care, Miss McConnell, or you will soon be floating above us. The drink can get away from you."

Annoyed at what she took as a concern she might embarrass herself or him, Tara turned back to her hostess and took another large sip as the men conversed.

"You have a lovely home, Mrs. Albouy," Tara said. "It seems so much cooler here than the harbor in Hamilton."

"You are right, my dear. Bel Air has a breeze even in the worst days of our oppressive summer. It is why we love it here. Come; let us take our drinks to the veranda. It provides a lovely view."

The four of them walked through the opened front door, Tara next to her hostess. "Did Bermuda experience the recent storm?" Tara asked, curious to know, as the island seemed unaffected.

"We had enough of it to require workers to clean up many downed tree limbs the next day, though the reports suggest the worst of it was elsewhere."

Captain Powell must have overheard them because he interjected, "I think the storm might have hugged the coast of America. We only got one side of it where we were."

"Summer hurricanes are rare but not unheard of in these parts," offered Mr. Albouy.

"It was the worst storm I've experienced," said Tara, thinking of young Billy, "but my oldest brother, George, who sailed with my father years ago, told me of one that was even more frightening."

"Ah yes, they can be that," Mrs. Albouy admitted. Then smiling, she added, "But you are safely arrived and we can be thankful for that."

"Yes, well, a young member of the crew was washed overboard when a lightning strike hit the foremast," said Captain Powell. "All of us were saddened by his loss."

"Oh!" exclaimed Mrs. Albouy. "How dreadful."

"Yes, dear, but such things happen at sea," said her husband, patting her arm.

Still mourning Billy's death, Tara moved to the white lattice railing of the large covered gallery that ran the entire front of the house and wrapped around both sides. She looked down on a magnificent view below the hill on which the house was situated, and she felt her spirits rise. Green lawns and gardens bounded by trees stretched away from the house, and farther in the distance the entire harbor lay before them, including the small islands, which appeared as green tufts in a sea of blue. It was as if the storm had never happened.

She felt more that saw Captain Powell approach behind her.

"Could you have saved him, Captain?" she asked without turning to face him. Tara still felt a tinge of resentment at his having let the seaman slip into the sea.

"I don't think so. The crew had to cut the fallen rigging loose for the sake of the ship. In any event, I knew I could not save you both."

Tara inhaled deeply and slowly let out the breath. "I am sorry but I had to ask. I keep seeing his pleading eyes."

"You know as well as I that the sea claims some nearly each voyage."

"Yes, but somehow this time it was more real, more frightening, to lose a lad like Billy." *It was almost like losing Ben again.*

"I'm proud of you, Miss McConnell, for allowing our hosts to see your enjoyment of their home when you are still feeling the loss of the lad."

"It would be rude not to do so." Then, allowing her eyes to scan the harbor, she spotted the ship. "There's the *Wind Raven.*" Moored at the dock, gently rocking at anchor was the black-hulled schooner, its sails furled as if tucked in for the night.

She tried to ignore the heat of the captain's broad shoulder nearly touching her as he said, "She's beautiful, even with the beleaguered foremast." His voice conveyed his adoration for his schooner. If he loved any female, Tara thought, it was likely his ship. He was more tied to her than a wife. He might want Tara's body, but a man like him wouldn't give his heart to a mere woman.

"Yes, she is," Tara agreed. "Of course, I'm used to seeing the masts more raked and the hull a dark blue, but any schooner is an awesome sight, particularly when the wind has billowed her sails."

"I like that about you, Miss McConnell," he breathed in her ear. "A woman who understands ships is rare." Tara felt the tickle of his breath against her ear and shivered. This man, this English captain, was not so easily handled as the other men she had known. He was not father, brother or fellow crew. He was a mystery, and at that moment she wanted nothing more than to lean back into him.

The Albouys were at the other end of the gallery studying a rose apple tree overlooking the main lawn when she turned to gaze into the captain's golden eyes. "There are many things about me that are rare for a woman, Captain." Why she had said that she did not know. Perhaps it was the swizzle she'd hastily consumed—or perhaps it was the man himself. But she so wanted him to see her for herself.

"Certainly there is more to you than first appeared, Miss McConnell."

"Is there?" Tara asked, holding his gaze. She felt a current flowing between them that made the moment seem to last forever.

"Oh, yes, I think so," he said, sounding amused. Tara wondered if he'd had more of the drink than she had. Why was he being so nice? Was it being away from his mistress of the heart, his ship? They were so close she had only to tilt her head up to bring her lips to his. She resisted the urge and turned back to the sweeping view.

"You can see the dockyard from here, Miss McConnell," Mr. Albouy remarked from far on her left, where he stood gesturing into the distance.

She went to join the older man and his wife at the railing, searching with her eyes beyond the harbor to the farthest land she could see. She heard the captain's boots on the wooden porch as he followed. "Are those the masts of the English Navy's ships?" she asked.

"Why, yes," explained Mr. Albouy. "There are several in port now." He glanced at the captain. "Shall I tell her the history of the island where the dockyard is located?"

"If you must," said Captain Powell, leaning against the nearby white post, one booted foot crossed over the other, his arms crossed in front of his chest, one hand holding his half-finished swizzle.

"Well, it seems about two hundred years ago, a ship under the command of a notorious pirate by the name of Powell ran aground on the main island, and accordingly he was banished by the colonial governor to Ireland Island, where the dockyard now stands."

Tara looked at the captain to glean his reaction. She could see only amusement in his golden eyes.

"I've assured him," Captain Powell drawled, "no relation of mine would run his ship aground, but I must confess one can never be certain when it comes to pirates and privateers. My family has both." He smiled and his white teeth set against his bronzed skin and black hair gave him a rakish look, making it easy for Tara to believe he had descended from pirates.

Mrs. Albouy cast a glance at Tara's now-empty glass and said to her husband, "Francis, I think it's time to let our guests have a bit of a rest before dinner, don't you?" Then to Tara, "We have two guest cottages, my dear. You shall have one, and Captain Powell, the other. They sit right next to each other in the extensive gardens behind the house. Hannah, my maid, can show you to the one we've selected for you and see to anything you might require."

"Thank you, Mrs. Albouy. That is most kind." Tara felt a sudden trepidation at the thought of having a small guest cottage next door to the captain's abode, but then she realized it wasn't much different from their adjacent cabins on the ship. But here there was no Jake watching over her, no watchful eyes of the crew.

* * *

Nick had stayed in one of the cottages the year before, so he was unsurprised when their hosts saw fit to assign them to him and his passenger. But to be so close to the fetching Tara McConnell sleeping right next door would test his resolve. Already he'd turned down Chloe's offer to spend time in her arms, not something he would have normally done after a long crossing. It was not a good sign. He was a man who took his pleasure wherever he found it and quickly moved on. To be enthralled with the American was a mistake. But knowing that and resisting temptation were two different matters. How long he could keep his hands off her he did not know. It was a battle he feared he would lose, for he was certain he could seduce the young American. She was not immune to his kiss, nor to his touch.

He followed Tara McConnell and the maid, Hannah, as they veered from the path toward the cottage on the left. As the maid opened the door and Tara turned to bid him good-day, he said, "I will escort you to the main house in, say, two hours. Would that be acceptable?"

"I shall be ready when you call, Captain."

Chapter 10

When she dressed for the evening, Tara reached for the coolest gown she possessed, fine white muslin with a Pomona green sash and flowers of the same color dancing on the hem and short sleeves. For once she had been pleased at the pins that allowed her to secure her long, thick hair off her neck. It was too warm to wear it any other way.

Just as he'd promised, a few hours later Captain Powell knocked on the door of her cottage, offering his arm in escort to the main house.

"Good. You're ready," was all he said, but his gaze lingered on her gown and she thought she saw appreciation in his eyes. She was too stunned by his appearance to mind the lack of a compliment.

The cinnamon-colored coat fit snugly over his broad shoulders, an ivory silk waistcoat adding an elegant touch. Tight nankeen pantaloons left no doubt of his male virility. And his ebony hair, grown nearly long enough for a queue, fell in waves to his collar. Even her oldest brother, George, who took pains with his dress when he was at home, had never looked so well attired, nor so handsome. Tara had to force herself to don a calm demeanor when he held out his arm to her.

"Good evening, Captain," she said, placing her fingers on his forearm.

He covered her hand with his, causing the familiar shiver no other man's touch had produced. "Is your cottage acceptable?" he asked as they walked down the path toward the main house.

"Oh, yes. And the windows are a welcome change."

At her words, he smiled. "You could always read in my cabin aboard ship. The afternoon light is better there."

Tara was tempted to leave his offer hanging in the air but instead said, "I don't think that would be a good idea."

He gave her a brilliant smile. "Probably not." He seemed amused. Whether it was at her or himself, she could not tell.

They walked through the gardens, passing well-trimmed hedges and bushes that reflected careful planning. But against such well-groomed greenery there were also splashes of random color. Bright purple bougainvillea spread over the walls of one of a handful of outbuildings, including a stable she could see in the distance.

They entered the Albouys' parlour as the other guests were gathering. The happy chatter filled the room. It was a lively group that gathered that night in the elegant home called *Bel Air* on the small island nearly six hundred miles off the coast of the Carolinas. Except for the warm, tropical breeze wafting through the open windows and the scent of exotic flowers and the sea, they might have been in any parlour in Mayfair.

A servant paused before them and offered a silver tray bearing the golden drinks of which she was now quite fond. The captain took one and handed it to her. "Like these, do you?" he said, seeing her grin when she enthusiastically reached for the beverage.

"Yes, I do. They are the perfect antidote to the island's muggy weather. I shall have to introduce them to my family in Baltimore, as our summers can be wretched."

He was still chuckling as their hostess approached. "My dear," said Mrs. Albouy, "you must not allow Captain Powell to dominate your evening. I want you to meet our other guests. Besides, the good captain is already acquainted with them from his previous visits."

"If you don't mind, Mrs. Albouy," said the captain, "I'll leave you to the introductions. I see the governor across the room, and I must have a word with him."

"Of course, Captain Powell. You run along," their hostess said in kind dismissal.

The captain bowed briefly and departed. Tara felt the loss of his presence as she watched him join an older gentleman standing alone by the window. While Mrs. Albouy rattled off the names of the invited guests who had gathered in the parlour, Tara listened, counting three women and five men, including her and the captain. Eight for dinner, she mused. A nice intimate gathering of the English—and their one American guest.

The first gentleman to whom Tara was introduced was Mrs. Albouy's nephew, Samuel Harvey, who had been quick to approach when the captain left her side. Mr. Harvey's aunt explained he was a merchant like his uncle; both had spent time in the West Indies. Tara thought him of an age with Thomas, who at twenty-nine was now the youngest of her brothers.

"Miss McConnell," said Mr. Harvey eagerly, "how delighted I am to meet you." His eyes focused intently on her like a pirate spotting a golden doubloon. His quick smile was a nice compliment to his sun-streaked brown hair and sparkling green eyes. He was a fine figure of a man attired in the clothes of a successful gentleman, and his bronzed skin suggested he was often outdoors. Tara had noted there were few English on the island who were able to keep their pale skin so prized in London. Even bonnets and parasols did not prevent a bit of color from appearing on the women's faces.

Mr. Harvey took her offered hand. His touch caused no reaction, no shivers up her spine. As he bent to press his lips to her knuckles, she looked over his inclined shoulder to see Captain

Powell frowning in her direction. What could have set the brooding man off now?

"I do hope you will be staying long enough for us to get better acquainted," said Mr. Harvey, bringing her attention back to him.

"I believe we are here just for repairs to Captain Powell's ship. It was damaged in the storm. And I am anxious to return to my home as my father is unwell."

"Please accept my hopes for his recovery," said Mr. Harvey sincerely. "I would be delighted to show you around the island while the ship is being repaired. Then, too, my business often takes me to New England. Perhaps I might call upon you there?"

"Certainly. I would be happy to introduce you to my family."

At her words, Samuel Harvey's eyes lit up. "I would look forward to such a meeting."

Tara hoped he did not misinterpret her offer of hospitality. She would have offered the same to anyone under the circumstances.

Mr. Harvey remained at Tara's side as Chief Justice Christie Esten and his wife, Esther, joined them. Tara thought the judge to be in his mid forties and dressed as fine as any successful English barrister.

Ann Albouy introduced her to them. "Mrs. Esten is the sister of Captain Charles Austen's late wife, Fanny." Tara had no knowledge of the man and perhaps that failure was seen on her face, for Mrs. Albouy added, "He is an English naval officer, dear, who lived here for a time. His sister Jane is quite well known as the author of novels most beloved by the ladies."

"Perhaps you would like to read one of Jane's novels while you are here?" inquired Mrs. Esten, a woman of slight frame with dark hair and gray eyes, who was very obviously with child. "My younger sister was quite fond of them. She was married to the author's brother, Charles, and when she passed away, she left me several. I can have one delivered to Bel Air tomorrow, if you like."

Then as if to persuade her, Mrs. Esten added, "Jane's novels are favored by the Prince Regent, you know."

Though Tara knew the gracious woman thought it a grand endorsement that their monarch enjoyed the novels, Tara was more impressed that the other woman read them. "You are most kind, Mrs. Esten. Yes, I would be grateful for a novel that you recommend. I always welcome good books."

Mr. Harvey chose that moment to make his excuses and left to speak with Mr. Albouy standing nearby, but before he departed, he leaned in and with an eager smile said, "I will return shortly to escort you to dinner, Miss McConnell."

She watched him walk away and wondered why she'd never met such a charming man in London. Though English, there was a different air about him, a warmth to his personality that was lacking in the men of the *ton* she had met, who, for the most part, seemed like stiff dandies. Perhaps it was that he lived in Bermuda or that he'd been engaged as a merchant with his uncle. But for all his charm and friendly manner, Samuel Harvey did not stir her emotions like the *Wind Raven*'s captain. Nicholas Powell was a man cut from different cloth than any man she'd known, save perhaps for her brothers, and they were Americans.

"I was educated in your fair country, Miss McConnell," said Justice Esten, drawing Tara's attention back to the couple, who were sipping swizzles next to Mrs. Albouy. "I studied law at Yale." The justice seemed sincere in his praise for America as he told her stories of his time in Connecticut.

"You have two sons?" Tara asked the justice and his wife at the conclusion of one such tale.

"Yes, though we've another on the way."

"You can be glad you are free of our boys this evening," interjected Mrs. Esten. "John and James have been brought up properly to dine with adults, of course, but they have so much energy at eight and eleven. I'm afraid their squirming can be quite distracting."

"I do know what you mean about the energy of boys. I grew up in a family of boys," said Tara, liking the justice's wife. She could well imagine the woman as the happy mother of two rowdy sons.

Captain Powell chose that moment to return to their small group. As before, his presence rendered her flustered and unable to concentrate on anything but him. Such a reaction to the overbearing captain, over which she seemed to have little control, was unsettling.

"Miss McConnell tells me she's sailed as crew on her brothers' ships," said the captain. "Most unusual, don't you agree?"

The Estens's expressions showed surprise and Mrs. Albouy's eyebrows rose, but after their initial reaction of incredulity, Mrs. Esten smiled in apparent admiration. "What an unusual woman you are, Miss McConnell." She cast a studying glance toward the captain, who appeared greatly amused at the controversy he'd stirred.

"Americans are an adventuresome people, I know," said Justice Esten. "I've had the privilege to consider many my friends—and still do, notwithstanding the last unpleasantness between our two countries."

"I want to hear all about your time on your brothers' ships," remarked Mrs. Esten, "and all that you've experienced aboard Captain Powell's ship."

Tara was delighted the elegant woman was interested and realized at that moment that she was enjoying herself, despite the fact she was surrounded by people who were all English.

Before Tara could attempt to describe her experiences, William Smith, the governor of Bermuda, joined them. The distinguished-looking man with gray hair bowed slightly. "It is an honor, Miss McConnell. My wife, sadly, is unable to be with us this evening. I know she would want to meet you, but unfortunately she is down with a summer ague. Must have been all the rain that came with the recent storm."

"Please convey my hope for her speedy recovery," said Tara sincerely.

Captain Powell added, "Please do give Mrs. Smith my greeting as well. I am sorry to have missed her this trip." Tara could not but admire the captain's easy manner with the English gentry on Bermuda and the respect they obviously had for him.

"I will do that," said the governor. "And she will want all the news from your travels, Captain." Then turning to Tara, "What brings you to Bermuda, Miss McConnell, other than Captain Powell's ship, of course?"

"I am returning from my aunt's home in London. My father is ill."

The older man expressed his earnest desire that her father would soon recover, and Tara found herself charmed. Perhaps stepping into the lion's den was not so terrible after all. Indeed, the English men and women gathered around her acted as if the war of only a few years ago had never happened. Except to acknowledge the "unpleasantness," no mention was made of the attack on her home city. It might be they were just being polite, but she couldn't help liking these far-flung members of English society.

She took a deep breath and sighed, daring a glance at the captain, who turned his head at the very same moment and returned her smile, causing her cheeks to warm. As much as she might prefer to seem indifferent to the arrogant captain, she couldn't stop looking at him. And she remembered his kiss and the night she'd spent in his bed, albeit innocently.

After finishing their drinks, the eight dinner companions ambled through the arched doorway leading to the dining room. Mr. Harvey returned to escort her to her seat; however, Captain

Powell had already offered his arm, so Mr. Harvey, expressing his disappointment, trailed behind them.

Having seen much of the house already, Tara expected to see a dining room with furnishings like those in her family's home in Baltimore and was not disappointed. The wall paneling rising from the polished cedar floors was painted a deep rose, casting a warm glow on the long, oval, cherry wood table taking up half the room. Beneath it was an Axminster carpet of blue and red design. Above the table hung a crystal chandelier, and though there was still daylight remaining, all the candles were lit. At one end of the room there was a fireplace with wooden mantel and above that hung a gilded mirror. There must be only a few months of the year, she thought, when it was cold enough to warrant its use.

Tara was seated between Mr. Harvey on her left and Governor Smith on her right. The captain sat directly across from her, flanked by Justice and Mrs. Esten, leaving Mr. Albouy at one end of the table and his wife at the other.

In the middle of the table was a beautiful arrangement of tropical flora, dominated by a plethora of yellow hibiscus flowers with rose-colored centers the same color as the walls. Tara lifted her gaze above the flowers and was suddenly confronted with the captain's golden eyes staring at her from across the table. His intense perusal caused her heart to race wildly and her stomach to fill with butterflies. She looked away and allowed Samuel Harvey to distract her with stories of his merchant business in the colony of Demerara on the north coast of South America.

As they talked, the servants glided inconspicuously around the table, serving the guests a spicy, cold fish soup. Their presence recalled to Tara's mind the great number of people of African descent she'd seen on the island since arriving in Hamilton. It appeared to her they outnumbered the English. She wondered if they were slaves or free, for while some Maryland planters had freed their slaves after the War for Independence, not all had done so, and the states to the south still maintained large numbers for their plantations.

In her usual forthright manner, Tara asked the governor, "Are the servants free in Bermuda?" Tara didn't miss the captain's raised eyebrows. Likely he thought the topic unsavory, but the governor took up the subject with apparent relish.

"Ah, well, that is an interesting question, Miss McConnell," said Governor Smith, shooting a glance across the table at Justice Esten. "England ended the slave trade ten years ago, believing it morally wrong, but the existing slaves in Bermuda were not freed with that action, so no, not all the servants you see are free."

"It is my hope," said Justice Esten from across the table, "that soon we shall see to their freedom."

"Much of America is divided on the issue, as you probably know," she offered.

"That is what I have also learned from correspondence with my American friends," said the judge thoughtfully. "I admire those in Maryland who took action to free their slaves."

The conversation ended when the servants brought platters of thinly sliced roast pork surrounded by slices of mango, papaya and banana. Tara accepted a portion and took a bite to discover the meat had been flavored with an unusual blend of spices that was quite pleasing to the palate. Accompanying the pork was a dish of roasted sweet potatoes flavored with cinnamon.

"The pork is delicious, Mrs. Albouy, as are the sweet potatoes," Tara remarked. "Such an unusual blend of spices."

"You will find that in Bermuda we draw not only from England for our recipes but also from America and the West Indies. The spices come from the places Mr. Albouy and my nephew have traveled. And, of course, one can now obtain them in Bermuda.

"Do you like the taste of the islands?" asked Mr. Harvey solicitously. The young man, having been engaged in conversation with Mr. Albouy, suddenly turned his attention on Tara. Across from her she saw the captain watching the younger man.

"Why, yes, I do," said Tara. "It's so much better than the often-bland fare served in London." With these last words she looked at Captain Powell, letting him know she did not find England's food to her liking. The amusement in his eyes told her he might think the English food bland as well.

Mrs. Esten laughed. "You have the right of it, Miss McConnell. We have found once you become used to island food, there is no returning to the former way of cooking."

"The syllabub you will have for dessert," said Mrs. Albouy, "in addition to the traditional cream and sugar, contains mango jam and rum instead of brandy and white wine. It is different from the syllabub they serve in London, and we quite like the change."

"Indeed we do," said Mr. Albouy cheerfully, "perhaps too much for the fit of my waistcoat." He patted his paunch, which pressed tightly against the brocade fabric. "Mrs. Albouy oversees a well-stocked kitchen."

Turning to the captain, Justice Esten said, "Our conversation earlier about slavery on the island reminded me, Captain Powell: There is a boy about whom I would like to consult with you. He was born to a free man of color ten years ago, and though his mother was freed by her master prior to the boy's birth, there remains some confusion about the boy's status because the manumission papers were not found when the former master died. The boy and the mother are at risk for being sold."

"Ah, I see," said Captain Powell.

"I know the papers exist, as I helped draw them up. The boy's father has approached me, knowing of my sympathies, and based upon our conversation, I think it might be best if the lad were taken off island. Might you be in need of a cabin boy?"

"Not I," said the captain. Tara looked at him with anxious eyes, hoping he could help the boy escape an uncertain future. The captain held her gaze for a moment and then said, "However, it is possible my first mate, Mr. Ainsworth, will soon be wanting one, as he's sailing the *Raven* back to London from Baltimore and will have a separate crew." This was the first Tara realized the captain didn't plan to be aboard his ship when it left her home city, and she was curious as to why.

"Joshua is a fine Christian boy who is intelligent and eager to please," Justice Esten urged, continuing his conversation with the captain. "I can commend him to you. And from what I recall of my meeting with Mr. Ainsworth the last time you were in port, he is a gentleman who would do well by the lad."

"Should he prove acceptable to Mr. Ainsworth, Joshua can be trained by my own cabin boy on the voyage to Baltimore," said the captain to Tara's relief, "though we've an errand to attend to first in the West Indies." At the justice's raised brow, the captain added in a quiet voice, "One of Prinny's tasks." No more was said and Justice Esten did not pursue the subject.

Governor Smith mumbled under his breath something about it being past time to end the plague on merchant ships. Tara wondered what the errand, as the captain had called it, might be.

"When might I bring Joshua by to meet you?" asked Justice Esten.

"I must attend my ship tomorrow morning to see about some needed repairs and some painting before we leave port. Perhaps you could have him brought to the ship then to meet Mr. Ainsworth?"

"I might just bring the lad myself," said Justice Esten contemplatively. "My own sons have been pleading to see your ship." The justice faced the captain with a mischievous twinkle in his eye, as if daring the captain to entertain the two boys. "If you are willing to have two boisterous lads climbing over the decks of the *Wind Raven*, I'd bring them along as well."

"I think the crew is up to the challenge," said the captain, smiling confidently. "Sure, bring them along."

Satisfied that the boy Joshua would be seen to, Tara turned to Mr. Harvey to ask about his time spent in the West Indies. "Did you sail with your uncle?"

"Yes, in the sugar trade. And it is good we made our fortune during the war with France because sugar prices have since fallen."

"Why, yes," said Mr. Albouy from the head of the table, "that is so, but as England's demand for sugar grows, which I expect it will, our shipments will increase."

"My brothers would be happy to hear you say that, Mr. Albouy," said Tara, "as they ship sugar and molasses from the West Indies to the coast of America."

"And what do they ship to the islands, Miss McConnell?" asked the governor.

"Flour, meat and lumber, though not to Bermuda," Tara replied. "You have no need for our lumber with your fine cedar."

"Do they sail to England?" inquired Mr. Harvey.

"They have begun to, yes. It seems England is hungry not just for sugar and rum from the West Indies but also for America's tobacco, cotton and lumber for ships."

"Have you sailed with them to England, then?" the young man asked eagerly.

"I have, most recently last year when they brought me to visit my aunt."

"You are amazing, Miss McConnell," he said, his eyes growing bright with apparent interest. "It is most unusual for a young woman such as yourself to know so much about the shipping trade."

"My family's business has been my life until last year, Mr. Harvey. I find the shipping business fascinating." From across the table she heard the captain pause in his conversation with Justice Esten to look at her with an amused expression.

"Have you had a chance to see much of our island, Miss McConnell?" asked Mrs. Albouy from the other end of the table.

"Only what I could see from the carriage. We came directly from the ship."

"You simply must have a jaunt about before you sail. Elbow Beach, not far from here, is lovely, a wonderful spot for a picnic."

"I'd be pleased to show you around," offered Mr. Harvey. "'Tis no trouble to take an afternoon for a beautiful lady. It would be my pleasure."

Tara opened her mouth to accept his invitation, but the captain spoke first. "I'll see to it when I return from the ship tomorrow, Mr. Harvey. You needn't bother."

There was silence for a moment and Tara, not wanting to embarrass the young Harvey, said, "That is very kind of you, Captain." And then to Mr. Harvey, "I am most grateful for your invitation. Perhaps if we remain a bit longer, I could accept another."

Samuel Harvey gave a hopeful look in Captain Powell's direction but did not receive the assurance he obviously sought. "I'm hoping the time here will be short," said the captain, "only what it takes to set the new mast and acquire supplies. We should be finished tomorrow."

"Well then, I will await your pleasure, Miss McConnell," said Mr. Harvey. "But please do not hesitate to call upon me. I am at your service."

With that, the empty plates were collected and the syllabub set before them.

"Ah, my favorite!" exclaimed Captain Powell. Tara stared across the table at the man with the golden eyes who seemed very different from the one his crew called "the Raven." He was relaxed and clearly enjoying himself. And excited over a dessert. Recalling how he'd enjoyed the tarts served on the ship, she thought he might have a sweet tooth. His demeanor seemed lighter as well. Perhaps with the burden of the storm behind him and being among friends, he could be at ease.

As he began to eat, Tara couldn't help but observe how well-shaped his lips were, and her mind recalled the times they had been pressed to hers. Suddenly he looked up at her, and she realized her gaze had lingered too long. Looking down at her plate, hoping he hadn't read her thoughts, Tara focused on her syllabub. The dessert made with mango and rum was wonderfully sweet yet had a slightly pungent taste that was more appealing than its blander cousin. This island way of cooking pleased her greatly.

"Do you like it?" asked Mr. Harvey.

"Oh yes, very much," she said, and licked a bit of the delectable confection from her bottom lip, where it had strayed. As she did so, the captain paused in his eating and diverted his gaze to her, making her wonder if what she had done was improper. Perhaps not, for then he gave her a small smile and resumed eating.

When dinner was concluded, instead of the men retiring for port and brandy, and the women remaining for tea, the men joined the women on the veranda, where they together enjoyed drinks and the view of the harbor below. Captain Powell walked to where she stood at the gallery's railing next to Mr. Harvey. In the distance, Tara could see light from the lanterns on the ship.

"Do you suppose the men are singing on deck tonight?" she asked the captain.

"Depends on which men Mr. Ainsworth held back. Some will be having a night in town, singing bawdy songs in the taverns of Hamilton."

"Hamilton Harbor has some lively taverns to offer your crew," said Mr. Harvey.

"Yes, I've been to several," said the captain, making Tara wonder if he would visit one tonight once he'd seen her to her door. It bothered her that she should care.

The three of them were quiet as they watched the full moon rising low in the sky. The huge yellow moon seemed overlarge. Its light, cast onto the calm waters of the harbor, turned them into a shimmering lake of silver. It was one of the most beautiful sights Tara had ever seen.

"'Tis a beautiful night," she breathed.

Speaking quietly into her ear as Mr. Harvey turned to answer a question posed by Mrs. Esten, the captain said, "'Tis a beautiful woman who watches it." Tara shivered at his words and turned her head to glimpse his veiled expression. She had no time to thank him for the compliment because Mr. Harvey, having finished his brief conversation with Mrs. Albouy, drew her attention with a question.

"Do you live in Baltimore, if I might ask?"

Since Tara could see he was genuinely interested, perhaps recalling her invitation for him to visit, she told him. "I do. On a hill above Fell's Point on the north shore of the harbor." The captain seemed to show interest in her answer, perhaps because their destination was Baltimore, but he did not seek to know more.

The sky darkened to reveal the brightest of the stars and the conversation stilled once again. The guests strolled back to the parlour, where the Estens, the governor and Mr. Harvey, the latter with admitted reluctance, said their good-byes. Captain Powell offered his arm to escort her to her cottage, and they walked up the slight hill together in the moonlight.

"I'm glad you agreed to consider the boy Joshua for Mr. Ainsworth's cabin boy," she said, recalling their dinner conversation.

"I saw the plea in your eyes, Miss McConnell, but you should know I would have offered in any event. It was a small favor to grant a man I greatly admire and, in truth, Mr. Ainsworth will have need of the lad."

Then remembering what had raised her curiosity earlier, she thought to ask, "Will you not sail your ship back from Baltimore to London?"

"Not the *Raven*, no. I'm picking up a new ship in Baltimore." He said no more and Tara was reluctant to ask. There were many shipbuilding concerns at Fell's Point and other places around the harbor. But recalling Mr. Ainsworth's comment about the captain favoring the ships sailed by the American privateers, she wondered which shipyard had his order.

At her door, they paused as she reached for the handle. Turning to bid him good-night, the captain took her hand and, raising it to his lips, kissed the inside of her palm, his warm lips sending a wave of pleasure through her. Familiar shivers traveled up her spine as he kissed her wrist.

"Captain, whatever are you doing?" And suddenly Tara realized he did not intend to stop.

* * *

Nick had watched the American girl charm Samuel Harvey all evening and resented the younger man's growing attraction for what Nick considered to be *his* passenger. Tempted by her aquamarine eyes and honeyed hair glistening in the candlelight, Nick had wished they were alone. And when her tongue reached out to sweep a drop of syllabub from her bottom lip, it was all he could do not to reach for her. It reminded him of their first dinner in his cabin, when she had done the same with a cinnamon and raisin tart. Walking to her door in the moonlight, seeing her golden skin reflecting the light from the full moon, he could no longer resist sampling her sweet mouth.

Pressing his lips to hers, he held her close and breathed in the scent of jasmine as he felt her breasts press into his chest. She resisted for only a moment, and when he deepened the kiss, she responded. In her innocence she could not know how enticing she was. Her hesitant manner was alluring. He did not want to let her go. But when he finally did, he realized, with some shock, there was more to his feelings for the girl than simple lust.

Raising his head, he looked into her passion-glazed eyes. "I've been wanting to do that all evening."

Tara McConnell sighed but no words came from her kiss-swollen lips. He could see she was new to this, likely overwhelmed by what she was feeling. Perhaps he had been the first to sample her lips. The possibility pleased him.

Using all the determination of mind he possessed, Nick stepped away from the seductive young woman. He would take no more than kisses.

"Well then, until tomorrow, Miss McConnell."

Chapter 11

Tara awoke to sun streaming in through the lace curtains of her one-room cottage. It was brightly painted in colors of yellow and coral—a small but cheery room. The windows, left open in the balmy air, allowed the chattering birds to inform her she had slept later than she normally would aboard ship. As she lay in her soft bed staring at the ceiling, her mind was flooded with the memory of the captain's kiss of the night before. It had kept her awake long after she should have been asleep. She was wise enough to know that she should have been more disturbed by his actions than she was. She was worried that with each passing day, she was becoming more entranced with him. There could be no future with an Englishman, especially one who would likely want only a brief and very improper affair.

Rising to a sitting position, she reached for her brush on the side table and began to take the tangles from her hair. She had forgotten to plait it last night before she'd gone to bed. Perhaps it had been the captain's drugging kiss combined with the swizzle and the wine. A deadly combination to be sure.

She stepped from the bed and donned her dressing gown just as Mrs. Albouy's maid knocked on the door, offering her water to wash and a cup of tea.

"Is Captain Powell about?" she asked Hannah, in what she hoped was an unconcerned manner.

"No, mistress. He rose early and said he was leaving for his ship. Mrs. Albouy said to tell you he'll be back around noon to take you to Elbow Beach."

Tara thanked the girl, then quickly dressed in a muslin walking gown with a square neckline edged in blue ribbon. Tying the matching ribbons of her straw bonnet and tugging on her gloves, she walked to the main house. At the front door, the butler took Tara's bonnet and gloves and showed her into the dining room, where Mrs. Albouy was just eating breakfast.

"Ah, my dear, your timing is perfect! Come join me. There is bacon on the sideboard as well as fruit and egg dishes. The rolls and butter are here," she said, gesturing to a silver tray. The arrangement of yellow hibiscus flowers still graced the table from their dinner.

Tara took a plate and, fighting a yawn, began to select from the offerings on the sideboard. "I love the tropical fruits you have in Bermuda. There are so many varieties."

"Try the cooked plantains. They are very sweet and one of my favorites."

Tara studied the long, browned slices of pale yellow fruit dripping with butter and what appeared to be cinnamon and sugar. "Very tempting," she said and took some onto her plate.

"There are some other local specialties," said Mrs. Albouy. "You might like the conch fritters. They are quite good."

Tara decided to try some of the fritters along with her eggs. Joining Mrs. Albouy at the table, Tara settled in for a delightful meal as the footman poured tea.

"I thought perhaps after breakfast you might like to take a walk through our gardens. We've many unusual plants from the West Indies."

"Oh, I would like that," said Tara. "We have few tropical plants in Baltimore and it's been a while since I was in St. Thomas."

"There is a lovely fishpond, too, which you may not have seen, and a nice bench where we can rest and enjoy a view of the house."

With the slight Mrs. Albouy by her side, Tara strolled through the structured gardens of Bel Air. Like the food, they were a blend of England, America and the West Indies. Up a low, sloping hill were terraced walls, complete with pillars and a decorative iron fence surrounding the fishpond her hostess had mentioned. Lily pads sporting beautiful pink flowers floated on the calm green water. Though very different from those at her home in Baltimore, they reminded Tara of the bright colors of the rose garden her mother had once so lovingly tended.

"It is lovely here," she said, taking a seat next to Mrs. Albouy on the cedar bench with the high curved back. Yellow hibiscus like those gracing the center of the dining table grew in profusion on a long hedge behind the bench. The two women sat looking down on the large pink house and, beyond it, to the blue waters of the harbor. Birds of varied colors made their presence known, chattering away in the trees behind them. To Tara, who had just come through a violent storm, lost a friend in the process and was now struggling with her feelings for the captain, it was an island of much-needed tranquility.

"I see you have bluebirds as we do," remarked Tara.

"Yes. The first men coming to these islands brought many birds and animals that were not native. I'm told the bluebirds we have are a bit different from yours. The bird's breasts are more cinnamon in color and the blue plumage more purple."

Tara studied the bird on the hedge closest to where they were sitting, observing the differences, though they were subtle. The gardens here were similar and yet different from the gardens in London. "Your gardens are truly beautiful, Mrs. Albouy."

"I have lived my whole life in Bermuda," the older woman said, "and still I love the weather that allows us to enjoy the exotic plants all year long. It was my intention to combine the best of what I pictured an English garden to be with more unusual flowers of the island."

"I have lived my whole life in Baltimore," said Tara, "except for the times I've gone to sea and the last year I spent in London. But this last year allowed me to see those gardens you speak of. Still, yours are more exotic and quite unique."

"Thank you, dear. Captain Powell always remarks about our gardens. England has beautiful gardens, of course, but nothing quite like ours."

"Have you known Captain Powell long?" Tara asked as her thoughts turned, once again, to the enigmatic man who acted the harsh captain one moment and kissed her with such care the next—and for the first time last night had called her *beautiful*.

"For a few years, yes, since he first began coming to Bermuda, I should think."

"I was told he was a privateer for England before he was a merchant sea captain."

Mrs. Albouy's next words confirmed what Nate had told Tara. "Yes, he and his father took many French ships as prizes. The Prince Regent was most pleased, I understand."

For a while longer, they sat on the bench enjoying a companionable silence and then, at Mrs. Albouy's suggestion, meandered through the gardens. They arrived back at the main house just as a messenger arrived. "A package for Miss McConnell from Mrs. Esten, ma'am," said the footman, dipping his head.

Tara accepted the small package and opened it to find a book. The cover read, "Pride and Prejudice, by the author of Sense and Sensibility." It was the promised novel written by the sister of Captain Austen. Inside the cover she found a note:

My dear Miss McConnell,

As promised, here is one of Jane's novels you might enjoy.

Sometimes first impressions can be wrong. You might consider giving Captain Powell an opportunity to prove himself.

I do not believe you will be disappointed.

Most sincerely,

Esther Esten

Tara wondered just what it could mean and why Mrs. Esten thought she had the wrong impression of the captain's character. Could the English captain be anything other than what she'd observed him to be in the weeks she had known him? Could he be more than an overbearing, but competent, captain, and what the *ton* called a rake? Her brother George had warned her of such men when she'd left for London. Could Mrs. Esten really be recommending him to her?

* * *

Seated in the parlour an hour later, Tara heard the voices of boys at play and hastened to the front gallery to see Captain Powell flanked by what she surmised were the Esten sons, since they looked very much like their parents. Both had the dark hair of their father and the finely drawn features of their mother.

Captain Powell smiled up at her from where he stood at the foot of the stairs. "It seems we have companions for our outing to Elbow Beach." The two boys stopped their gallivanting to stare up at Tara.

"Miss McConnell," the captain said in what Tara took to be mock formality, "allow me to present James and John Esten.

James," he turned to the older boy on his right, "and John," he said to the younger boy, "make your bows to the lady." Tara came down the stairs and the boys very properly bowed to her.

"I'm delighted to meet you," she said, greeting the two boys, who were dressed in breeches and shirts, absent their jackets, obviously prepared for a day of play in the sun. "Did you enjoy your morning on Captain Powell's ship?"

The boys' wide grins told her all she needed to know. "He let us climb into the rigging!" exclaimed the older James.

"Well, that's more than he will allow me," said Tara, looking at the unapologetic captain, who seemed amused at her comment. "Is all well on your ship?" she asked him. The boys scampered up the steps in front of them.

"The mast will be swayed up tomorrow so we can leave the next day with the tide." He looked relieved to know his ship would soon be restored to rights and they would be on their way. Apparently the mast was taking longer than he'd believed the night before. Tara was glad they would soon resume their trip; she was anxious to see her father. She had even considered seeking a ship sailing northwest from Bermuda. But since she had already defied her aunt in leaving without her maid, she was reluctant to leave the one ship her aunt had insisted she take. Moreover, she could not very well travel alone on an unknown ship. Those were perfectly good reasons—her *only* reasons—to stay with Captain Powell and his ship. Or so she told herself.

They walked up the steps to the front door. "If you agree, Miss McConnell, I thought to pack a picnic lunch and take the boys with us to the beach. The rascals can romp while we enjoy the scenery."

"Mrs. Albouy's cook is a step ahead of you, Captain," Tara replied. As they entered the house, the butler took the captain's hat and Mrs. Albouy greeted him.

"Good morning, Captain. I have shuffled the Esten lads into the parlour. They seemed quite eager to tell me about their morning adventure. Why don't you join them while I ask Cook to add a bit more food to the picnic fare—we don't want those boys to go hungry—and then you can be off?" She left them, saying over her shoulder, "You'll have your hands full, I expect."

* * *

Elbow Beach, named, as Mrs. Albouy had told her, for the gentle curve of the cream-colored sand that stretched between the tree-topped cliffs and the blue waters, was the most beautiful beach Tara had ever seen. In the pale blue sky overhead, puffy white clouds drifted slowly as if lethargic and reluctant to be on their way. The water closest to shore was the blue-green of the turquoise ring her father had given her when she'd left for London, but farther out, the deeper water appeared indigo. Mrs. Albouy had told her the coral reefs around the island had sent many an unwary ship to the bottom. But today all was calm, and the palette of colors and the breeze rustling through the palm fronds were an elixir to her senses.

The boys scrambled out of the carriage, doffing their stockings and shoes to run across the wide expanse of untouched sand to where small waves were breaking on shore. Captain Powell watched them for a moment, then set down the picnic basket in the shade of a palm tree, and quickly shed his own stockings and shoes to leave his muscular calves bare below his breeches. The skin on his legs was bronze like his face, making her wonder just how much skin he showed to the sun when he was with only his men. She had seen her brothers frolic in the waters off Fell's Point and when they were anchored off some island, but she'd not seen them naked. Somehow she thought the captain did not observe the niceties.

"I hope you will forgive my partial disrobing, Miss McConnell, but I may as well join the lads. It is far more comfortable to have one's toes free, don't you think?" He said this with a smile that Tara was certain held a dare. Not to be daunted, she sat on a nearby rock, and with up-turned brows waited for him to turn his back. When he did, she took off her gloves and then removed her stockings and shoes and, covering her legs with her skirts, sank her feet into the warm sand and wriggled her toes.

"It feels wonderful."

He whipped around, chuckled and held out his hand. "Come, sea nymph, let us walk to the water. After the hot sand, the waves will feel even better." He was not wrong. By the time they reached the shore, her feet were on fire and she was happy to lift the edge of her white muslin gown to let the water rush over her bare feet.

The boys splashed each other, playing in the shallow water up to their knees. Staring down at their feet, they shouted with delight when they saw their toes through the clear water. The captain joined in their fun, splashing them with seawater only to dart away. The boys took it as a challenge and raced after him, the three of them running down the beach. She could see them in the distance engaging in a game of tag.

Had she worn her breeches instead of a gown, she would have joined in their game. But instead she was content to watch, amazed at the captain's lighthearted frivolity with the two boys. Once again she marveled at how different he seemed away from the responsibility of his ship and its crew.

Eventually the three tired of their game and began to return to where Tara was waiting. Giving into a sudden desire, she lifted her skirts and ran barefoot down the beach toward them. The captain picked up the younger boy and carried the lad on his shoulder while James walked at his side, chatting away. As she approached, James raised his face to the captain's, hanging on every word the man uttered. Watching them, and the captain's patience with the boys' antics, Tara realized he was very fond of these children—and obviously they idolized the English sea captain.

For a moment Tara wished it were her family, her boys and, to her surprise, her man. Her feelings for Captain Powell had changed. The arrogant, unbending captain had softened, along with her resentment for the Englishman. Standing on Elbow Beach, Nicholas Powell, captain of the *Wind Raven*, was different from the man she'd first encountered. He was so much more.

"You seem the exuberant one today, Miss McConnell," the captain remarked when she caught up to the three of them. His golden eyes pointedly looked at her bare toes peeking out below her gown. He set John on the sand and the boys each took one of his hands.

"I'm just enjoying this place." *And you.* For he'd become a charming and winsome man. Why would he show her such tenderness now? Was it only being free of the burden of command?

"Are you hungry yet, lads?" the captain asked. "Shall we see what the Albouy cook has prepared for us?"

With glad agreement and shouts of "I'm starved!" the boys ran to the shade, where the picnic basket waited. Once there, the captain spread the picnic cloth on the sand in the shade. The meal the cook had prepared was, indeed, a feast: roast chicken, mussels in a spicy sauce, sliced cucumbers and, for dessert, apricot tarts.

"Tarts!" shouted John when Tara set them on the cloth.

"Tarts last," said the captain, gently chiding the boys, who sighed in compliance and accepted the plates Tara handed them, which she had piled with chicken, mussels and cucumbers. There was fresh fruit juice, a blend of orange and mango, for the boys and white wine for the captain and her.

After luncheon, the boys played near the water's edge, building a castle in the damp sand, while Tara and the captain reclined in the shade looking on. It was very peaceful with the birds chirping in the palm trees above them and the soothing sound of the rhythmic roar of the waves rushing to shore. Leaning on one elbow, Nicholas Powell stretched his legs before him. A lock of ebony hair blew across his forehead as he watched the boys, who were now playing in the water. The lines of concern in the captain's face were gone. Instead, the face of a contented man emerged.

Tara glanced at his hand lying on the cloth. Eager for something to fill the awkward silence, she remarked, "That's a beautiful ring you wear."

He looked at the blue stone, glowing in the dappled light filtering through the palms. "It's my mother's. She gave it to me when I earned my ship, in recognition of my becoming a man in my father's eyes, or so she said. It's a blue moonstone, and was a gift from her father when she turned seventeen."

"Ah, a family heirloom."

"Yes, I suppose it is."

"If you don't mind my saying so, Captain, you seem a different person in this place."

"So do you, Miss McConnell," he said smiling, his golden eyes glinting. "So do you."

For a moment, she openly returned his gaze. But she was not so unwise as to allow him to see she might care. She had been raised around men who loved the sea, as indeed she herself did, and she recognized only too well this English captain was content with his lot as a man, having no ties save those to his ship and his crew. She would not allow him to see the change in her feelings.

Like the small shimmering shell she had picked up on the beach and tucked into her watch pocket, her growing feelings for Captain Powell would remain her secret.

Chapter 12

The Tres Puertas tavern in Cabo Rojo was crowded as Roberto Cofresí and a few of his men stepped through the open door. A reception as warm as the night air greeted them. They were expected, it being their custom to celebrate a prize when there was plenty to share. A drink among friends after a good dinner was also a welcome tradition. The patrons who knew his crew lifted their heads to shout words welcoming them home as they wound their way through the tavern.

"Ah, Roberto!" the *tabernero,* Ramón, shouted, a wide smile on his round face as he began pouring them rum from where he stood behind the bar. "I have heard the fishermen of the *Retribución* had a good catch today, no?"

"*Sí,* Ramón, a good day," acknowledged Roberto as he headed toward his table in the rear of the room, the one always reserved for him and his men when they were expected. There he could sit safely with his back to the wall, watching all who entered.

The tavern keeper himself delivered the rum, setting the four tankards before them. "So there will be much sharing with the people of Cabo Rojo?" Ramón inquired.

"*Sí,* spoils enough to buy your wife that dress she's been ogling, and coin enough to feed even your growing brood."

Ramón gave a hearty laugh and leaned in to whisper. The men sitting with Roberto discreetly looked away. "I came to your table myself to deliver a message."

Roberto studied the tavern keeper's face, which had suddenly grown serious.

"There was a man asking about you yesterday."

Roberto sensed the tavern keeper's determination to remember the smallest details. His loyalty, like that of the others, reminded Roberto it was not only vengeance he sought in his piracy, but a better life for the people of Cabo Rojo and the island that was his home.

"He's an old man with graying hair, and a foreigner, *sin duda*. Not a Spaniard, and not from here. More likely English," Ramón speculated, twisting his mouth as if he chewed on something distasteful. "Though his accent was hard to place."

Roberto turned to Portalatin, who he knew had been listening. "See what our spies have to say. Perhaps the man has also been asking elsewhere."

Portalatin took a swig of his rum and rose to depart. "*Sí, Capitán.*"

Roberto had many spies around Porto Rico, most in Cabo Rojo, ordinary people like shopkeepers, a school teacher, even a priest— people who owed much to El Pirata Cofresí and whose gratitude was reflected in the information they provided concerning merchant ships. They would not miss a foreigner asking about him or his men. Nor would they fail to send him word.

Turning back to Ramón, he inquired, "What did the man seek?"

"Information on your ship. He wanted to know when the *Retribución* was expected in port. He must know this is your home."

"Was he followed when he left?"

"*Sí*, I put José on the man but he disappeared in the market crowd and José was unable to find him. I thought him a wily one." He paused and looked briefly toward the bar as if thinking, and then back to Roberto. "I remember now. José thought the man seemed to know he was being followed."

"We will find him. I cannot imagine he is alone. Could be someone seeking vengeance for a lost ship." Roberto rested his chin on his upturned hand, his elbow on the table. It would not be the first time. That was one reason he maintained a network of spies in the various ports.

Cabo Rojo was not a large place. He would soon have the man's identity.

* * *

Nick watched his passenger as she stood at the prow gazing into the orange and red sky, the large glowing disk slowly sinking into the Caribbean Sea. The light turned her tawny hair into strands of shimmering gold. He had watched her many an evening as they sailed south to Porto Rico, never growing tired of gazing at the beautiful girl, as she never grew tired of gazing at the sea.

The *Wind Raven*, now bearing the name *Viento del Cuervo* and flying the flag of Royal Spain, had been anchored on the far side of Boquerón Bay on the west coast of Porto Rico for two days, and he could see his passenger was growing restless. He had confined her to the ship for her protection, though he had refused to answer her many questions about the changes made to the schooner. He did not want her to be aware of his mission concerning the pirate Cofresí for fear she would insist on becoming involved.

She leaned against the rail, her stance proud and fearless as if she were daring the world—or him—to stop her should she take a fancy to leave the ship. He expected a further rebellion, and soon.

He could not envision Tara McConnell as one of the ladies of the *ton*, content to while away her time in the drawing rooms of London as Caroline had been. Caroline would have hated the life that this American girl loved. Why had he never seen that before? In her own way, perhaps Caroline had recognized the truth he'd denied. They were never meant to be together; they were only an interlude in each other's lives. Tara was different. At some level, he had recognized it the first time she'd climbed into the rigging, assured and smiling before his men. Even in Bermuda, where she had delighted his British friends, she had shone like a sparkling gem, willing to try foods that were new to her and conversing on all manner of topics. He remembered her running barefoot at Elbow Beach, lifting her skirts as she splashed in the small waves rushing to shore. Like a mermaid suddenly given legs, she embraced life. He had fought to act the gentleman in front of the Esten boys when what he had wanted to do was lay her down in the sand and make love to her. Since then, his eyes had often found her in the evening as she stood at the rail gazing into the setting sun. What would he do about her when they reached Baltimore?

She had persisted in acting as one of his crew, defying him at every turn, but with a subtle difference. Since their time in Bermuda and the kisses he'd pressed upon her, there was something new between them, though aside from a greater desire to have the woman in his bed, he could not have said what it was. He knew he could seduce her if he persisted. His crew likely expected it of their captain.

His thoughts were interrupted as his attention was drawn aloft to the top of the new foremast. Some of the attachments set in Bermuda had been jury-rigged and Jake Johansson, fastidious as always, intended to re-led and re-splice the rigging before they sailed to Baltimore. He made a mental reminder to ask Jake if the job had been completed.

Out of the corner of his eye, he saw Nate coming over the side, his agile movements belying his years as he walked toward Nick, mumbling under his breath.

"Any news?" Nick asked, anxious for information on the pirate and his ship.

"None, Cap'n. But the way the hair on the back of me neck is standin' on end, I'd swear we're being watched. When I left the tavern yesterday, a man followed me. I lost him in the crowd in the market, but I begin to wonder. I hope yer not planning on stayin' long."

"No, but I'd like to have a chance to cripple the pirate's ship when he is otherwise occupied. Tonight, I think, we must seek the *Retribución* in earnest. There will be no moon."

* * *

Tara looked away from the setting sun, past the blue waters of the bay glistening with the last rays of light, toward the shore and the palm-strewn hills above the long stretch of beach. The gray cat brushed against her skirts, having adopted the habit of following Tara up on deck in the early evening. Reaching down to scratch Samantha's ears, Tara chided herself for wearing a gown, the change she had made in her apparel since Bermuda.

It was for him she had begun dressing the lady and the realization caused her to frown. Somewhere on the voyage she had become uncomfortable with her boyish behavior and she liked the way the captain looked at her when she wore the frippery. Though she still wore her breeches in the morning while helping the crew with their chores, by the afternoon she would be wearing a gown, albeit the modified ones with her breeches underneath. Still, from her outward appearance she was dressed in the feminine attire that would have been welcomed in any parlour in London. All for the sake of a captain who paid her little attention except to steal kisses whenever the fancy took him. But their time in Bermuda had told her that beneath the rogue there was a man of intelligence, mirth and honor.

With days rocking at anchor in the bay, she had become bored with the ship, which surprised her, but then there was less to do when not at sea. In the time Joshua had been with them, she'd often helped the second cabin boy with his knowledge of the ship when Peter was occupied. But even that was not enough. And she was most anxious to know why the *Wind Raven* was now decked out like a Spanish merchant ship. Her questions posed to the first mate had produced only vague answers, something about avoiding issues with the local officials. Still, she thought it odd.

From what she had seen from the deck as they'd sailed along the island's coast, Porto Rico was lush with greenery and dense stands of palm trees. But Cabo Rojo on the west coast was drier, with ragged cliffs rising above blue waters. The bay where they were anchored seemed an exception with its sandy beach running the full length of its long shore and green vegetation beyond. Small villages dotted the coast, the last rays of the sun making their brightly painted cottages glow.

Her attention was drawn to Nate, who had just come aboard and was striding toward the captain. As the two men talked, the captain's dark brows drew together. With a concerned look, he gave instructions to Nate that she could not hear from where she was standing. The old sailor nodded and went below. It was time for the evening meal and Tara strolled toward the captain as he watched her.

"Will you dine with me this evening, Miss McConnell?" the captain said, disclosing nothing of his conversation with Nate. Lately she had taken to eating in her cabin so the invitation was unexpected, though not unwelcome.

"If you wish, Captain."

"I do. I will be going ashore later with a few of the crew and want your agreement to remain aboard the ship."

Seeing his dark brows draw together, she took his request as an order. He was concerned about something. They walked toward the hatch as Tara considered her position. She was a passenger not a prisoner, but they were in foreign waters and, as the captain he'd be concerned for a passenger getting lost, or worse.

"Captain, I grow tired of this confinement while we are anchored. I would very much like to go ashore with you tonight."

They descended to the lower deck as he responded. "That will not be possible, Miss McConnell."

Something was amiss, of that Tara was certain. Something Nate and he had discussed. Something the good captain did not want to tell her. It made her worry, too. Still, he could not hold her captive forever.

"Tomorrow perhaps I will go ashore, Captain, whether you approve or not."

"Tomorrow, Miss McConnell, we will sail."

* * *

Later that night, Nick crouched behind a small rise on a hill above the cove where the pirate ship rested at anchor a few miles down the coast. At his side were Russ, Jake Johansson, Charlie Wilson and a half dozen other members of his crew, all dressed in dark clothing. They had walked in so they could approach by land. Stealth had been their plan and it seemed as if fate was with them. Based upon their intelligence, he expected to find only a skeleton crew.

He peered over the top of the rise to see the small schooner looming like a dark specter in the moonless night, its deck lit only by a single lantern. Midnight had come and gone as they waited for any activity aboard the pirate ship. Nick had seen only a few shadows moving about earlier, but now, other than a single man on watch, all was quiet. It was time.

Slowly Nick and his men wound their way down the hill, pausing behind rocks to be certain they were not being observed. Finally they reached the longboat the pirates had hauled on shore to afford them access to their ship. Nick's men slipped the boat from the sand and, without a sound, scrambled over the side and quietly rowed across the dark water. In addition to his saber and pistol, lying next to him in the boat was his Baker rifle, which he could use to take out the pirate watch if they were spotted from afar.

Nick cocked his pistol. "Keep your weapons ready as you board," he whispered. "They'll soon be needed."

They arrived at the pirate ship without incident, the waters of the bay smooth as glass, and climbed up the side using the manrope. Nick was the first to drop onto the deck, landing in a crouch; his men followed. The snoring sentry amidships suddenly woke.

"*Sangre de Dios!*" he shouted, drawing a machete from his waist, but before he could wield the weapon, Russ fired his pistol and the pirate dropped to the deck, dispatched to the next world.

Four pirates emerged from the main hatch at a run, machetes raised. Nick drew his saber and a skirmish ensued, but it was clear from the start the pirates were not prepared for the attack. Nick's saber quickly drew blood from the swarthy pirate who'd lunged at him. Seeing he and his companions were greatly outnumbered, the pirate surrendered, dropping his machete and raising his hands in the air. His companions soon followed suit.

Nick summoned Charlie Wilson. "It seems most of the pirates have gone ashore. Have these three said anything about Cofresí's whereabouts?"

Charlie, who understood Spanish, had been listening to the pirates speaking among themselves. "No, Cap'n. Each is blaming the other for failing to see us before we were upon them."

Hearing Charlie's words, Russ said, "These men are as loyal as yours, Nick. They'll not be speaking of their captain, not even under penalty of death."

"Well, based on the description we have, Cofresí isn't one of these," he replied. "Spike the guns and take what powder they have. At least we'll remove his claws for a time."

When the job was done, Jake reported the hold contained no cargo, save for food supplies and the gunpowder the crew of the *Wind Raven* would take with them. Nick ordered the balls thrown over the side.

"Tie up the pirate's men and leave them in the hold for their captain to find." Nick ordered, glancing at the one who was dead and the one who was wounded in the shoulder.

"We could sink her, Nick," offered Russ, "but then we'd have these bilge rats to deal with."

"An intriguing idea. I suppose the Prince Regent would prefer that, though I expect the pirate would soon procure another ship with his wealth."

"More likely he'd seize one," said Russ.

As Nick was considering whether to take the time to sink the *Retribución*, he suddenly had a sense of foreboding, the urge to return to his ship nearly overwhelming. "I don't want to blow up the ship with the powder we ourselves can use, and to do more would take time I'm unwilling to allow. We've lingered overlong."

* * *

Nick and his men arrived on the beach where they'd left their longboat, but it was gone. A sinking feeling came over him as he gazed across the gray water toward his ship. Small currents of the bay lapped at his boots as the light of the early dawn allowed him to see two longboats rowing toward the *Wind Raven*. Together they carried at least a dozen men.

Cofresí had discovered their presence.

Tara.

"The freebooters are headin' toward the ship, Cap'n!" one of his men said in a raspy whisper.

"I am aware," he said, his voice cold as he examined his options. Nick was certain his watch would see the pirates advancing through the waters, but taking no chances, he took out his muzzle-loaded rifle and fired a shot. He could not reach the pirates before they arrived at his ship, but he could be certain his men were warned.

"Quickly," he urged Jake and the others, "bring one of the boats from there under the palms." He gestured to where he'd earlier seen the boats overturned under the canopy of trees. The bos'n ran to the boats with the others following to do their captain's bidding.

Russ and Nick helped put the boat in the water and the men leaped in, save for Jake, who waited for Nick. Nick climbed over the side and Jake shoved the boat from shore and vaulted over the side.

"Have you a plan when we get to the ship?" Russ asked while the men pulled oars and they skimmed over the water.

"Only to kill as many of the pirates as I can," said Nick. *And to save Tara.* "Pistols first while we have them."

Nick heard the sound of pistols being fired on board the *Raven* as they rowed toward the ship. Not all of his men had pistols. In the early light of dawn, the white smoke from those that had been fired could be seen billowing above the deck.

Most of the *Raven*'s crew would be fighting with their long-knifed cutlasses, the sailors' weapon of choice. Though well matched with machetes, few of his crew could wield them well. They were merchantmen, only some former privateers, and of those, only a few had engaged in hand-to-hand fighting.

They were too late to prevent the pirates from boarding, as Nick knew they would be.

Arriving just after the clash of blades began, Nick climbed over the rail and into the lingering cloud of smoke. He breathed in the sharp odor of spent powder and sulfur as he unsheathed his saber and pulled his cocked pistol from waist, searching for a place to dive into the fray. His crew was waging a desperate attempt to fend off the fierce, machete-wielding pirates, but some had already fallen. The deck was awash in blood.

Pirates were cutting down his men, one after the other; the clash of metal and the grunts of men filled his ears. In front of him, Jake stood like a tower of strength, a long knife in each hand, as he protected the boy Joshua huddled behind him. Nick slashed his saber across the back of the pirate facing Jake, and the tall bos'n leaped in to cut the pirate's throat.

"Joshua! Up the mast and quickly!" shouted Nick, swiveling to meet a pirate rushing toward him. Sidestepping the downward thrust of the machete, he avoided all but a superficial graze of his left arm. Catching the pirate in the side as he turned, Nick braced himself for the sickening feel of his blade sliding through flesh.

Mayhem was all around him as he paused to take in the battle.

Standing amidships he saw the profile of a tall pirate, a machete in one hand and an axe dripping blood in the other. Blood ran down his bare chest and dripped from loose strands of his long blond hair. Surrounded by his dark crew, the pirate stood out like a beacon drawing Nick's gaze.

Cofresí.

The pirate captain advanced toward old Nate, who was holding his own near the aft hatch on the quarterdeck. Diving into the fray, Nick fired his pistol with one hand while cutting down an approaching pirate with his saber. The ball exploded into the air, hitting the left arm of the blond pirate. Cofresí's machete fell to the deck with a thud, and the pirate captain turned, his face a mask of seething rage, his glare aimed at Nick as he raised his axe.

All sound ceased for Nick as a huge hulking beast of a pirate stepped through the aft hatch, dragging Tara with him. She was fighting him tooth and nail.

The blond pirate turned his gaze to follow Nick's and the men fighting nearby stepped back and looked toward the beautiful girl in the white muslin gown held in the grasp of the hulking pirate.

* * *

"Let go of me, you scurvy beast!" Tara yelled, kicking the shin of the beefy pirate who held her. But the man's muscled arms were like bands of steel. Seizing upon the one action left to her, she bent her head and sank her teeth into his fleshy forearm. It only made him grip her more tightly to his wide chest, forcing the air from her lungs.

"So it's to be like that, is it, *sirenita?*" the corpulent pirate expelled his foul breath into her ear and moved his hand to cover her breast.

Incensed, Tara shoved her elbow into his paunch, hoping to hit his ribs buried beneath. He grunted, then laughed and turned to one of the other pirates. "Look what I found, Capitán—a spitting mermaid!"

Suddenly a knife flew past Tara's head, embedding itself in the neck of the pirate who held her. Blood spurted over Tara and she wrenched away. The pirate slumped to the deck as he reached for the knife in his neck. But his hand slipped away, his head hitting the deck, his dark eyes vacant and staring into space. Tara wiped the blood from her face with her arm and looked around for her knife-wielding savior—and into the eyes of the *Wind Raven*'s captain.

That he had thrown the knife became clear when one of the pirates, seeing his dead companion, threw his fist into Captain Powell's face, causing the captain's head to whip to one side. The pirate followed it up with a sharp blow to the captain's ribs and he sank to his knees. Two pirates grabbed the *Wind Raven*'s captain and stretched him between them even as the captain struggled to gain his freedom. To Tara's horror, blood dripped from the captain's lip and his left arm as he moaned. With great effort he rose to stand, glaring his disgust at the two pirates holding him.

At that moment, Tara had never been more proud of the captain—his courage, the strength he imparted to his men. Never had she felt more love for him.

Tara's eyes were drawn to the blond pirate whose presence dominated the deck; his piercing blue was gaze fixed upon *her*. Silence replaced the sound of clashing steel as the pirates, who she could see were prevailing, looked toward the blond giant as if awaiting an order. Powerfully built, his shoulders broad, the pirate wore a black scarf around his neck, but his bronze chest, splattered with blood, was bare. Down his left arm ran blood from a wound, and in his right hand he wielded an axe with a blood-smeared blade. He was terrifying.

Fear gripped her as she stared at his eyes and then at his axe. Would she be next?

"You will die for slaying my man, Captain Powell," the blond pirate said in perfect English, his voice harsh, all the while never taking his eyes off Tara. His gaze was devouring, making Tara feel as exposed as if he'd stripped her of her clothes. To the other pirates, he ordered, "Round up the English crew and put them in the hold, the captain and the first officer in chains. And, Portalatin, send some of the crew to bring the *Retribución* into the bay so we can transfer the cargo."

In rapid movements, so fast she barely took them in, the pirates disarmed the rest of the *Wind Raven*'s crew and began shoving them toward the cargo hatch.

The pirate captain turned his gaze on Captain Powell, who was still straining against the two pirates holding him fast. With a cynical grin, he said, "Did you think I was unaware you had come to my waters, Englishman? I am not so ignorant as you might believe. I know well the stories of the *Wind Raven* and her captain, no matter the language in which you choose to cloak your ship or the flag you choose to fly. You are a living legend in the West Indies. And soon, Captain Powell, you will be a dead one."

Stunned, Tara could only stare. Nicholas Powell could not die! *God, please keep him safe.*

She cast her gaze over the bodies strewn about the deck, nearly vomiting when she saw one of the *Raven*'s crew with a deep gash across his neck, his head almost severed. A few of the dead were pirates bearing pistol wounds in their chests, their bodies tangled with those of the *Raven*'s crew. Smitty was sitting against the main mast, his eyes closed. She could not tell if he was dead. Some of Captain Powell's crew lay wounded. She breathed a sigh of relief when she saw the familiar faces of Russell Ainsworth and Jake, both being shoved toward the hatch. Nate was being dragged to join them. She knew Peter had been below decks with her and hoped the lad was unharmed.

Lastly, following his crew, Captain Powell was prodded with a machete toward the hatch. He looked back at Tara. The fire in his eyes gave her courage. He had not surrendered; neither would she.

The blond pirate faced Tara, his voice suddenly gentle. "*Ven aqui, mí cariño.*" Wiping his axe blade on his pants and slipping the instrument of death into the sash at his waist, he extended his hand to her. Tara didn't need to understand Spanish to know he was calling her to him; it was in his eyes. His startling blue gaze was more frightening than the bloody axe he had sheathed. She did not move, only stared, frozen with fear.

"Come to me, sweetheart," he said in English, "I will not harm you."

Chapter 13

Cofresí stood on the quarterdeck of the English ship watching the girl as she walked to the prow, her arms wrapped tightly around her as she faced away from him. Her golden hair reflected the sun's rays like some mythical being, drawing him to her. He knew from her voice she was American, perhaps one who had longed for liberty as much as he did. He had admired her bravery when, unafraid of his men, she had fought to be free. From the moment he first saw her, he wanted her, his desire an immediate, tangible thing.

For some time, he had thought he should take a wife. His older brothers expected him to marry. Disappointed with his maritime activities, and abhorring his piracy, they hoped if he were to wed, he would settle down, leaving behind his days at sea.

He would not marry any of the cantina girls in Cabo Rojo who freely offered themselves to him, nor one of the village girls whose eager mamas shoved them toward him. And none of the docile daughters of the distinguished European families with whom he'd been raised appealed to him. No, he must have a woman with a strong will to match his own, a woman of courage, a woman of passion. Perhaps this golden-haired girl was the one for whom he'd been searching.

But why was she aboard the English merchantman? Was she Captain Powell's woman?

Roberto vowed to discover the truth. Soon he would know all her secrets. If it was as he hoped, she might be the one. For someone like her, he could almost imagine setting aside his pursuit of vengeance and leaving the sea as his brothers desired. He could still fight for his island country's independence and assist the cause of his friend Simón Bolívar in Venezuela. And he would have a woman of his own at home to raise his sons.

More than an hour passed before the *Retribución* sailed into Boquerón Bay to be joined to the English ship. As soon as the plank was in place, Portalatin crossed and came to Roberto.

"Capitán," said Portalatin, "the English captain made a visit to the *Retribución* before returning to his ship. They spiked our guns and put the crew into the hold."

"Hmm," Roberto was both angry and amused, "so that is where the English captain was while we were attacking his ship. Ah well, Captain Powell will pay with his life. Were any killed?"

"Enriquez. Juan was wounded but he will live."

Roberto paused to remember Enriquez, the man who had served him from his early days as a pirate. With a resigned sigh, he said, "I suppose I should not be surprised that Powell was seeking my ship while I was taking his. It is the way of things. I am grateful he did not choose to sink her. That would be most inconvenient."

He paused to consider what next to do. He had intended the English ship for his compatriot in Venezuela. "We cannot very well send a ship lacking guns to our friend in South America, now can we?"

Portalatin shook his head in agreement.

"Leave the guns on the English ship. We will have to replace those on the *Retribución*. Perhaps some made with bronze this time, eh, Portalatin? The ones on that small Dutch ship we took a few days ago should serve well. It sustained damage but the guns are in tact. Once you remove them you can sink her. Go ashore and make the arrangements. While you are gone, Manuel can see to the transfer of the English cargo and clean whatever blood is on the deck of my ship. When you return, you can hold the English ship for me."

"*Sí*, Capitán. Will you leave the *Retribución* here for the night?"

"No. I have plans for the beautiful *señorita*. I will take my ship and return tomorrow so you can install the new guns. Look for me at midday."

Once Roberto's men had transferred the cargo from the English ship to the hold of their schooner and washed the *Retribución*'s deck of blood, Roberto crossed to his ship to bathe and don fresh clothes. He had decided to take the rest of the day and the coming night to become acquainted with the golden American girl. There was much he wanted to know.

When he returned to the English ship some time later, Roberto found the girl standing in the stern, as if trying to remove herself as far from his men as possible. She had been allowed to clean herself and don a fresh gown. Though he had ordered she be given her freedom on deck, she was not allowed to remain below. He did not want her to feel like a prisoner, but he could not have her interfering with his decisions concerning the English captain and his crew.

She watched him as he approached, her gaze steady, her stance proud and unbending. "You are well?" he inquired.

"Well enough," she said, defiance in her eyes, the same eyes he'd noticed earlier were the color of Boquerón Bay.

"*Bien.* There is a place I wish to show you. So you will come to my ship, *cariño*, and while we dine, you will tell me who you are and why you were aboard an English ship."

* * *

Tara had been biting her knuckles, worrying over the *Wind Raven*'s captain and crew. But try as she might, she could not see a way to help them at present. She needed to buy some time till she could steal a weapon to help them escape. The captain could not die at the pirate's hand.

She supposed it would make no difference to the pirate captain if she did not wish to comply with his instructions, so she said nothing when he informed her she'd be coming to his ship. After all, there was little she could do to thwart him, at least for now.

Hoping she could believe the pirate when he said he would not harm her, she followed him to his schooner. His Porto Rican crew, much darker in coloring than their captain, looked on, scrutinizing her every move with curious eyes. She, too, was curious—about their captain. How had a blond European who spoke with the cultured voice of an educated man become a ruthless pirate?

By the time he collected her from the deck of the *Wind Raven*, he had rid himself of all traces of blood. It was midday and the sun was now high in the sky. The air was warm and sultry, though an occasional welcome breeze stirred the wisps of hair around her face. In the time since he had disappeared onto his ship, the pirate captain had attired himself more in keeping with his speech, returning to the *Wind Raven* wearing dark blue breeches, black boots and a white shirt open at the neck. His blond hair was reined into a queue at his nape.

As they entered his cabin, he took a dark blue jacket from the back of his desk chair and threw it around his shoulders. Though he looked like a gentleman, she knew he was not. Unlike Captain Powell's warm golden eyes, there was no mercy in the pirate's steely blue gaze.

Tara's trunk and valise lay on the deck of the pirate's cabin. Seeing them gave her chills. It did not appear he intended to return her to the *Wind Raven*, but then the pirate's plans for Nicholas Powell spoke only of death.

Quickly glancing around her, Tara noted his cabin was furnished more sparingly than that of Captain Powell, and it was smaller and more cave-like. Still, it contained the things she'd expected to see: a desk, table and chairs, and a shelf bed set against the bulkhead. It was neat and clean, but it lacked the higher ceiling of Captain Powell's elegant cabin and it lacked his many books. The thought occurred to her the pirate likely didn't spend much time on his ship. His home was on shore and probably not far.

"I have forgotten my manners, *mi cariño*. We have not been properly introduced. I am Roberto Cofresí y Ramírez de Arellano." He bowed with his left arm stretched to the side and his right arm across his waist. The wound in his arm did not appear to be paining him much or he hid it well. At her raised brow, he added with a smile, "Many in Porto Rico call me *Cofresí*, and my men call me *Capitán*, but you may call me *Roberto*."

Tara said nothing.

Her reticence to engage in conversation seemed to amuse him. "And you would be?" he asked with a smile.

"Tara McConnell. But you may call me Miss McConnell."

The pirate captain chuckled and she knew in that moment that he had already decided that no matter her wishes he would call her whatever he liked.

"What do you intend to do with Captain Powell and his crew?" It was the most pressing thought in her mind.

He sat with one hip on the edge of his desk as he studied her in a long appreciative look. In a very matter-of-fact voice, he said, "Captain Powell will die for unnecessarily taking the life of one of my men. Others may have died in the fight but Tomas died for nothing. Still, I did not wish to distress you, so I waited." He shrugged, apparently unconcerned. "It can be done in the morning." She opened her mouth to protest, and as if to anticipate her, he said, "I would have disciplined my man for his rough handling of you. And though I must apologize for Tomas's bad manners, he would not have hurt you. His death was unwarranted. Each man in my crew knows not to harm a woman on a ship I have taken as a prize."

"You are a pirate! Captain Powell could not have known I would remain unharmed when that…that boar was mauling me and would not let me go. Surely you see that?"

"I see you defend the English captain. Are you his woman?" His blue eyes bore into hers and Tara realized he considered the question of great importance.

"Certainly not. I am merely his passenger." She looked down at the deck, not wanting the pirate to see the desperation in her eyes, to see how much she cared about the fate of Nicholas Powell. "It is just that I do not wish to see him die for defending my honor."

"I see. It is good you do not belong to him. But he will die all the same."

The possibility of Nicholas Powell dying at the pirate's hands chilled Tara to the bone. Trying not to think of such an occurrence, and not wanting to convey all she felt for the Englishman, she forced herself to ask, "What about Captain Powell's crew?"

The pirate captain rose from the desk, walked to a small wooden table set against the bulkhead and poured a deep amber liquid from a wide-bottomed carafe. "May I pour you some Madeira?"

"No, thank you." Concerned she might anger the pirate, she added, "Perhaps later."

"To answer your question, they will live. I will sell them as slaves to serve on other ships."

With a sharp lurch, Tara felt the ship move beneath her feet. They were underway. "Where are we going?"

"As I told you, I have a place I wish you to see. We sail south and east around the end of the island to one of our bays that glows in the night. You have not seen it before?"

"No." Tara could not recall having seen such a bay.

"Then I have chosen well, for it is a beautiful sight, and I would share it with you." Tara had no desire to sail anywhere with the pirate, but she needed time to think of what to do to help the *Wind Raven*'s captain and his men. Perhaps she could buy them some time.

"You will not do anything tonight with Captain Powell or his crew?"

He took a sip of the wine and set down his glass, then slowly walked to her. She could feel her heart pounding in her chest as he neared, afraid of what such a man might do, aware they were alone in his cabin. She would be powerless to stop him. But when he reached her, he lifted her hand to his lips and pressed a kiss to her knuckles. "No. Tonight I intend only to enjoy your company, Tara—*mi cariño.*"

Though he appeared a gracious host, Tara wondered if he were perhaps insane. She was acutely aware she was Cofresí's prisoner, held on his ship and sailing toward some bay where the waters glowed. Apparently he thought it a small matter he'd been dripping in blood only hours before.

He had allowed her run of the deck as they sailed and she was grateful. The wind off the water cooled her fevered brow and sharpened her wits as she pondered her next steps.

They sailed past jagged cliffs covered with sparse green vegetation rising from turquoise waters, the pirate crew watching her from the deck and the rigging. Despite her situation and the looming question of what might lay ahead for her and the *Raven*'s crew, Tara could not deny the beauty of the island the pirate called home.

As evening settled around them, he bid her to enter his cabin once again and to sit at his table, where one of his men served a simple meal of fragrant stew. She looked down at the bowl placed before her to see a tomato sauce filled with all manner of shellfish. The spicy aroma wafting to her nostrils told her the meal would be delicious, but Tara was too worried about Captain Powell and his crew to do more than dip her spoon in the stew.

Another dish arrived. Cofresí called it *mofongo*, a mash of plantains, garlic and oil cooked with spices.

Tara had no desire for food.

As the pirate captain ate, his appetite seemingly unaffected by the day's events, he spoke of his home and his family, as if he wanted her to know him. He had an older sister he spoke of in gentled tones, in contrast to his comments about his older brothers. Tara could not think of the pirate as having a family.

The light from the lantern reflected off the silver and black earrings that dangled from his ears as he spoke. She had noticed them before when she'd first seen him on the deck of the *Wind Raven*, but now, seeing them close, she observed they were round in shape with four points, like bejeweled compasses, each set with a large faceted crystal. Tara thought the stones might be diamonds, so great was their sparkle. For a fleeting moment, she wondered if he wore them as a vain decoration or a distraction for his victims. Perhaps it was both.

Though beautiful, the jewelry did not render him feminine. Instead the earrings made him seem all the more the pirate. Despite what she suspected was a proper upbringing, he had chosen to act the renegade. His orders to kill, given with confidence and void of remorse, would be quickly obeyed.

"You are not eating, *cariño*," Cofresí said, setting down his spoon. "You will need your strength for the days ahead. Eat, *por favor*."

Tara looked up at what she had to admit was a handsome and very masculine face with strong cheekbones and a high forehead. Could such a man be deranged? She dipped her spoon into the bowl set before her. Lifting the spoonful of stew, she held it in front of her mouth for a moment, and then dropped it back into the bowl.

"Surely you must realize that under the circumstances I have no appetite." How could he expect her to eat when the deck of the *Wind Raven* was coated with blood and the life of her captain, the man who now held her heart, was threatened with death? "I am worried about the men of the *Wind Raven*, and for that matter, what is to become of me?"

"Tonight you shall not worry," he commanded in his deep melodious voice, as if he expected his orders to always be obeyed. And she supposed they were. "For tonight, there is only my ship and the sea and the stars." Tara felt the ship slowing and heard one of his men on deck shouting orders in Spanish. She assumed it was an order to douse sail. Perhaps they had reached their destination.

Wiping his mouth with a napkin and downing the last of his wine, Cofresí rose and offered his hand. "Come. I will show you a most mysterious sight and you can tell me more about how you, an American, came to be on board an English ship."

They arrived on deck as his men were furling the sails and setting the anchor. Tara scanned her surroundings. They had entered a bay. The muted shades of scarlet and purple in the fading sunset were quickly giving way to a darkened sky as the stars emerged above them. Slowly they walked the length of his schooner as he told her of his youth. She did not want to hear about the lad who loved the sea, who defied his father and older brothers to sail his first small boat. It reminded her too much of her own youth.

When the sky was a midnight blue, Cofresí uttered something to one of his men, then led her to the rail and pointed to the anchor chain. It was pulled taut, a dark shadow. Around the chain where it entered the water was a circle of blue-green light radiating out in all directions. Cofresí picked up a small piece of wood on the deck and tossed it over the side. At the sound of the splash, there was a flash of the same blue light, its rays spreading out in all directions from where the object had plunged into the water.

Gazing into the distance, she could see the small waves rushing to shore erupting into sparking points of blue light as they encountered the sand. It was, as Cofresí had said, a mysterious yet most magnificent sight. And for a moment, it distracted her. The entire bay was alive with glowing blue color patterns, fluctuating with the disturbance in the waters. The shimmering blue color reminded her of the ring Nicholas Powell wore on his little finger, as if the stone had captured the same light. Suddenly her mind was back with the captain and his crew. How were they faring?

"Is it not romantic, our Porto Rican phenomenon?" the pirate captain asked. When she nodded, he elaborated. "We have three such bays in different parts of the island. Always there is a mangrove swamp nearby." He reached for her hand and brought it to his lips. "I wanted to share it with you."

His touch disturbed her. His knowledge and his educated manner of speech impressed her. He spoke English with ease and only a slight accent. At times his speech flowed in and out of Spanish with his men, as if both languages were frequently crossed in his thoughts. It would not surprise her to learn he spoke other languages as well. Facing him, she said, "Tell me, how it is you, being a pirate, are so well spoken." Tara would remind him he acted the pirate; she did not want the magic of the glowing blue waters or the stories of his family and his youth to allow her to forget who he was, what he had done or what he planned to do with Captain Powell and his men.

"You are surprised that I am so learned? Do not be. My father was born of an aristocratic family in Austria and came to Porto Rico from Spain as a man of some wealth. He changed our family name of Von Kupferschein to Cofresí because it was easier for the Spanish to pronounce. My mother, who was of a similar family, died when I was a small child, but my father saw that my two older brothers and I attended a private school where we were taught languages, literature, geography and arithmetic."

"We have the early deaths of our mothers in common," she noted. "But why take up piracy?" Tara could not imagine any man with that background, education and wealth becoming a pirate, preying on merchant ships, no matter the lack of a mother's love.

"Ah that is another story, *cariño*, one of brutality demanding revenge. I would not speak of it tonight and steal from our precious time together. Tell me why you were with Captain Powell. I have long known of the English captain they call *the Raven* who sails the waters of the West Indies. But why are you his...passenger?"

"If you must know, I am returning home to America from my aunt's house in London, where I spent the last year. Captain Powell's mother is a dear friend of my Aunt Cornelia. My father in Baltimore is ill, perhaps even dying." Tara spoke the words, reminding herself as she did of the man she had worried about since she left England. "But why do you ask? Surely my troubles cannot be of importance to you."

"Everything about you, *cariño*, is important to me." With his long fingers, he brushed a strand of hair from her cheek, where the night wind had blown it. She stiffened as he placed his hand on her neck and curled his warm fingers about her skin, making her shiver. He drew her to him and before Tara could object, brushed his lips across hers.

She pulled away. "I do not wish your advances."

"I will not force you, *cariño*, as I would force no woman. But in time you will see I am the man you need."

Tara nearly sputtered. "A pirate? Why would you think that?"

"Some things cannot be explained just now. Then, too, you might consider that I will not always be in my current…profession. But know this, *cariño*. I, Cofresí, will win you, of that you can be certain."

Chapter 14

Nick was glad he had insisted the hold of the *Wind Raven* be kept clean. He did not fear rats, and besides, the gray cat had found her way to where his crew sat nursing their wounds. But even with his standards of cleanliness, the hold stank of bilge water, and his nose never dulled to the rank odor.

They'd had no food since being thrown in the hold, but at least they had the water the pirates had not removed, which was stored in casks. Somewhat surprisingly, the pirates had also left the spare canvas, spars and anchor cable, for which Jake had expressed relief. Optimistically, Nick thought, the bos'n looked toward a day he might need them.

Nick's only injuries were some badly bruised ribs, a cut lip and a bruised jaw. But others of his crew did not fare so well. They had lost a half dozen men to the pirates' machetes, and most of the rest were wounded.

It had taken them a while to assess the injuries. There was only one lantern in the hold and the light was dim. John Trent had taken a slash to his arm from a machete. Augie Adams had received a blow to the head and was still unconscious. Charlie Wilson had various cuts on his limbs, including a slash to one arm. Smitty had a deep gash in his side. Thankfully, little Peter was unharmed. Jake and Russ were also without major injury, along with Nate. That is, if he didn't count the cuts. The wizened older seaman tended the wounded in his usual competent manner, using their shirts and what little cloth was to be found in the hold to clean and bind wounds. Nick's medical kit was still in his cabin so they made do with what they had. Peter scurried between the men, offering them water. The other cabin boy, Joshua, who also survived unscathed, having been defended by Jake, trailed behind, trying to do what he could to make the men comfortable even though he was still wide-eyed from the pirate attack. The cook, McGinnes, was wafting eloquent about the wrath of the fairies. Nick was of little use to them as both he and Russ had been bound in chains.

"How are the men, Nate?" he asked, still favoring his side where he'd taken the blow. His left arm caused him only a little pain where he'd been grazed by the machete. Lifting his chained hands to wipe the side of his face, he came away with a streak of blood from the cut on his mouth.

"Holdin' their own for the most part, I think. I'm worried about Smitty, but he's still out so at least ye'll not hear him groanin'. Last I checked he'd stopped bleedin'. Yer next on me list. I must clean that wound in yer arm and I've some torn strips to bind those ribs ye've been holdin'. I know ye don't think I see how they're painin' ye, but I do."

The older seaman wound the cloth strips tightly around Nick's ribs. Thankful for the lessening pain, Nick leaned back to consider their plight as Nate tended his arm. If it hadn't been for Tara's appearance on deck, and all that followed, they might have fought on to the end. But that opportunity had passed. Looking over at Russ, he asked, "Have you been thinking of an escape?"

"They'll have to bring us topside at some point," said Russ. "We've enough men left we might start a scuffle sufficient to gain the upper hand if we can take their weapons. Won't be easy, and may not succeed, but it may be our only chance."

"I've considered that. If we choose that course, we'll have to make sure Peter and Joshua and the badly wounded are brought up last."

Nick's thoughts were full of Tara; he worried what the pirate had done with her. Along with his ship and his cargo, Nick was certain Tara would be counted as spoils. He could still see the look on Cofresí's face as he said, "*Ven aqui, mí cariño.*" The gleam in the pirate's eyes had been possessive when he had beckoned her to come to him. The pirate had repeated the words in English, but it had been unnecessary. Nick well understood the meaning. Cofresí had claimed Tara McConnell just has he had claimed the *Wind Raven*. It jarred Nick to hear the pirate call her *sweetheart*. His gut had twisted in alarm. Though the pirate had said he would not harm her, Nick did not see how a man with so few scruples could be trusted to keep his word.

Nick's feelings for the American girl ran deeper than he wanted to admit. He would gladly die to see her safe.

* * *

As Cofresí had assured Tara the night before, his ship remained anchored in the luminous bay overnight. The pirate captain had given her his cabin, and though she had locked the cabin door and stretched out on the bunk, she slept little. Worried about Nicholas Powell and his crew and wondering what the pirate meant by his statement that he intended to win her, or why he would want to try, Tara was a frazzle of nerves when he knocked on the cabin door the next morning. She had just changed her gown to a clean one, the special one with breeches beneath, and pulled her hair back into a knot, when she opened the cabin door. The tall blond pirate stood there grinning.

"It's a glorious day, *cariño*. Come. I will show you, and when we return to my cabin, breakfast will be ready. You ate so little last night you must be hungry."

Though she was beyond hunger, her head hurt and a sick feeling in her stomach told her she needed to eat or she would have no strength. Still, it seemed wrong to eat anything when the captain of the *Wind Raven* was bound in chains in his hold. She had spent the dark hours of the night trying to think of a way to get a weapon to his crew, even searching the pirate's cabin in the hope of finding one, but had not been successful. In truth, she'd thought of nothing, save tossing a weapon to them when they were brought up from their prison, assuming she could get her hands on one.

She followed Cofresí up on deck, where clear blue water surrounded his schooner, rocking gently at anchor in the calm waters of the bay. His men, busy about their chores as they prepared to get underway, leered up at her. At their captain's harsh glare, they went back to their work.

Hearing the sound of a sail luffing in the wind, Tara looked up to see a strange blue, red and white flag flying from the main mast. It was divided in the middle by a white cross, the two lower corners were red and the two upper corners were dark blue with one white star in the left blue corner.

"What is that flag?" she asked Cofresí.

He smiled and his blue eyes lit with a fervor she'd not seen since the first time he'd looked at her on the deck of the *Wind Raven*. "The flag of the Free Republic of Porto Rico."

"You do not fly the flag of Spain?" Tara was surprised. Porto Rico belonged to Spain.

"No, I do not, though I am not so foolish as to prey on the ships that do. For my forbearance, Spain looks the other way when I take my prizes from the merchantmen of other countries. The flag I fly is that of my real allegiance, the fight for Porto Rico's independence from Spain. I give my best prize ships to my friend El Libertador Simón Bolívar, to help the cause of independence in Venezuela and South America. Have you heard of him, *cariño*?"

"Yes, my brothers who were privateers in the last war with England have spoken of him."

"He is a great lover of liberty, as am I." Then looking at her with sudden tenderness, he said, "He greatly admires America and the war you waged with the English for your independence."

"You are not only a pirate, but also a revolutionary?"

"We are not so different, you and I, *cariño*. I capture prize ships and give the bounty to my countrymen and those fighting for freedom, just as did your American privateers. We both wish to be free of the European powers, no?"

"America has fought to be free of the British, yes." She would concede that and no more. "But England and Spain are not at war. How do you justify taking Captain Powell's ship?

His blue eyes flared for a moment, conveying the passion within. "Spain may not be at war with England, *cariño*, but I am."

Tara wondered what that could mean and why he would declare a personal war on a country, but she wanted to ask another question more.

"Do you intend to give the *Wind Raven* to your friend Bolívar?"

"Exactly my plan, *cariño*."

"And you would tell me of your plans…why?"

His lithe movement brought him close, barely inches away. She took a step back and he followed, capturing her elbows in his hands and looking deeply into her eyes. "Because I want you to know my heart and to share my life."

* * *

Tara was horrified at the pirate's plans for her. She could never do as he wished.

She managed to force down a small bit of breakfast before they sailed back to Boquerón Bay, where the *Wind Raven* was anchored. Anxiety for the fate of Nicholas Powell and his men left her stomach unsettled. She set her eyes on the horizon and sighed with relief when the larger schooner came into view.

"Bring up the crew of the English ship," ordered Cofresí as he stepped on board the captured ship. Tara followed closely behind him, wanting to be assured the men of the *Wind Raven* were as she'd last seen them, or at least no worse. "But leave their captain in chains below," added the pirate captain.

Nicholas Powell was still in chains. She had to think of a way to help him. *But how?*

As the *Wind Raven*'s crew came up on deck, blinking their eyes against the blinding sun, the pirates stood guard, machetes unsheathed and ready. Tara watched the eyes of the men she had grown to care about. They looked tired and hungry. Some of their clothing showed the signs of the fight the day before, torn and splattered with dried blood. A few were limping or bearing cuts, and some had makeshift bandages. Their shared glances told her they were planning something. Fear for them washed over her like a wave as she thought about what the pirates might do to the unarmed men should they attempt to regain control of the ship.

One of Cofresí's men approached him with a look of urgency. "Capitán, there is a problem with the rigging on the English ship." Gesturing high into the shrouds near the top of the main mast, the pirate said, "Something is wrong in the lines near the crosstrees and Manuel discovered a broken tie chain."

The pirate captain scowled and squinted into the sky, looking toward the crosstrees high above them. "Watch the English crew. I will see this for myself."

Cofresí's long legs ate up the deck as he strode to the side of the ship, deftly swung onto the shrouds and swiftly climbed. Tara watched, as did the crews of both ships, as the pirate captain muttered what sounded like a Spanish oath and scaled the rigging. It was clear he was frustrated as he reached the crosstrees and hauled himself up the futtock shrouds, leaning backward, precariously perched over the deck a hundred feet below.

With a visible effort, he swung his weight up over the edge, reaching for the shroud above—and grabbed only air. At that moment, Tara remembered Jake had not finished the repairs aloft and the shroud was not properly rigged. Cofresí could not have known and now there was nothing for him to take hold of. Tara gasped as he fell back, dangling from the crosstrees by one hand, flailing his other arm wildly as he sought to gain purchase and prevent a fatal plunge.

Should she try and save him? And if she did, would it gain the freedom of Nicholas Powell and his crew? She could only hope. Tara ripped away the bottom portion of her gown, leaving her in breeches. Hearing the fabric tear, Cofresí's men turned their attention from their captain to her. Ignoring their shocked faces, she raced around them and leapt into the rigging. She could hear one of the pirates following as she climbed to where the pirate captain dangled high above the deck. She had always been fast climbing the rigging, faster than any of her brothers. It had served her well when she'd rescued Billy; it served her now.

Holding onto the doubling, Tara leaned out, stretching as far as she could, and grasped the leather of one of the pirate's boots. As she took the heel into her hand, her foot slipped and she fell back onto the doubling. Gasps sounded from the deck below. Her heart racing, she fought to control her fear. Righting herself, she reached again, this time without losing her footing, and again took hold of the pirate's boot.

"Will you free this ship and all who sail her if I do not let you fall to your death?"

The pirate captain grimaced, his hold loosening. "Will you stay with me if I let them go?"

Tara knew in an instant what she would say. There was no choice, not really. If the pirate fell to his death when she could have saved him, both she and the *Wind Raven*'s crew would be slaughtered. If she stayed with him, the captain and his men would go free.

"Yes." She pulled Cofresí's dangling feet back to the rigging, first one booted foot and then the other, setting them firmly onto the ratlines. Tara could feel Cofresí's legs shaking; she could see the sweat beaded on his forehead as he turned his head and looked down to see her below him.

"*Madre de Dios*," he said, expelling the breath he was holding, "you saved my life, *cariño*. And for that I will keep our bargain." No one had heard his words, save the pirate who had followed her into the rigging and who was now just below her. He gave his captain a troubled look.

"It is all right, Manuel," Cofresí shouted past her. "The woman rescued me from the faulty rigging. It was good that she did, *sí*? You would have been too late."

"*Sí*, Capitán, I am glad for the *señorita*'s quick thinking and quicker feet." The pirate Manuel gave her a steadying gaze. He knew the bargain she had struck.

From the looks of the *Wind Raven*'s crew as she descended to the deck, they were not pleased she had spared the life of the pirate. To them, she had aided the enemy. Little did they know of the promise she had won by giving the pirate his life.

Once they were both standing on deck, Cofresí took her hand without a word and led her across the plank that had been laid between the two ships. She felt the hard stares of the *Wind Raven*'s crew following her. She could see they had known of the dangerous situation on the crosstrees and had hoped Cofresí would fall to his death. Had counted upon it. Still, Tara did not regret her action, not if it led to their freedom.

Once on his ship, Cofresí led Tara to his cabin, where he poured two glasses of Madeira and handed one to her. His blond hair had come loose from his queue and hung around his shoulders, framing his silver and black earrings. "Drink, *cariño*, and celebrate with me the life you have saved. As it is mine, I am very grateful." Then with a smile spreading on his face, he took a large swallow of wine and said, "It appears I owe you the *deuda* you forced me to." When Tara's brows drew together, he explained, "A debt. Or perhaps as you might think of it, I owe you a boon. And I will pay it."

"You have promised the life of Captain Powell and his men—and their freedom."

Staring at his Madiera, the pirate seemed to reconsider what he had agreed to. For a moment she feared he would renege. Narrowing his gaze to study her, he finally said, "You may trust I will not break my word to you, though it will anger my men and I would relish killing Captain Powell. But I will have you for consolation and my crew will have Captain Powell's cargo."

The look he gave her was cunning; it sickened Tara. She had no desire to remain the prisoner of the pirate and all that could mean. But no matter the cost to herself, she could not bear for him to take the life of the man she loved, even if that man did not return her love. Nor could she allow the crew of the *Wind Raven* to be sold into slavery to spend the rest of their days at hard labor on foreign ships. There had been no doubt when she'd scaled the rigging that their freedom had been her goal.

"I will hold you to your promise, Captain."

"I expected no less, *cariño*. But you must convince the Raven and his men. You must make it appear you are staying with me from your own desire, not as a bargain for their lives. Perhaps they can be made to believe we are already lovers, no?" The look he gave her said he expected it would be true soon enough.

"I will never willingly become your lover."

"We shall see."

Tara swallowed her fear for the future. She could not think about the gleam in the pirate's eye. He was right to insist she make the men of the *Wind Raven* believe she wanted to stay with him, lest Nicholas Powell risk his life and the lives of his crew to preserve her honor and her safety. How else could he explain to his mother what he'd done with the niece of her best friend? No, the pirate had the right of it. She must make it convincing. Captain Powell must believe it was her decision. And what would happen to her after that? She shuddered to think. She had to get back to her family—to her father. In her mind, a plan to escape the pirate was already forming. Though she would go with the pirate to save Nicholas Powell and his crew, she would not remain with him.

The pirate stared into his wine. "We will return to the *Wind Raven*, but not today, I think. No, tomorrow would be better. Let the good captain believe you have spent another night in my arms. And tomorrow you will show your affection for me. You will smile when I speak of our being revolutionaries. You will be convincing, no? And they will believe you have chosen to remain with El Pirata Cofresí."

Once again, Cofresí acted the gentleman. He had given orders to have the crew of the *Wind Raven* taken back to the hold, and then he gave her time alone to change her clothes before joining him for dinner. They dined as they had before, only this time Tara ate, for the knowledge that the *Wind Raven*'s captain and crew would be freed buoyed her spirits immensely. She did not doubt the word of the pirate captain. For some reason, she believed he could be trusted once he had given his word. And she had been careful to extract his promise to do all he had said. Tomorrow he would release Nicholas Powell and his men. Tara did not think overmuch about what would happen beyond that. It seemed both captains wanted her, though neither spoke of love. She would endure what she must and one day she would find a way to be free and return to her family.

* * *

Nick was surprised when his men returned to the hold. So, it seemed, were they. Russ and Nate were the first ones to join him in the dimly lit space, his first mate no longer in chains. Seeing Russ was about to explain what had happened, Nate turned his attention to helping the wounded find a comfortable resting spot.

Nick could wait no longer. "What has happened?"

"I'm not certain," confessed Russ. "You know that rigging for the new mast the bos'n wasn't happy with? Well it seems more pressing work drew Jake's attention elsewhere and he was not able to see to it. It was fortuitous as Cofresí chose this morning to go aloft and take a look. He was reaching above the crosstrees to grab the foretopmast shrouds, but since they weren't fully rigged, he lost his footing and was left dangling backwards over the deck. We would have been short one pirate captain had not our passenger intervened. Just like with Billy, she scrambled into the rigging and righted the pirate's footing before he could fall to his much-deserved death. Nearly fell herself doing it, too."

"She saved the pirate?" Nick asked, disbelieving.

"She did. While most of the pirate's men stood around gaping at her breeches, she scaled the rigging. 'Twas a sight to see, I must say. There were many open mouths in our own crew as well."

"Why would she save the pirate?" Nick asked, frowning. *Why indeed?*

"No one knows. But you know her propensity for saving seamen from death. Still, it looked as if she and the pirate were on very good terms when they came back to the ship together this morning."

"She spent the night with the pirate aboard his ship?"

Seeing his expression, Russ looked apologetic. "Sorry, Nick, it appears she did."

* * *

The next morning, Nick and his men were brought up on deck and Nick's chains were promptly removed. He and his crew were then gathered together on the quarterdeck as Cofresí stood with Tara at his side amidships looking back at them. The pirate crew watched from the railing and some from the shrouds as their captain addressed Nick and his men.

"Tara McConnell, an American revolutionary sympathetic to the cause of a free Porto Rico, has decided to stay with me. We have found pleasure together."

There were gasps from Nick's crew and loudly voiced objections by some, but the pirate crew uttered not a word.

"Because Tara has decided to stay with me, I, Cofresí, will be generous to the Raven and his crew. You may take your ship and leave my waters. It would be wise not to return." Then putting his arm possessively around Tara's waist, he pulled her close.

Nick was seething at the pirate's words and his hands on Tara McConnell, but he forced himself to look carefully at the faces of the pirates. They were unsurprised. Obviously they had been told this would happen. Before Nick could respond, Cofresí kissed her, to the cheers of his crew. At first Tara remained still, though compliant. Then she lifted her hands to the pirate's shoulders, pulled him close and ardently returned his kiss.

Nick felt a slow burn forming deep inside. So, the American girl had given to the pirate what Nick had resisted taking for himself. As he'd feared, she had spent the last two nights in the pirate's bed. No ordinary pirate, he reminded himself, but a pirate all the same. Rage consumed him at being betrayed once again by a woman. Battling to overcome his anger, he told himself Tara was just another Caroline but of a different kind. One left him for a title; the other left him for love. *Love of a pirate, for Christ's sake.* An educated, smooth-talking pirate. *Fool.* Tara had never been his. They'd not become lovers. Why that should grieve him, he did not question.

He'd known Tara McConnell had no love for the English. Just like the pirate. So what if she chose the pirate's cause? Let him have her.

Nick moved to the front of his men. "I thank you for my life and for our freedom, Captain Cofresí," Nick said, graciously bowing before the pirate with a sarcastic smile. He would not let Cofresí or Tara see his dismay. "And I wish you and Miss McConnell well. I understand you have already had her chest brought aboard your ship, so my crew and I will say our good-byes and bid you smooth sailing." There were murmured objections from those of his crew who had grown fond of the American girl. He ignored them. They were too protective of the hoyden. "Be still!" he commanded in a whisper sent over his shoulder. "The girl has chosen her fate. I will not intervene."

Nick watched as the pirate's men slowly filed over the plank back to their ship, a silent and brooding group. They might support their captain but they did not like losing their prize. Of course, they had the cargo of the *Wind Raven* to assuage their loss, though if his hiding place were still secure, the pirates had not found the gold Nick always carried.

After the pirate crew departed, Nick watched Cofresí take Tara's hand and lead her across the plank to his ship. She looked back only once and then only to the somber group of the *Wind Raven*'s crew, where her gaze lingered for a moment.

With dispatch, the grappling hooks were removed and the sails of the *Retribución* unfurled to slowly catch the wind. Soon they were sailing away from the *Wind Raven* still anchored in the bay. Nick watched from the starboard rail as the tall blond pirate stood proudly on the deck of his ship, his arm around Tara's shoulders, a tether to her future. The gaze of the two golden-haired beings was fixed on Nick as they sailed away.

Chapter 15

Tara never took her eyes off the *Wind Raven* or her captain as the pirate's ship carried her from them. Tears flowed down her cheeks as she silently said good-bye to the man she loved, the one to whom she had given her heart.

"Come, *cariño*," said Cofresí. "Our new life begins." Tara looked away from the dwindling sails of the other ship. Had she a spyglass she might have stared longer into the horizon, hoping for a last glimpse of the schooner she'd called home for so long. She never had a chance to say good-bye to the first mate or the gunner or McGinnes or Nate or Peter or Jake. Intentionally, she had not said good-bye to their captain. It was for the best. She would not have been able to keep up the pretense with him. He would have seen the tears in her eyes and known she loved him. Known it was all a lie.

"What do you intend to do with me now?" she asked.

"Why, I plan to introduce you to my family as the woman I intend to court."

"I do not encourage your suit, nor would I want to mislead your family."

"I am a patient man, *cariño*. And I do not think it proper for you to linger aboard my ship. I will see you safely to my home in Cabo Rojo and clothed in a manner that befits a Cofresí. Do not tell my sister of your past tendency to wear men's clothing. She is a good Catholic and would not approve. Juana will take you to church and act the part of the chaperone until we are wed."

"I will be a prisoner, you mean."

"A protected woman, *cariño*. You will not need to sail again. My family's home is one of the finest in Cabo Rojo. It will be there that we will raise our family."

Tara felt the walls closing around her. From the stifling London ballrooms to the elegant prison of the pirate's home, she had traveled far. But she was determined to travel still farther, to escape and return to her family.

*   *   *

"I've known ye for a heartbroken lad when Caroline left ye for the earl, and I've known ye as a rogue and a privateer—more pirate at times than even yer namesake—but I've never known ye for a fool," scolded Nate.

Nick and the old seaman stood at the helm, Nate's sure hands on the wheel, as the *Wind Raven* sailed from Boquerón Bay, heading for the open sea.

Nick had heard the old seaman's counsel before, and though he would prefer not to listen to his chiding now, Nate's standing as an old friend of the Powell family dictated he give the man the respect he was due.

"I suppose I'm partly to blame," Nate said, shaking his head. "All those years ago, I watched it happen and said nothin'. Many a time I wanted to talk to ye, but I thought ye'd not be wantin' to hear what I had to say. 'Tis to my shame I kept quiet."

"What are you talking about?" said Nick, full of anger at Tara and anger at himself for caring about her still.

"When that woman hurt ye, ye buried the wound deep and never grieved. Swept it away like dirt 'neath a rug. Then to make sure ye'd never hurt like that again, ye made your heart unbreakable, cold and distant." At Nick's raised brow, he added, "Oh, yer a man loved by women, to be sure—many women 'tis said—but in truth ye love only your ship, yer family and yer crew.

Ye must change that, Nick. Ye must risk yer heart again. Give it to her." Nate looked in the direction of the pirate ship growing ever smaller in the distance.

"She is gone, Nate. Chose the pirate. You saw it yourself. My God, she spent two nights in his bed!"

"I've been wonderin' about that."

"Russ said she saved him—"

"I saw it meself. But ye know as well as I do that lass would save any man, as she once saved Billy and would have saved him again, though she nearly died tryin'."

"She was kissing the pirate, Nate."

"Listen to yer heart, son. I'd swear me eyes saw the lass playin' the greatest role of her life. When she looked back at us as she left the ship, her heart was in her eyes."

Stepping to the rail and gripping the brightwork to anchor himself, Nick stared into the horizon, watching Cofresí's sails now a mere dot in the distance. Likely the pirate was headed for some cove in Cabo Rojo to be alone with his prize. A deep ache settled into Nick's chest. Losing Tara felt like dying, like he couldn't get enough breath into his lungs.

Was Nate right? Had Tara been pretending? Viewed in that light, many things suddenly became clear. Why she wouldn't look at him, why she had not said good-bye, why she had hesitated before kissing the pirate. He wanted to believe Nate's words, oh so badly. Nate had no need to urge him to give her his heart. She'd claimed it one night on the deck of his ship when the dying sun bathed her in golden light.

"Ye've always been like yer father, Nick, and never more so than with this woman."

Nick whirled around at the words of his old friend. "What do you mean?"

"He's a one-woman man and so are ye. But until now, ye'd not met that woman. Well, now ye have. If ye let Tara McConnell go, I promise ye'll feel the loss for as long as ye live."

Nate gestured for Nick to take the wheel as the older seaman lit his pipe, a small smile deepening the many wrinkles on his timeworn face. A few strands of his gray hair blew across his forehead, carried by the wind coming off starboard. "She reminds me of yer mother, that one does. The wild Claire Donet," he said wistfully.

"My mother is a lady. Tara's the wild one, a hoyden who wears breeches."

"Ah, yer mother is a lady *now*, but ye'll recall I knew her when she was the pirate Jean Donet's daughter. A bit o' the banshee she was then, though she was convent-raised. She nearly broke up yer father's cabin throwing things at him when he abducted her and refused to let her go. Don't forget, lad, I may have gray hair now, but I was once yer father's cabin boy. I was there when he stole her from the convent where Donet had her stashed in France. Ye'd be wise to take a lesson from yer father and do the same."

"Why should I risk the *Raven* for Tara McConnell? She's made her choice."

"Well, for one thing, ye love her. 'Tis plain as the nose on yer face. And for another, if my instincts are right, she went with Cofresí but she was not happy about it. There was deep regret in those sad eyes as the lass took her leave. I've been thinkin' about it and I believe she went with the pirate only to free you—and yer crew."

Nate's words sank in. *Only to free you.* Had she had done it for him? Like a forbidding black cloud, Nick sensed the wrong that had been done hovering in the background and the desperate need to right it. He had been freed with no explanation save the pirate's whim. What if it hadn't been a whim? What if it had been...*a bargain*—her willing compliance for his freedom and that of his crew? If Tara hadn't wanted to leave, if she didn't want the pirate, Cofresí would take her against her will. The thought of the pirate's hands on her made the anger rise within him like gale-force wind.

"How did my father do it, Nate?" he asked in a slow, deliberate voice.

"Ah, now that'd be a story."

Over the next few minutes, Nate told him the story of all that had happened the night of the daring raid leading to the capture of the wild Claire Donet.

* * *

Tara felt like a bird in a gilded cage. She had been in Cabo Rojo for a week, and the few words of Spanish she had picked up barely allowed her to manage halting conversations with Cofresí's sister, Juana, much less the fast-flowing conversations in the marketplace when Juana took her shopping. Thankfully, Juana spoke English. Like her brothers, she had been educated in several languages.

Juana reminded Tara of the pirate, with her golden hair, only a shade darker than her brother's, rendering her an attractive woman. She had welcomed Tara into their home, an elaborate two-story structure built around a central courtyard containing a lush garden. It was pleasant to sit in the shade of the trees on hot afternoons, and Tara had often gone there to think, to plan and to dream.

Though his brothers looked askance when Cofresí told them he met Tara on an English merchant ship, Juana had questioned little, seemingly delighted to have Tara living with her in their family home, no matter she was neither European nor Catholic. Tara had the impression Juana approved of her, and that made their time together pleasant. Cofresí's sister seemed starved for the company of another woman. Her brothers, especially the pirate captain, were very protective of their sister, and except for her regular visits to the marketplace, Juana did not often leave her home.

Juana had confided to Tara that Roberto was her favorite of the brothers, and she expressed a desire to see the two of them wed. Tara did not encourage the idea, but she suspected the pirate had told Juana of his intentions. Tara's heart belonged to an English sea captain, though there had never been any words of love between them. She missed him terribly. Where was he now? Likely on his way north. Tara thought only of escape and of going home to her family in Baltimore. Still, reality did not stop her from dreaming. And when she sat in the garden and dreamed, it was of Nicholas Powell.

"What are you making for tonight's dinner, Juana?" asked Tara, smelling a wonderful spicy aroma as she entered the kitchen.

"Roberto's favorite, since he is returning tonight."

Tara had not seen the pirate captain for most of the week and, knowing he was to return, she wondered if he would still act the gentleman. Before he had left, the pirate had begun dictating orders as to how she was to dress and conduct herself, as if she were one of his crew, or worse, one of his possessions.

"Oh? And what is it he likes?"

"*Empanadillas.*" At Tara's blank look, Juana explained, "Small pies filled with lobster and crab and a sauce made with many spices. I serve them with rice and fruit and sometimes cut greens."

"It sounds tasty. I've never had them. May I help?"

"Would you be willing to go to the marketplace for me? I have need of a few more tomatoes and some *cilantrillo.*"

Tara had purchased both with Juana once before and knew which stands sold them. She thought she could manage enough Spanish to secure the items.

"I'd enjoy the walk." Juana never considered Tara would try to escape, and in truth, Tara had not figured out how she would accomplish her goal to be free. She had no money of her own, no transportation and, except for a few words, she did not speak the language. She had thought perhaps she might find a ship sailing to America that would grant her passage for the promise of payment in Baltimore. The idea presented many risks, and she'd not seen any American ships in port, but it was the only plan she had. Cofresí was too well known and too well liked for her to seek help from anyone in Cabo Rojo.

"I could send a servant, but I know you like to get out in the afternoons," said the thoughtful Juana.

"You are right. I do." Juana always provided the money for any shopping they did, telling Tara that Roberto gave her coins aplenty. Tara didn't doubt it and wondered if he'd yet sold the cargo he'd seized from the *Wind Raven*. In the time he'd been gone from Cabo Rojo, she assumed he was arranging to dispose of his stolen merchandise or making one of his runs to capture a merchant ship. She shuddered to think what might be the fate of the crew. She had personally witnessed death at the hands of the pirate.

Cofresí was a paradox: On the one hand he was gentle with her and his sister, and on the other, a ruthless pirate who thought nothing of slicing into a man's neck with his axe. He treated Tara like she was some idealized woman. While praising her courage, he was doing all he could to stifle her spirit. It was clear to Tara what he really wanted was a compliant Catholic wife. He would make her into that woman if she allowed him the opportunity. She had no intention of succumbing to such manipulation. Yes, a walk to clear her mind and some simple shopping would be good. Perhaps there would be a captain of a merchant ship in the square.

Tara left Cofresí's home, where only Roberto and Juana now lived, their father having died three years before, and hastened along the village street. Walking briskly, thinking of the ships she'd seen in the bay, she was suddenly grabbed from behind and pulled into an alley. She twisted in the man's grip, desperate to get away, but he lifted her from the ground and held her against his powerful chest, his hand stifling her screams.

"Hush."

She froze. It was the voice of Nicholas Powell; it was Nicholas's arms holding her. She breathed a sigh of relief, but her heart was still pounding in her chest. *He had scared her to death!* As she stilled, panting out small breaths, he relaxed his hold and set her feet on the ground. Tara turned to see fury in his golden eyes. And maybe worry…

"Captain, what are you doing here?" He was dressed in the clothes of the local Porto Ricans, a muslin shirt open at the neck to reveal a black mat of chest hair, black pants and a sash at his waist. His black hair blended with the men on the street, though no one would mistake Nicholas Powell for a villager if they looked at him closely.

"I should have thought it was obvious. I am rescuing you. Or would you rather I didn't?" The sarcastic tone of his voice and his frown told her he was unsure of his welcome. But no matter his gruff mood, she was elated. He had come for her!

She looked into his golden eyes. Did he see in them the love she harbored for him? Truthfully she said, "I never thought anyone would come."

"Well, I did, though I may yet regret it. We must go—now!" He began to pull her along with him out of the alley.

"Wait! Where is the ship?" she asked, hoping it was not far.

"In a cove some distance north. I could not very well take the chance the pirate would see the ship in the bay."

"You need not worry. He won't return until tonight."

"Were you eagerly awaiting him?" he asked sarcastically.

Her Irish temper flared until she remembered the last time he had seen her she was kissing Cofresí. "No, I was dreading it."

"It's a damned good thing I found you today. My men and I have been watching, but you were never alone until now." He took her arm. "Come. Nate and Jake are waiting."

Tara went willingly, his hand holding hers tightly. It was the lifeline she'd been craving since she'd left the ship.

They kept to the shade of the trees as they hurried along the few streets to where Nate and Jake stood near a small carriage. It was black and looked a bit worse for wear but to her it was a carriage to freedom. The driver, a young man, held the reins of the one horse. The older seaman, like Jake and the captain, was dressed in the clothes of the common men of the port city, pants and a muslin shirt with a sash at his waist.

A smile spread across Nate's leathered face when he saw her. "How good it is to see ye."

"And you," she said, returning his smile as tears spilled from her eyes.

Jake beamed a smile at her. "*Ja*, we would not go without you."

They had come! She wondered if the captain had urged them to do so or if it was Nate's idea. No matter his suspicions, the captain still held her hand. He helped her into the carriage and the boy climbed into the driver's seat.

"So 'twas as I suspected," said Nate as he joined them, followed by Jake. "Ye never wanted to leave us, did ye?"

Tara wiped away the tears with her hand and the older seaman leaned forward to pat her shoulder. The captain still held her hand in a savage grip, saying nothing. Instead, he stared out the open window, appearing to brood. Jake, who sat next to him in the cramped quarters, looked on awkwardly, as if he wanted to say something but had no idea what it should be.

"It was the only way…"

The remainder of the bumpy ride to the ship was a silent one. Occasionally, Nate and Jake shot the captain a glance but neither ventured into the stony silence that surrounded them. Tara dared not look again at the captain's brooding face. She was afraid of what she would see.

As they neared the cove where the *Wind Raven* lay at anchor, its sails furled, Tara's thoughts drifted to Juana, who had been so kind to her. Cofresí's sister would not understand why Tara had not said good-bye.

And what would Cofresí do when he learned she was gone?

Chapter 16

The sun was beginning to set when they reached the small hill overlooking the *Wind Raven*, anchored in a cove north of the blue-green bay of Porto Real. Tara's heart thrilled at the sight of the black-hulled schooner, its masts bared of sail and gently rocking with the swells of the ocean. She felt a nervous anticipation at the thought of soon being alone with the captain.

She stepped down from the carriage, tucked the stray hairs falling around her face into her straw bonnet and smoothed the wrinkles from her plain muslin gown, chosen for its suitability for an afternoon of shopping in the hot and muggy weather of Cabo Rojo. Most of her other clothes were at Cofresí's home, along with her books. She did not expect to see them again. A few of her gowns had been left behind in her cabin and she was glad of it for she would need them. She had been wearing her turquoise ring, else it too would have remained with the pirate.

Nate handed a coin to their young driver, who turned the carriage around and headed back down the rutted road.

Soon the captain, the two men and Tara had crossed the water in the boat that was left waiting for them hidden in the trees. Reaching the ship, the captain was the first one up the rope ladder. He helped her on board and said, "I'll see you in my cabin as soon as you've given your greeting to the crew. They've been waiting to see you."

When the captain descended the aft ladder, the air erupted in loud cheers. Looking around and seeing the warm smiles on the faces of the crew, who had become her very dear friends, she felt her eyes fill with tears.

Charlie Wilson sheepishly stepped forward to ask, "Is it true what Nate's been saying, that you did it for us, so the pirate would set us all free?"

Tara suddenly felt shy around the gunner she had come to like. "Yes," she said, grateful to see the crew nodding their heads in acceptance. Even the ones who had been unfriendly before now smiled warmly. Among them was Smitty, nodding from where he sat off to one side. "I bargained with him that day on the rigging. He merely took advantage of a situation that was to his liking."

"Thanks be to you, Miss Tara," said Charlie. The others murmured their agreement.

Mr. Ainsworth seemed to be speaking for the whole crew when he said, "Nate told us we could have seen it in your eyes if we'd only been watching you instead of the pirate. Forgive us for thinking what we did."

Tara smiled, happy to be among them. She did not fault the crew for believing she had willingly gone with the pirate. It is what she had wanted them to think. But she loved them all the more for believing she had done it for them.

At her side, Jake said, "The captain wanted I should bring you to his cabin as soon as you spoke with the crew, Miss Tara." Jake was a large man known for his fists, but to Tara he was a gentle soul. She thought he'd walk through hell for her.

"That won't be necessary, Jake. I know the way."

"It is good you are with us again," said the blond giant as she turned toward the aft hatch. "We were happy when Nate told us what you'd done and that the captain was going to fetch you." Then he added proudly, "I volunteered."

Tara looked back and couldn't resist a smile for her guardian angel. "I'm so glad you did, Jake."

The other men began drifting back to their work as Tara went below. She entered the familiar companionway and walked the short distance to the door of the captain's cabin, remembering the first time she had done so. She had been nervous then to face the captain who had scowled at her from the quarterdeck. She was nervous now for an entirely different reason. She loved the captain who was on the other side of the cabin door and she had not a thought as to what to do about it. Even if he had loved her, she could not marry an Englishman and suffer again the parlours of London. It would only be another kind of cage. And she wanted desperately to see her family.

Besides, Captain Powell's only use for women was in his bed. He had kissed her, more than once. Perhaps that is where he wanted her, too. She doubted he cared more, though she knew he had been concerned for her safety as a passenger.

Taking off her bonnet, she knocked once, and hearing a muffled "enter," opened the cabin door. He was standing at the window with his back to her, looking toward shore.

"Was I correct in assuming you wanted to be rescued?" he asked, slowly turning to face her. "Or did you wish to remain with the pirate?" His face was a mask of indifference as he continued, but she sensed there was anger just beneath the surface. "It's too late now in any event. I won't waste my crew's efforts and relinquish you to him again so easily."

Tara observed him carefully. His golden amber eyes were looking at her with a disturbing intensity she'd not seen before. His jaw was clenched, his expression that of a man about to begin yelling. Even having to pay the price now, she was glad he and his crew had accepted her lie. It had saved their lives.

"You were meant to believe I went with him of my own accord," she felt compelled to explain. She stepped farther into the cabin and laid her bonnet on his desk. "In truth, I did."

His eyes narrowed at her words.

"I bargained my freedom for your life and the lives of the crew. Cofresí required I go with him voluntarily. I made the only decision I could."

"You should have told me!" he bellowed. Was he angry at his own powerlessness? Or did he blame her in some way for her capture?

"And what would you have done if I had? What *could* you have done? You were bound in chains, what was left of your crew wounded and with no weapons. I was afraid he would kill you that very morning."

"And the kiss? Was that also necessary?"

He was jealous! It was a good sign, and it made Tara hope for more.

With a great effort, she held back her temper and explained, "Cofresí made clear I had to be convincing. He assured me you would never believe it otherwise. He even kept me a second night aboard his ship to make you think—" Tara could not finish the thought, but she could see from his wince that he knew of what she was speaking.

"And did you go to his bed to make it even more convincing?" His hands fisted at his sides as he spoke the words with sarcastic emphasis. Tara closed the small distance between them and raised her hand to slap him.

He caught her hand just before it struck his cheek. She glared at him, now as angry as he. "I did not go to his bed at all, if you must speak of it. And for your further information, Cofresí did not demand that of me." *At least not yet.* At the captain's snort of disbelief, she pulled her hand from his grasp. "Yes, he wanted me. He made that clear. But he intended to make me his wife, though I gave him no encouragement." She resented all the explaining she was doing when his crew had accepted her word without question.

"The thought of that pirate touching you—" he said, looking to the side.

"Why should I be explaining this to you? You care nothing for me. I am merely unwanted baggage, a passenger who has caused you much trouble."

When he turned to face her, there was a different look in his eye. "Perhaps I—"

A knock sounded at the door, ending their conversation abruptly. "Enter," the captain said.

Peter and Joshua stepped through the cabin door, carrying trays of food.

Dinner had arrived.

The silence was awkward. Peter filled it. "McGinnes thought you'd be hungry, Miss Tara." Then looking at his captain, "Is it all right if we set the table for your dinner, Cap'n?"

"Yes, Peter, you and Joshua can set the table. Please thank McGinnes for his consideration. I am certain after her long journey to the ship Miss McConnell has an appetite."

In truth, Tara was too angry to be very hungry, but since McGinnes had gone to the trouble to welcome her back in his own way, she would force herself to eat. "Please tell him for me, Peter," she said, smiling at the boy and his companion, "that I am most grateful for his kindness."

Dinner was a silent affair, each too proud and still holding too much anger to speak. Yet between them was a current Tara felt through her skin. Had she hoped he would welcome her back with open arms, confessing his love? As she considered her daydreams in Cofresí's garden, she now thought them ridiculous.

When the meal was over and they finished their wine, he rose. As if the argument had never happened, he offered, "How about a turn on the deck? We might even catch the last of the sunset."

"Do we sail tonight?"

"I would like to but we can only make ready. The wind is not with us."

Tara was glad for the suggestion to go up on deck, as the light had faded in the cabin and the air in the smaller space was hot and still. Besides, she had a need to walk.

The moment she came through the hatch, Tara breathed deeply of the night air. It was still warm but cooling, and without the hot sun beating down, not as oppressive as it had been earlier. The sunset had faded to a blend of dark red and violet. She was only vaguely aware of the watch as she and the captain walked to the prow and gazed west.

"A fine fix we're in," Tara said, looking first at the captain and then at the night sky. The stars began to show themselves in the darkening canvas above, giving her the sense she stood on a precipice at an auspicious moment in time. It had only been a short while ago she had gained the insight she had now about the two of them. She should have realized the truth long ago.

"What do you mean?" he asked, coming up behind her, so close she could feel the heat of his chest. His warmth had always drawn her, and it was pulling her to him now like a strong undertow.

"Each of us withheld from the other the one thing we wanted," she remarked, staring into the night sky.

"And what would that be?" He put his hands on her arms, drawing her back against his chest. She shivered with his touch but allowed it, while fighting the urge to turn and fall into his arms.

"You wanted my body and, fool that I am, I wanted your heart."

He spun her around so fast her vision blurred. "My heart? You wanted my heart?"

"Yes, but I cannot seem to touch it." His eyes carried a look of astonishment. "Well, you can keep it," she said emphatically. "I don't want it anymore. And you shall never have me!"

He stared at her for only a moment. "Oh, yes, I will." As if she had defied one of his many orders and he was having none of it, he brought his mouth down on hers in a kiss that was claiming. One of his hands closed on her nape and his other arm wrapped tightly around her waist, holding her to him, trapping her with his powerful strength.

Exasperated with his seeming indifference and angered at his lack of trust in her, she had taunted him. But now that she was in his arms, she realized it was where she had longed to be. Wrapped in the overpowering passion that flowed between them, the passion he could draw from her in an instant, she didn't want to fight her love for him any longer. His kiss was hungry, devouring, sweeping her away. She leaned into him, accepting his kiss, desperately seeking to join together what had so long been held apart.

"Tara, oh, Tara," he breathed as he pressed kisses down her throat. He had never said her name before. It was like a caressing breeze, making her giddy with the joy of it. It sounded to her like a lover's words, tender and sweet. She wanted to believe they were.

"Perhaps I should call you *Nicholas*," she whispered as his kisses fluttered over her ear.

"Perhaps you should," he whispered back as he raised his head to look into her eyes. "I think it's time we admitted what lies between us. I want you, Tara McConnell, and I think you want me, my black heart notwithstanding." With that he lifted her into his arms and carried her to the hatch. Once inside his cabin, he drew her to his bed, gently shoved her down and joined her, drawing her into his arms.

He leaned on one elbow, pressing kisses to her lips, her eyes and her throat. Entwining his fingers in her hair, he set the pins to flying, and when her hair was free, his hand traveled up and down her body as if learning every curve.

Excited by his touch, Tara returned his kisses, reaching her fingers into the waves of his ebony hair. His palm closed over her breast, his gentle kneading soothing the ache that had been growing since his first kiss. She had not known this was what she wanted, but she did now. She wanted more.

He slid on top of her and she welcomed his weight, holding him tightly to her. She wanted more. Holding his head with her hands, she pulled his mouth to hers and kissed him deeply. No matter their future, she loved this man.

She wore only the muslin gown and her underthings. He moved to one side and, in deft fashion, removed them, kissing each new part of her his efforts revealed. His lips as they touched her skin awoke feelings she had not experienced before. Soon, her garments had all fallen to the deck.

She was naked but he was still clothed. Wanting to feel his bare chest against her breasts, she tugged at his shirt. He rose briefly from the bed to shed the shirt and in the dim light she saw the white bandages wrapped around his arm and his ribs. Then she heard his boots and trousers fall to the deck. Briefly she caught a glimpse of his tanned chest and the black thatch of hair. Her gaze slid down to his white skin, untouched by the sun. She was startled by what she saw. He did not look like her brothers who, as youths, had frolicked in the waters of the Chesapeake. Here was a grown man who was naked and...aroused. The sight of his hard flesh frightened her.

Then he was back, his heated flesh touching her from lips to legs. She was excited and willing, yet the passion was so new to her. But this was the man she loved, the man she had dreamed of kissing. He kissed her again and moved his body to rest between her thighs. He rubbed his aroused member against her tender flesh, bringing a warm wetness and an urge to be joined with him. It was a consuming thing, so long had she wanted this man.

"Tara, there is no turning back once I make you mine."

It wasn't a question, but Tara knew he was waiting for her to object. Did she want him to stop? To turn back the tide of these feelings, this passion rushing at her like a tidal wave, seemed near impossible. She had already given him her heart. It was only the next step to give him her body, to make them one. Shoving aside her concern for what he might feel for her, she said nothing but willingly accepted what she knew he wanted to give.

He kissed her again and slipped his hand from her breast to her hip. The aching wetness lodged in her woman's center increased as he began to touch the tender place with his fingers while drawing first one breast and then the other into his mouth. Every nerve of Tara's was alive, aware of his every move. "Oh," she moaned when she felt herself reaching some new height. It was then he removed his fingers and replaced them with his hardened flesh.

She could feel him enter the tight passage as he spread her thighs to take more, driving through the maidenhead she had long protected for the man she would love.

Tara gasped at the sudden rending and he stilled, breathing heavily in her ear, as he remained suspended on his elbows above her. The pain was small and subsided quickly. Then he began to move, plunging in, and then withdrawing, then plunging still deeper. Tara wrapped herself around him and hung on, still kissing him, as he moved in long strokes. She was overwhelmed with the joining. The two of them were now one.

Their breathing grew labored and heavy as Tara felt another crest building, this time from deep within. Their bodies were slick with sweat from the heat of their loving and the tropical night as she raised her hips to receive him, wanting all he could give. The crest rose and the wave broke, carrying her with it. She heard him groan as he joined her in a final release.

It was more than she'd ever dreamed, this uniting with the man she loved. It was everything.

Nick pulled her close to his body and held her. "At last you are mine," he whispered.

* * *

Tara woke while it was still night, the lantern casting its frail light about the cabin. She barely noticed the gentle rocking of the ship on the calm sea. His arm was draped across her chest, and his hand loosely cupped her breast. The touch of his fingers against the sensitive skin made Tara's nipple harden.

In the cold reality of the dark cabin, their passion only a memory, her mind asked, *What have I done?* She'd given him not only her heart but also her virginity—when she was still unsure of his love. Sharing everything with him only left her more aware how vulnerable she was if her love was not returned.

Tara turned her head on the pillow to look at Nicholas. He was awake and his golden eyes staring at her.

"You love me," he said, a confidant grin forming on his face, the moonlight revealing his white teeth.

"Yes," she admitted, turning her face away. She had told him she'd wanted his heart. Did he need to remind her? It made her feel like just another conquest of the handsome English captain.

"Marry me, Tara," he said, pulling her chin back to face him.

Never thinking to hear those words from him, she sat up, pulling the sheet across her breasts. "Why?"

His warm hand slid to her back.

"Well, for one thing, I've taken your maidenhead. You're quite ruined, at least in my circles. As a gentleman I would expect to marry you, of course." To Tara his words sounded glib, even if they were true. "And it's time I marry and raise a family. I'm not a bad catch, you know, even if I am English."

She sighed. Did men always think so logically, so devoid of emotion? He spoke as if he were arranging a new shipping contract, not gaining a life's mate, a woman to cherish. She knew it was the way things were done in England, but she was having none of it. Her heart sank. She had truly been a fool to expect more from the brooding captain with the jaded heart. She would be no man's broodmare, especially not one who lived in London. "That's not good enough."

"But you love me. You admitted it."

"Yes, I love you. And just now I hate that I love you. The question is, Nicholas Powell, do you love me?"

"Well, I…" He ran his hand through his hair and looked down at the bed.

"I thought so." Rising from the bunk, she turned her back to him and grabbed her clothing from the deck. She could feel his eyes on her naked form. Quickly dressing as best she could, she searched for her shoes.

"Where are you going?" he asked in a gruff voice. "It's the middle of the night, Tara. Come back to bed."

He reached for her, but she avoided him. She needed to leave, to be alone with her thoughts. Finding her shoes, she pulled them on and walked toward the door. "I think I'll return to my own cabin if it's still there for me. I don't want Peter or your men to find me in here."

"They all know," he said, rising on one elbow. "There are no secrets on a ship, Tara. The watch would have seen me kissing you and then carrying you to my cabin. They wouldn't need to be told what happened next."

Tara's cheeks heated as she remembered just what did happen next. His crew would know, too. They knew their captain well.

Some of his men had no doubt watched with interest as he swept her into his arms and carried her below. By now his entire crew would be aware of her fall from grace. They would know their captain had taken the American passenger to his bed. Some probably thought the pirate had already claimed her, so what was one more? She could hear the ribald comments now. But not all would be making such comments. Some would be wondering why. Others, like Jake, would be disappointed, perhaps even angry.

"Tara—" She left her name on his lips as she slipped through the cabin door. Though she had intended to return to her cabin, somehow it seemed too small to contain all she was feeling. She walked to the companionway and climbed the ladder to the weather deck. Breathing in the cooler air, she passed the watch, who barely acknowledged her, and strolled to the prow. She wanted to get as far away from Nicholas Powell and the eyes of his crew as she could.

She gazed up at the black sky. The stars were still there where she'd left them, only there were more of them now. How could the stars still be set in their places when her world was crumbling? She drew comfort from seeing her favorite constellations. Like returning friends, they were there to remind her she'd survive even this. She would always have the sea, and now that she'd been rescued, she would soon be with her brothers.

She'd known loss before. The death of her mother, Ben and others in the war—and Billy. And she'd known sadness when she had said good-bye to her father and brothers the year before. But this pain was new. It was as if a part of her dreams had died. And she supposed they had. In the week following her arrival in Cabo Rojo, while sitting in Juana's garden, she had foolishly dreamed of a life with Nicholas Powell, of sailing the seas with him on his ship. But in her dreams he loved her beyond reason. In reality, he would marry her, but only because that is what a gentleman did when he had *ruined* a virgin. He could not even say the words she'd longed to hear—not even when she'd asked. She would not go to his bed again. She could only hope there would be no child of their passion.

Wrapping her hands around the rail, she heard the sound of something hitting the brightwork. Looking down, she saw his blue stone ring on her left hand. *When did he put it there?* She tried to pull it off, tempted to throw it into the sea, but it would not budge. What did it matter that he'd given her his ring when what she wanted was his heart? She would not be dragged back to England only to be left at his home to while away the hours sipping tea like Aunt Cornelia's friends. It would be just another prison.

A tear slipped down her cheek and she quickly wiped it away. There would be time enough to cry when she was home.

* * *

Nick lay in his bed with his arms folded under his head staring at the overhead above him. The lantern was sputtering, but the moonlight filtered into his windows, casting a soft light about the cabin. That had not gone as he'd planned. While Tara had slept, he'd put his mother's ring on her finger—the ring his mother had told him to give the woman he would eventually marry, the ring he *never* gave Caroline. He'd planned to ask Tara to be his wife when she awakened. He would not have taken her to his bed had that not been his intention. What did the woman expect?

He'd said something wrong, but what? She should have been pleased with his offer of marriage. He owned ships and she loved ships. They could sail together, at least until the children came. That thought made him smile. Tara, big with his child. A son perhaps. Most women he'd taken to his bed wanted nothing more than an invitation to be Mrs. Nicholas Powell. So why had it not been enough?

He cared about her, of course. Nate said it was obvious he loved her. Why else would he risk his ship to rescue her? To offer to provide for her? To want her to be the mother of his sons? Yes, he'd been angry with her, but that was because he'd been afraid he'd lost her. Afraid she really wanted another. Afraid the pirate had touched her. He blamed himself for allowing Cofresí to take his ship and his woman. And she *was* his woman. He'd claimed her with his body, and he'd put his ring on her finger as a sign to his crew the lady was his.

Women were difficult creatures to understand, Nick mused. He'd never tried. When he'd made love to Caroline, he'd expected to marry her, yet without a second thought, Caroline had cast him aside for another. Tara was perhaps the most difficult of all to understand. Intriguing from the beginning, she was unlike other women in so many ways. Making love to her had been different as well. Never before had he loved a woman while giving her pleasure. Well, not since Caroline, but he wondered whether he had ever really loved the English girl, or had merely been obsessed with her. Until Tara, he had never wanted to stay wrapped in the arms of a woman through the night. Even now, it felt somehow wrong that she was not here beside him.

There was nothing for it; she would have to see reason. He would talk to her.

Chapter 17

Roberto stormed about his home, desperate to know what had happened to Tara. His *cariño* had disappeared off the streets of Cabo Rojo just before his ship had arrived the evening before. So far, no one had seen her, though he'd sent men out to search the town and the harbor.

Where can she be? If another man touches her—

"Roberto," said Juana, entering his study, where he stood staring out the window waiting for the return of his messengers, "there is a lad here to see you."

"Send him away. I'm in no mood to visit with the village boys."

"I don't think he is here for a visit, brother. He says he has a message for you about the American girl. He must mean Tara."

Roberto did not wait for the youth to be shown to him, but strode to the front entrance, where the lad waited, worrying his hat in his hands as he stared down at the tile floor. Roberto recognized the boy as one of the village lads who followed him and his men about, always seeking to do them a favor. "Pablo, what message do you bring?"

"I waited until I knew you would be awake, Capitán," explained the hesitant lad. "Last night my father told me some men had hired our carriage. Papa asked me to take them to their ship. It was anchored in a cove north of Porto Real. I was waiting with two men when another joined us. He had a girl with him. Since I had seen this one with Juana in the marketplace, I thought you would want to know."

"What ship was it, Pablo? Did you see the name?" Roberto asked anxiously.

"The *Viento del Cuervo*. It was still light enough for me to see the name on the hull. And it flew the flag of Spain."

"When was this, Pablo?"

"Early in the evening, Capitán. I know this because I returned home late and almost missed my dinner."

Roberto thanked the boy and handed him a coin. He would make a fine and loyal spy one day.

When the boy had gone, Roberto turned to his sister, who had heard the conversation. "It seems Captain Powell did not take my advice to stay out of our waters. And now he has taken from me the woman I want. For that he will pay."

"Be careful, Roberto." She placed her hand on his arm. "I do not have a good feeling about this. If the English captain would take her from you, he will fight to keep her."

"I would expect no less from the English captain," said Roberto, his mind already planning how he would capture the English ship. He couldn't sink her outright because Tara might be harmed. But there were other ways he could cripple the Raven's ship.

Juana again urged caution. "It may be that Tara wanted to go with them, Roberto. I could tell she was sad that she was not going home to her family. Perhaps you should let her go."

"No, Juana. This is the woman I want. And what I want, I take, *verdad*?"

* * *

Nick never got the chance to talk to Tara, though he tried. When faced with him directly, she was polite but distant. She took her breakfast in the galley with McGinnes and a few of the crew, who now embraced her as one of their own. Then later on deck, surrounded by his men, it was easy for her to avoid him. When word spread that he had taken her to his cabin, the crew became protective of Tara. Nate just shook his head each time he looked Nick's way, like a schoolmaster dismayed at his pupil's poor progress. Nick was feeling a bit guilty himself. He had taken her maidenhead and she had rejected his proposal. But she still wore his ring and that encouraged him. If his men thought he intended to treat Tara as one of his other women, they would be wrong.

It was early morning when the wind rose and Nick gave the order to set a course west from where they were anchored toward Mona Island, and then north, northwest around Porto Rico. They had reached open sea and he was just about to give the order to set a course east toward St. Thomas, where he intended to stop for supplies and cargo for their trip north, when he heard the lookout's cry. "Sail ho!"

"Where away?" his first mate, standing amidships, shouted back.

"Dead astern!" came the reply on the wind.

"Mr. Greene!" Nick yelled, his eyes searching for his cabin boy. Peter came running with Joshua behind him.

"Yes, Cap'n?"

"Fetch my spyglass from my cabin and be quick about it!"

Peter flew down the hatch and, a moment later, returned, handing him the brass cylinder. Climbing a short way into the rigging, Nick extended the spyglass to its full length and held it to his eye, focusing on the horizon. The small patch of white in the clear blue sky grew larger until it became the sails of a small schooner. *Cofresí.*

"Make all sail!" he shouted as he jumped to the deck and cast Nate a look that told the old salt what to expect. Nick handed the glass back to Peter and ordered, "All hands on deck!" His crew clambered up the rigging to set the additional sail that would allow them maximum speed.

"You think it's Cofresí?" asked Russ.

"Almost certain. I'm going to try and outrun him, but I don't expect we'll be successful. The *Retribución* is much lighter and faster."

"But they have fewer guns and, unless they've replaced the ones we spiked, they have none at the moment," said Russ, obviously attempting to be encouraging.

"He would not be pursuing us if he did not have guns, you can be sure of that."

Calling the gunner and bos'n to him, Nick told them of his suspicions. "It's the *Retribución* and we're going to try and outrun her, though I believe we'll soon have a fight on our hands. Should that become clear, we must try and stay upwind of her and heave to for the fight. Best to assemble a crew, Mr. Wilson, and see the guns are run out." Then looking at the eager faces of his cabin boy and Peter's companion Joshua, Nick said, "Peter, you set up a powder train to carry shot and powder from the hold for Mr. Wilson."

With a "yes, sir!" Peter returned Nick his spyglass and disappeared down the center hatch.

Choruses of "aye, aye, Cap'n" filled the air as his crew hurried to comply with the other orders he'd given.

Russ turned to Joshua. The boy had not moved as the orders were issued to the others, and now he looked to the man he would serve as cabin boy. "Lad, you'd best relieve the lookout and stay aloft."

The dark-skinned boy from Bermuda grinned. "Yessir, Mr. Ainsworth!"

Nick shared a smile with his first mate at the boy's delight at being sent aloft. The lad had come far in his training in the short time he'd been with them.

Nick left Russ and headed toward the helm, where Nate was already sending them into the wind. He came to a sudden halt when he saw Tara standing on the quarterdeck.

Striding to her side, he said, "It's the pirate, Tara. I want you below."

He was unsurprised when she objected. He'd expected as much. "But I may be able to help, and you know Cofresí won't allow his men to harm me." It took all of Nick's self-control not to carry her to his cabin and lock her in, but he had no time for that now.

"His guns won't know it's you, Tara. No, I want you below decks."

She looked at him searchingly, as if seeking another line of persuasion, but his stern countenance allowed none. Letting out a quick breath, she said, "All right," and turned toward the hatch. Nick breathed a sigh of relief. Her obedience might be grudging, but at least he had it. It was best. He wanted her far from the fighting, where she could be hit with some object hurling across the deck. He had to keep her out of the fray—even if he lost to the pirate and Cofresí took her from him, at least she would be alive.

The members of his crew who had served in the British Navy now demonstrated their experience as they smoothly moved through their paces, preparing the ship for the fight Nick instinctively felt would soon be upon them. They picked up speed and he braced for the roll of the ship as the added sails billowed above him. Raising his spyglass, he looked again at the ship that followed in their wake. The sails of the smaller ship grew larger as the pirate drew closer, sailing close to the wind. Nick hurried below and armed himself with his saber and pistol. Then he paused. He had to see Tara one last time.

He didn't knock before opening the door to her cabin. The memory of the night before was still fresh in his mind and he didn't care in what dishabille he might find her. She whipped around as he entered, a knife in her hand and still wearing her breeches. Crossing the short distance, he took the knife from her, set it on the bed and pulled her into his arms, kissing her deeply. As if knowing this kiss might be their last, she did not object but returned his ardor, fervently clinging to him. He wanted to stay with her and hold her, a last effort to convince her how much he cared, but he had no time. "I can't stay," he said, pulling away, "but God willing, I'll be back. As long as I live, Tara, I won't let him have you." Her blue-green eyes looked long into his, telling him she believed him.

He turned and hastened above decks to see the *Retribución* closing fast. His attempt to outrun the pirate had failed. Only three hundred yards separated the two ships. Very soon they would be within firing distance.

The smaller schooner pulled alongside, then began to circle the larger, slower ship. "Prepare to fire!" Nick shouted. Just as he gave the command, the pirate's guns belched fire and smoke as chain shot ripped through the *Wind Raven*'s sails. One of his crew screamed as he fell under the assault. Nick looked aloft, relieved to see Joshua still holding firm in the crosstrees.

Nick ordered, "Fire!"

Balls flew from both ships and found their targets, the exploding powder creating a thunderous roar and sending white smoke billowing around them. Shouting orders from the quarterdeck, Nick was gratified to see the foremast of the pirate ship shattered. But his own ship was taking on damage as well, two of his guns now disabled. The port bow had been smashed in, the gun there overturned and useless. The shot-riddled foresail strained in the wind and split clear through to the boltropes, torn into worthless strips of canvas. He heard a yard crack aloft as the topsail slewed around, rigging snapping like pistol shots as the lines parted under the strain.

Mr. Wilson's gun crew had successfully fended off many a French ship when they had been privateers for England, but Nick realized that would be of no avail as the small schooner circled around to their stern like a wasp harassing a bull.

Nick could see the tall blond pirate standing astride on the deck of his ship, his axe gleaming from where it was tucked into his red sash, a confident smile on his face. The ships were so close Nick could hear the shouted order from the pirate captain to fire at their rudder. A loud boom sounded and the *Wind Raven* shuddered, taking the hit below the water.

Nate had the wheel and one look was all it took to tell Nick what he'd already surmised. The pirate had clipped their rudder, leaving them unable to maneuver.

The real fight was about to begin. His men rained down musket fire on the pirate ship.

"Prepare to be boarded!" shouted Russ.

The pirates brought their ship alongside and soon the grappling hooks clawed the rail, locking the two vessels together. The fact that both ships had sustained damage wouldn't prevent the battle that was about to ensue. Nick drew his saber and then his pistol, his mind steeling for the onslaught.

Cofresí stepped confidently onto the *Wind Raven*'s deck, his axe held high, ready to strike, just as Joshua, in his role as lookout, yelled, "Sail ho off starboard!"

Nick's gaze shifted to starboard, where a large brig flying the flag of Royal Spain was rapidly closing on them. He recognized it as one of those that patrolled the shores of Porto Rico and the colony of Santo Domingo.

"Stand down!" he shouted. "Stand down, I say!" The crewmen of the *Wind Raven* froze in automatic obedience. One of the pirates made as if to lunge forward, but Nick raised his pistol and the pirate faltered and stopped. Nick glared at Cofresí. "Control your men, Captain. This fight is over."

* * *

Pacing restlessly in her cabin, Tara felt the ship shudder then heard the unmistakable sound of grappling hooks being thrown over the rail. Suddenly all was quiet. She felt helpless not knowing what was happening, not knowing if Nicholas Powell was lying in a pool of blood on the deck. She might have rejected his halfhearted offer of marriage, but she had not stopped loving the man. His kiss, only minutes ago, had nearly undone her.

Scrambling up the ladder, she came through the hatch to see Nick in front of her, poised to fight, a pistol in one hand and a saber in the other. Cofresí stood near the port side rail, some of his crew around him, as he stared toward starboard. Tara's gaze followed his to see a brig drawing alongside. It was flying the Spanish flag.

The pirate suddenly turned in her direction. "Tara, *mi cariño!*" He began to walk toward her, but Nick intervened, placing himself protectively in front of her.

"She's mine, Cofresí." Nick's voice was harsh to Tara's ears.

"No!" screamed the pirate, his face twisted in scorn. "Tara promised to come with me in exchange for your life. You have stolen her from me."

Tara stepped around Nick, looking into the pained blue eyes of the proud pirate. "I did go with you, Roberto, but I would not have stayed. Don't you see? I need to be with my family. Cabo Rojo is not my home, and I am not yours. Captain Powell did not steal me; I went with him willingly."

Nicholas reached his arm around her shoulders, drawing her back to his side.

From starboard, Tara heard the sound of grappling hooks and then the Spanish words, "*¡Cesen el fuego! ¡Y atención!*"

Turning her eyes in the direction of the shouted words, she saw a Spanish naval officer in a blue and red uniform embellished with gold braid on his sleeves crossing a plank stretched between the two ships. Men in uniform followed behind him. "What did he say?" Tara asked the *Wind Raven*'s captain.

"He commands us to stop firing and hear him." At Nicolas's words, the Spanish officer stepped down to the deck and paused, as if surprised to hear English.

Cofresí stared at the officer, a disbelieving look on the pirate captain's face.

"I am Captain Juan Gravina. Who is in command of this vessel?" demanded the Spaniard.

"I am. This is my ship," said Nick, stepping forward. "Jean Nicholas Powell, at your service. And may I add that your intervention is both timely and welcome as we were just about to defend ourselves from this pirate's unwarranted intrusion. As you may surmise from the damage to my ship, he was not invited."

Hearing Nick's speech, the Spanish officer said, "You are English, yet you fly the flag of Spain?"

"Ah, yes," Nick said, "the ruse was necessary, I'm afraid, to avoid Captain Cofresí. As you can see, I was not successful."

"Cofresí would attack your ship while flying the flag of Royal Spain?" At that the Spanish officer turned his frown on Cofresí. "You go too far, *mi compadre*."

By this time, others of the Spanish crew had taken a position behind their captain. "Arrest this man!" said Captain Gravina to his men, pointing to Cofresí. "He has much to answer for."

Cofresí stood proud and defiant, seeming to consider whether to resist. Then he shrugged. Tara thought the command he gave in a whisper to his pirate crew must have told them to go along with the Spanish authorities, for while there was murder in their eyes, they sheathed their machetes. Tara watched pirate's gaze as it shifted to her, a look of longing on his face.

"Tara, *mi cariño*," he said sadly, "how I could have loved you..." Then he turned and, having obtained permission from the Spanish officer to leave a few of his men to sail the *Retribución* back to the harbor, followed Captain Gravina onto the Spanish brig.

Chapter 18

The sun was just beginning to set over the *Wind Raven*'s stern when they limped into the dock in St. Thomas. Nick's eyes were drawn to Fort Christian standing guard over the harbor as he said to Russ, "I had planned to make a short stop in Charlotte Amalie for supplies, but it seems fate would have us stay longer. We've sustained some damage to be sure."

"I'm just glad there was enough of the rudder left to see us here," said Russ. "I thought Nate was going to have a fit when Cofresí's ball found its target."

"That rudder was his pride. Is Augie well enough to see to the new sails we'll need?"

"He's already making a list," said his first mate.

"I'm going to see Miss McConnell to an inn. I think I'll stay the night in town myself. I want a bath and a dinner on land." He ignored Russ's raised brow. "Can you manage the crew's visits to shore, and your own, till I return tomorrow?"

"Quite well. And you might raise a glass of Champagne in celebration of our causing the pirate not a little discomfort. Prinny should be happy about that. It may earn you a knighthood like the one he bestowed on your brother."

"Hadn't thought of that. The prince can be generous at times. Perhaps he'll do something for the entire crew. In any event, I'm hoping Cofresí will be out of the water for a while. The Spanish captain did not look pleased to learn his local pirate had fired on a ship flying the royal flag."

"I had never considered such a ruse would aid us with the authorities, but Gravina's face certainly showed outrage. No matter you're English, the Spaniard was furious."

"We were fortunate."

Tara came up on deck wearing a gown and a proper bonnet, looking every bit the lady. She carried the small valise he had asked her to pack. It was difficult not to stare at her beautiful face and he remembered their one night of lovemaking. In his mind she belonged to him. He left his first mate to close the distance between them. "I would have carried that up for you, Tara."

She met his gaze and then looked to one side. "No matter. I am here now. Where are you taking me?"

"Lavalette's. It's the largest hotel in Charlotte Amalie and a short distance from the harbor. It will give you a chance for a real bath and a fine dinner and some time on land while the ship is being repaired for the trip to Baltimore. The owner, a French merchant, is a friend of mine."

"Yes, I would like that very much."

"Shall we walk or would you prefer I get a carriage?"

"Oh, I would love to walk."

A few minutes later, Nick handed his own small bag to Peter, along with Tara's valise, and the three of them left the ship. The town of Charlotte Amalie was thriving and Nick noted the many importing houses added since he'd last been here. Red-roofed whitewashed homes and other buildings sat amidst green hills, making it one of the most beautiful ports in the Caribbean.

"Have you been here before?" he asked her.

Blue-green eyes looked into his for a moment then looked away. "Yes, once, a few years ago, but we did not stay long. I only left my brother's ship one time."

"I was here quite a bit in those days. Odd our paths never crossed."

"My brothers kept a close watch on me. But now I am glad for the chance to see more of the town."

They climbed the steps of the two-story white hotel with the lattice railing on the second-floor gallery. Peter followed with their bags. At the counter inside the entrance, Nick was pleased to see the desk clerk recognized him. "Ah, *bon*. Capitaine Powell. You return to us at last! M'sieur Lavalette will be so pleased."

"A room for the lady and one for me for two nights, I think, Philippe."

"*Oui.*" The clerk smiled at Tara and opened his book. Speaking to Nick, he said, "*Quelle belle dame!*"

Nick began to translate for Tara. "He just paid you a compli—"

"I know what he said. *Merci*," she said, smiling at Philippe. "*Vous avez une langue d'argent, m'sieur.*"

"You speak French?" Nick asked her, not having realized that before. He wouldn't have expected it from an American. But did she have to tell Philippe he had a silver tongue? It would only encourage the Frenchman.

"A little. You might recall that when England was America's enemy, France was her friend."

He was not able to avoid his hearty laugh. "Imagine *my* dilemma, for half my family is French and the other half is English—and the two countries are ever at war."

Tara laughed then, too, and the sound of it was beautiful. She had not laughed in a long time, not since their day at Elbow Beach.

Nick decided he owed Philippe a larger coin than usual when he discovered his room was adjacent to Tara's. Remembering Philippe's wink when he'd placed the two keys in Nick's palm and told them dinner would not be served for an hour, Nick decided it had been no coincidence.

"A bath for the lady and one for myself, Philippe."

"*Mais oui,*" he replied, "You shall have them directly." The French clerk disappeared down the steps, Peter with him. The cabin boy, who seemed delighted to be assisting his captain on land, was to pick up a few things for Russ and then return to the ship.

Nick escorted Tara into a room dominated by a dark wooden four-poster bed. His eyes lingered on the fine blue counterpane, imagining Tara lying there waiting for him. "This should be a welcome change from your small cabin," he said, watching her turn in a circle in the middle of the large room. He wanted to take her into his arms and toss her onto the bed and make love to her. Instead he took a deep breath. "I'll return in an hour to take you to dinner."

* * *

Tara opened the doors to the gallery and stepped out onto the balcony suspended high above Charlotte Amalie. Beyond the red roofs of the buildings crowding the streets of the prosperous Caribbean port were the waters of the harbor. The orange and red of the setting sun had turned them a shimmering coral. The beautiful picture presented brought a sense of peace to her troubled soul.

So much had happened since she'd left London; it felt to Tara as if she'd lived a lifetime. The feeling was not new; she had experienced such before when sailing with her father and then later with her brothers. But this time the source of the feeling was different. She had become a woman, been courted by a pirate and desired by a rakish English sea captain. Her father would not have approved of either man. He wanted her to wed an American patriot, no doubt one of the rising statesmen he was ever bringing to their home. Somehow, she thought any meeting between her father and Nicholas Powell, assuming her father's health allowed such an encounter, would be stormy.

Then another thought entered her mind. Would Nick have one of his crew see her to her door or would he escort her home himself? Given that she still wore his ring and he'd not asked for its return, she suspected it would be the latter. At some point she would have to find a way to return it. She supposed she could have asked McGinnes for pork fat to work the ring loose, but for some reason she had not done so. As she gazed at the harbor waters on fire with the blazing colors of the sunset, she experienced a sudden and wrenching sadness at the prospect of saying good-bye to the English captain.

Tara reveled in the steaming bath that the hotel maid arranged for her. The last one she'd had was in Cabo Rojo. Splashing water on her face for a wash while at sea grew tiresome. The hot freshwater bath was a luxury she was pleased to indulge in, as was the feather mattress in her room.

Soon she would be home, a wiser, sadder woman perhaps, and one uncertain of her future, but still she would be home.

An hour later, Tara had changed into a clean gown, this one with no breeches beneath it. She wanted to dress the part of the woman she had become, confident in her femininity. It was her choice, after all, and she had come to realize that looking the lady did not deprive her of her independence.

Fortunately, not all of her gowns nor all of her things had been in her chest when it was taken to the pirate's ship. So tonight she drew her hair up into curls at her crown and tied a sapphire-colored ribbon around her throat, fixing a small stone of the same color set in gold at the center. She had been saving it and had not worn it yet. It had been a gift from Aunt Cornelia on the occasion of her first ball. How long ago that seemed, and how far away. The ivory silk gown she'd worn then and now had a braided trim at the high waist in the same colors of blue and gold. It was the most elegant gown she owned, so she had been thrilled it was left in her cabin with her remaining things. For some reason, she wanted to appear the elegant lady for Nicholas Powell.

The knock at the cabin door came just as she slipped her feet into her silk slippers. She pulled the wooden door open to see the tall handsome captain with his midnight locks reined in for the evening and his golden eyes devouring at her. He wore the same jacket and breeches he'd donned for the Albouys' dinner in Bermuda, a dark cinnamon jacket over an ivory silk waistcoat and nankeen breeches. Instead of his black boots, he wore stockings and shoes. His cravat was more elegantly tied than it had been in Bermuda. Affixed to his lapel was a small white island flower with a yellow center, a frangipani, she thought, and absently wondered who had placed it there.

His sun-bronzed skin had deepened in color since leaving London. Observing the smile on his face, she knew with certainty she would remember his smile for the rest of her life.

Leaving behind her heavy thoughts, and looking for a lighter note, she said, "Hullo, Captain. How nice that you are so prompt and looking so very much the London gentleman."

"And you, Tara, are stunning." His perusal of her appearance said he approved of her efforts to please him. As he offered his arm and they descended the stairs to the dining room, she considered that his clothing, like the pirate captain's, was deceptive. Beneath the gentleman's clothes was a man hardened, like his heart, by his days at sea.

The dining room of the hotel was bathed in candlelight, each of the tables covered with a pink tablecloth and bearing a small candle. There were many other candles above them in the two magnificent chandeliers. Tara felt as if she'd entered the home of a wealthy European, save for the tropical flowers of red and yellow gracing the sideboards that made clear she was not in Europe. Tropical air wafted in from the open windows, providing a welcome breeze. From where she and the captain waited just inside the door, Tara could see several couples had already been seated.

A short older gentleman with dark brown hair and a well-trimmed mustache that curled up at the ends walked toward them wearing a very conservative black coat and trousers with white shirt and waistcoat, the latter embroidered with gold.

"*Bon soir*, Capitaine Powell!" the man said effusively, his French accent clearly displayed. "Philippe told me you had arrived. It is my great good fortune to host you and your lady." Then fixing his gaze upon Tara, he smiled. "*Quelle surprise, et très jolie!*" Quickly he looked to the captain. "Please to introduce me."

The captain gave a soft chuckle, seemingly amused with the little Frenchman. "Miss McConnell, meet my good friend Pierre Lavalette, the owner of this fine establishment."

The Frenchman beamed his pride, bowed and remarked in a melodious voice, "*Je suis enchanté.*"

The captain waited for him to rise. "Pierre, may I present Miss Tara McConnell of Baltimore."

"*Ah, une Américaine.*" The Frenchman gave Tara a slow appreciative smile while twisting the end of his mustache with the fingers of one hand. He was an interesting little man with elegant manners and gestures, who was obviously proud of his fine hotel and his acquaintance with the English captain. But then Nicholas Powell wasn't just a captain of his own ship, though that was achievement enough. In the last few days, Nate had told her the captain was heir to an English shipping empire and that his family sent many ships into the West Indies and to Eastern Europe for trade.

The captain surveyed the stylishly decorated room. "Business appears to be good, Pierre."

"Ze French merchants, my old friends and former partners, ze keep me *très occupé*." Then with a quick turn of his wrist in the air, he added, "I have no complaints."

"Do you have a table for Miss McConnell and me?"

"*Mais oui!*" he exclaimed, gesturing for them to follow him. "I have saved my best for you!" As they walked together, the Frenchman made an aside to Nick. "Ze kind you like, a quiet table, sheltered from the others."

The table to which Monsieur Lavalette led them was set off to one side, surrounded by palms set in pots forming a natural barrier between the table and the rest of the room. Though Tara was bothered by the idea the captain had previously dined with a lady in the secluded spot, she was glad she did not have to endure the curious stares of the other guests, for as they walked to their table, many heads turned in their direction.

* * *

Nick had seen the open expressions of interest in the eyes of the men as they stared at Tara when she crossed the dining room. He had expected it, for her honey-colored hair glistened in the candlelight and her skirts rustled as she glided to their table, even more graceful on land than she was on the deck of his ship. Her movements rendered the lines of her alluring body, a body he now knew quite well, nearly ethereal. It made him feel all the more possessive of the woman he had claimed as his. He was well pleased with the potted palms that provided a screen for the table Lavalette had selected.

He had not forgotten Russ's suggestion that they have Champagne, and knowing the Frenchman would stock it, he ordered them a bottle. He had much to celebrate. He had met the pirate head on and, though he had not emerged unscathed, he and most of his crew had their lives. And he was quite certain the

Prince Regent would be pleased with his efforts to remove, at least for a time, the threat to the British merchants plying the waters of the Caribbean. Then there was the beautiful American hoyden to consider. Though she continued to be coolly polite, always observing a safe distance between them, he knew she was not indifferent, not after their night together. He was her first lover and intended to be her last. Tonight he would wine and dine her and then, perhaps, he would make love to her—to demonstrate she was his and always would be.

The food Lavalette's well-trained waiters served them was very French and very good. It began with the rich, buttery taste of pâté de foie gras, followed by greens with cucumber, lemon and egg. The main course was a platter of crabs stuffed with breadcrumbs, minced vegetables and island spices. Side dishes of saffron rice and a yellow-squash soufflé complimented the meal.

He could see by the smile on her face Tara was enjoying herself. "You like the food."

"It is nearly like being at the Albouys', only with a French touch."

He couldn't resist the smile that spread on his face as he poured her more Champagne. "So it is."

Dessert consisted of mango tarts. He loved their sweet but delicate flavor, which reminded him of the syllabub the Albouys had served in Bermuda. After being confined to the hold of his ship with no food at all, and then forced to live on the rations the Spanish captain had shared with them, he was relishing the excellent food.

Tara, despite her praise for the French cooking, ate sparingly, as if making an effort to appease him when she had no appetite. He did not ask what troubled her, afraid it might be memories of the pirate and not wishing to remind her of those days. And yet, he wondered, was she sad to see the pirate go? Cofresí's parting words to Tara, speaking of his love, still had him seeing red. She was his and the thought of the pirate touching her made his temples throb. He didn't dare think they might have shared some tenderness of which he was unaware.

Soon they were thanking their host for the delightful meal and climbing the stairs to the corridor that led to their rooms and the gallery built on the front of the hotel.

He led her past the doors to their rooms, and she asked, "Where are we going?"

He took her hand. "To observe the view."

They stepped though the door at the end of the corridor out onto the gallery and into the night. The air was warm and sultry.

"It's so glorious with the lights from the ships in the harbor," remarked Tara.

"But not so bright as to dim the stars," he said, casting a glance at the sparkling lights set into the velvet blue sky, "or you."

He was looking at Tara now, not at the stars. Alone on the terrace and with Tara so close he could smell her familiar jasmine scent, Nick pulled her into his embrace. He would wonder later if her willingness had been the Champagne or the night itself, but she did not resist. He held her for a moment, content to feel her softness against him. Then he nuzzled her hair and began kissing her neck, working his way to her lips. Tenderly he kissed her, hearing her sigh. When she opened her mouth, he deepened the kiss, mingling his passion with hers. God, he had missed her.

"Tara, I want you," he whispered into her ear.

"You only desire me, Captain," she said, pulling back, "and that is not enough."

"It will be enough for tonight, and then on the way to Baltimore, we can explore the 'more' that lies between us."

Her blue-green eyes were glazed with passion from his kisses and Nick sensed she would not say him nay. He led her back to the corridor and to his room.

Once inside, he drew her to him.

"We should not do this...again," said Tara. "It can lead nowhere."

"Perhaps it can. And you want it. I feel you do, Tara. So do I."

"I cannot deny that I have little resolve when you are so close and kissing my neck as you are."

His lips were, indeed, on her neck as he trailed kisses along the ribbon she wore around that slim column, the ribbon that had tantalized him all evening. Slipping her small sleeves from her shoulders, he bent his head to kiss the ivory skin untouched by the sun. He didn't hurry—the slow seduction he had in mind would take some time. And when it was over, Tara McConnell would know with certainty that she had been claimed as his.

"I have much to teach you, Tara, but that will come later."

He ran his hands through her hair, freeing it from the pins. Then with deft attention to her gown, he undid the buttons. Her gown slipped to the floor, followed by her chemise. He lifted her onto the feather bed. Not wanting her ardor to cool, he quickly removed his clothing and joined her.

"You are mine, Tara. As I told you once before, there is no going back."

* * *

In truth, Tara knew once she had given herself to Nicholas Powell, the door to her innocence and to the past would be closed. She was a woman and tonight she would be his woman for she wanted him with all her being. She had missed his rough hands and his ungentle ways and, though he might want to marry her for reasons that left her wanting, she could not say good-bye without this one last night between them.

He was taking his time, seeming to love every inch of her. Though she'd had too much Champagne and not enough food, Tara was aware of his every touch, every caress. Lovingly he cupped her breast, sending ripples of current through her. Soon he replaced his hands with his mouth. Her fingers entwined in his hair; she drank drinking deeply of his kisses, holding him to her.

"Oh, Nicholas…" *I love you.* She would not voice the cry of her heart aloud but she could not help crying it in her mind. She did love this man, this English sea captain, and God help her, she would take what he offered, though it might be less than she wanted. Writhing beneath his hands as he teased her woman's flesh, leaving her wet and wanting, she heard herself moan as he said her name over and over. Perhaps he cared more than she thought. She wanted him to care.

The night breeze wafted in through the windows of his room as he rose above her. "Tara, my woman, my love—" He thrust into her and Tara felt her muscles tightly constrict to hold him there. Joined together they let their passion carry them to the heights they had reached once before. Only this time, Tara was a full participant, moving with him toward the precipice where, overcome by the wonderful spasms that gripped her, she cried out her release together with his.

Chapter 19

Tara woke to the morning sun streaming in the windows and realized with a start she was alone—in the captain's room and in his bed. Immediately she looked around for her clothes, though she had no desire to don the female frippery with all the buttons. It would delay her return to her own room.

Rising from the bed, she spotted his black satin banyan lying on the settee. She reached for the garment and pulled it on, securing the tie. Seeing the key to her room on the side table, she retrieved it, gathered her clothes and hurried to the door. Carefully, so as not to make a sound, she opened it and peered down the hall. Seeing no one about, she slipped into the corridor and into her room a few feet away, unseen by the other guests.

A short while later, a maid knocked on the door of her room. Glad she had changed into her own dressing gown, Tara greeted her as she carried in a tray of island fruits, rolls and coffee. Tara wondered if the servant had been waiting for her to return.

"I will see a bath brought for you, miss," the black woman said as she set down the tray. "The captain said you were to sleep as long as you liked, so I'd not come before now to be sure you had risen."

The explanation seemed overlong to Tara but she was thankful for the maid's discretion. Perhaps she was kindly allowing Tara to preserve her honor, or perhaps the captain had arranged it. Tara realized just then that she'd not hidden the captain's black satin robe. The maid's eyes darted to where it lay over the back of the chair. Fortunately the good woman said nothing.

"Captain Powell said I was to tell you he would return at noon," the maid said. "He wanted to check on his ship this morning."

So, he had not deserted her as she had thought, but had left word of his whereabouts. Tara supposed it was an act of kindness to allow her privacy after their night together. She could find no fault in him for that. But she did find fault in herself for once again falling prey to his practiced advances, a willing accomplice to his seduction. She had planned to give him the moonstone ring last night, but somehow forgot to do so at dinner, and then later, well, any thought of it fled her mind when he'd begun to kiss her. *Damn the man for being so attractive and damn me for loving him!*

Tara thanked the maid, and once she had eaten, she bathed and dressed. Unwilling to wait for the captain's return, she decided to walk to the ship. As she reached the last of the hotel's steps leading down to the street, Peter came up to her, a dimpled smile on his face.

"Were you waiting for me, Peter?"

The boy with the brown curls smiled more broadly. "Aye, Miss Tara. The cap'n told me I should. He thought ye might take a fancy to walk to the ship and he'd not have ye go alone. The docks can be a rough place even in the daytime."

She supposed it should bother her that Nicholas Powell knew her so well he could predict her actions. But she'd been more than a month on his ship and they'd had more than a few adventures together. It gave her pause to realize just how well he knew her after last night, for he had made love to her more than once. "That was thoughtful of him, Peter. I'll be glad for your company."

The busy port town was just waking up as they walked along together. Peter happily chatted away, telling her of all the changes to the ship.

"The cap'n's taking on more cargo for Baltimore and the crew's busy seeing to repairs. I've never seen old Nate so particular with fixing something. Ye'd think that rudder was his own babe the way he watched the workers like a mother hen. Mr. Adams, back at work after that blow to his head, has been yelling all morning about the damage to the canvas. An' the carpenter is cursing up a storm about the hole in the bulwark. Ye sure ye want to go there just now?"

She couldn't resist grinning at the boy. "Yes, I am sure, Peter. I want to see the crew and check on the wounded. Are they healing all right?"

"Well, aside from Smitty, who had a relapse. He's been confined to his hammock and ordered not to resume any duties just yet. The rest are coming along fine. McGinnes is complaining about having to bring Smitty his meals, but I don't think he really minds. We're all glad Smitty is on the mend."

* * *

Nick had risen early, feeling confident and satiated from the night before. Things would come right with Tara; they had to. Though, as he considered the thought a second time, he wondered if even a night of lovemaking would convince Tara to marry him. The hoyden could be stubborn.

He was just about to climb up the gangplank when he noticed a man standing on the deck of the ship docked next to the *Wind Raven*. He was tall and dark like Nick, and something about his movements seemed familiar. Nick glanced at the name on the schooner. *Sea Kitten*. It meant nothing to him. But as he studied the movements of the man, he thought he recognized him. Walking down the dock to get a closer view, he looked up—and into the eyes of his brother.

"Martin! It *is* you! I thought I recognized that way you have of standing on a ship's deck."

"Nick?" his younger brother asked with an astonished look on his face, so similar to Nick's own save Martin had the dark blue eyes of their mother. "I had no idea you were here! I thought you'd be in Baltimore or on your way home by now."

"I might have wished it so." Nick said, then raced up the gangplank and embraced his brother. "I thought *you* were still in London!"

"I had an adventure in the Midlands, my last task for Prinny. After that, much to Father's delight, I decided to return to the family business. What about you?"

"I've had a few diversions of my own. First there was the storm that took out a mast and lost me a man. Then Prinny's errand off Porto Rico had me tangling with a pirate. Cofresí—know of him?"

"I've heard of him. He's taken a few prizes among our fellow merchantmen. What were you doing with *him*?"

"It's a long story. If you've time, and some hot coffee, I can give you the gist of it."

"Sure, come to my cabin. God, it's good to see you! I can't believe it's been only months."

As they walked toward the aft hatch, Nick asked, "This is your ship? I didn't recognize the name as one in the family's inventory."

"Father's gift to me for seeing the light. As you know we are now reconciled. The name of the ship is another story. It may take more than one cup of coffee to tell you that tale."

As they reached the aft hatch, a woman's voice reached from the deck below. "Martin?"

Nick grinned at his brother. "Brought a lady along, did you?"

His brother's expression suddenly grew serious. "Do you remember the redhead you met the last time I saw you at home?"

"How could I forget a lady so fair, Martin? Surely you do not think I've changed that much in so short a time."

"Well, be on your best behavior," said his brother, reaching for the ladder. "That lady is now my wife."

"Oh, ho! You do have a tale to tell."

When they reached the deck below, standing in the companionway was the gorgeous redhead to whom Nick had been introduced the last night he'd been in London. "Hullo again," she said rather shyly.

"Nick, you met my wife before we were wed. She is now Lady Katherine Powell."

The redhead smiled and extended her hand. "Seeing as you are Martin's brother, you may call me *Kit*. All my friends do."

"I'm delighted to see you again, my lady," he bowed over her hand, "and even more delighted to learn you condescended to wed my brother, a mere knight to your ladyship." In his mind, Nick remembered the first time he'd met her. Martin had introduced the blue-eyed beauty as the Dowager Baroness of Egerton.

The woman who called herself *Kit* laughed and, facing her husband, said, "I see your brother has not changed, Martin. A rogue as charming as ever." Nick didn't know about the charming part but he'd not deny he'd often played the rogue.

They walked into Martin's cabin, where the smell of fresh coffee greeted them. "When did you two marry? Were the parents there?" Nick was thinking he'd missed a major family gathering.

"Just before we went to the Midlands, and no, the parents were still at sea with our two younger brothers. Kit has not yet met our parents or the twins. Only Lord Ormond and his lady and a few friends attended."

"Well, we can certainly celebrate now," Nick enthused. "And there is someone I'd like you both to meet as well."

Kit poured them coffee and Nick spent the next hour with his brother and sister-in-law recounting all that happened since leaving London, including the vicious storm and the pirates, but leaving out a few parts of the story that concerned Tara. He was surprised to learn Martin and his wife had become embroiled in a rebellion in the Midlands, but then, knowing his brother was a spy for the Crown, he supposed he should have expected some misadventure. It appeared both of them had led an interesting life since they'd last been together.

After Nick explained his desire to wed Tara, his brother shook his head and remarked to his wife, "I can't believe my big brother has finally succumbed to be leg shackled." Then to Nick, "You're not having me on?"

"No." Nick was becoming uncomfortable with his brother's teasing. "Is it so difficult to believe I might wish to marry?"

"Frankly, yes. But then some people say fairies still roam the earth—is she one of them?"

Nick considered his brother's question. McGinnes would say so. He had called her a *leanan sídhe*, or something like that. Then the words the cook had spoken that fateful morning they'd had the service for young Billy came back to him. *If a man can refuse her, she will be his slave, but if he loves her instead, he will forever be hers.* "Probably," he said in answer to Martin's question, and then added, "one never knows."

"She'd have to be one of the magical ones to have you in tow. Who is she?"

"An American. Miss Tara McConnell—and my passenger. It seems her aunt, a Lady Danvers, knows the mater."

"Oh, I know of Lady Danvers," said Martin's wife. "My mother often spoke of the dowager baroness. She is well thought of for her charity work." Nick's spirits sank. He'd have more than

Tara's father to win to his cause. He'd have to convince Tara's Aunt Cornelia he was worthy as well.

"The world grows ever smaller," he said resignedly. "In Bermuda, we spent an evening with friends of mine and fellow merchants, the Albouys, whose guests included relatives of that author mater likes so well."

"Jane Austen," said Martin. "You stopped in Bermuda?"

"Had to for the mast. You'll have to come to the *Raven* and see my new cedar foremast. It's better than the original made in England."

Nick saw his brother reach for his wife's hand and heard Martin say, "Kitten, are we boring you with all this talk of ships?"

Nick couldn't resist asking, "Is the new ship named after you, Kit?"

His sister-in-law blushed and looked at her husband. Martin answered for her. "Yes, the *Sea Kitten* is named for Kit." Then giving his wife a look of tenderness, he said, "I promised her a trip to some tropical isles before we settled down in London. But it seems our new status will have us in port for a time."

Nick shifted his gaze to Martin's wife, and she explained, "I'm expecting a child."

Elated for them and for his family, he exclaimed, "Congratulations!" Rising to slap his brother on the back, he added, "The first grandchild. Won't Mater and Pater be pleased?"

"I'm thinking they will," said Martin. "But the nausea that comes with the early days has made it difficult for Kit to take the swells on the seas just now."

Kit held up her cup and smiled, "Ginger tea."

"We'll be staying close to St. Thomas till this phase passes," said Martin. "Do you sail north from here?"

"Yes," Nick said, taking a swallow of his coffee. "As soon as the *Raven* is repaired I'm away to Baltimore. But first I want you to meet Tara. Though I have asked her to marry me, she's not yet decided to have me. In fact, she seems quite resistant to the notion."

"I can't wait to meet this woman," his brother said. "Quite a change for the man about London who, in his twenties, had women lining up to dance with him."

"You have my permission to ignore my brother," Nick leaned toward Kit, "he exaggerates."

* * *

Tara and Peter arrived at the ship to a hive of activity. The air was filled with the sounds of hammers, saws and men shouting their needs to the workers they'd hired in Charlotte Amalie. She scanned the deck looking for the captain but did not see him. Nate yelled from starboard, "If'n yer lookin' for the cap'n, Miss Tara, he's in his cabin, just came back aboard with some visitors."

Tara wondered if she should interrupt him in the midst of a meeting but in the end decided to go below. After all, the gray cat wasn't the only one on board who was curious. On her way, Peter trailing behind her, she greeted the men and inquired about the status of their injuries.

Feeling a bit awkward after their night together, when she reached the captain's cabin, Tara squared her shoulders, raised her chin and knocked. At the captain's familiar "enter," Tara opened the cabin door and stepped inside, leaving the portal open for Peter. Suddenly she was faced with two men who looked very much alike, standing on either side of a beautiful redhead. She blinked. Both men had sun-bronzed skin and smiles that revealed white teeth, but the shorter one had deep blue eyes.

"You must be Tara McConnell," said the man with the blue eyes.

"Tara," explained Nicholas, "this is my brother, Sir Martin Powell. And the lovely woman beside him is his wife, Lady Katherine Powell."

"Please call me *Kit*," the redhead said. "Martin and I don't stand on formality with friends."

"I would be honored if you would call me *Tara*," she said, remembering her manners.

Nick came to her side and placed a possessive arm around her waist, making Tara a bit uncomfortable. What must his brother and sister-in-law think?

"Nick tells me you've been his passenger," said Sir Martin, his eyes examining her closely, "and from what he's told us about the trip thus far, you must be a stalwart soul."

"Come," said Nick, playing the host. "Let's sit and have a cup of coffee." Then he turned to Peter, who'd been waiting patiently behind Tara. "See if you can get some ginger tea from Nate for Lady Powell. He usually keeps it around for seasickness." The cabin boy hurried out the cabin door to do his bidding.

Tara enjoyed Nick's brother and sister-in-law and soon the four of them were laughing at the antics of the gray cat with the very large white paws that had curled up in Tara's lap and gone to sleep.

"The cat used to sleep on my desk of a morning," said Nick, "but as you can see, she has left me for a softer setting."

With their light banter, Tara soon found she was enjoying exchanging quips with Nick's family. After a year in London and months at sea with an English crew, Tara no longer felt uncomfortable being surrounded by her one-time enemies. These were friends. Perhaps it was a reflection of her newfound maturity that she thought even her family would forgive the past for the kindness these people had shown her. It had been the same on Bermuda. They saw her not as an American, but as herself.

Sitting next to the captain, knowing in a matter of weeks they would part, Tara felt a sudden melancholy. But she would not change her mind. Nick's sister-in-law might be one to enjoy afternoons in an English parlour, but not Tara.

"Would you allow me to sketch you?" the beautiful redhead asked.

"She's very good," Sir Martin said to his brother and Tara.

"I would like a portrait of Tara," said Nick. "A sketch for my cabin would be very nice."

Sir Martin raised a brow to his wife, and Kit said, "If you're willing, Tara, before you sail, I'll do a sketch of you. Perhaps we can begin this afternoon. It doesn't take me long once I start."

"That's very kind of you, Kit." And so began Tara's friendship with the captain's sister-in-law. When the two brothers went back to their work, Nicolas sent Peter to retrieve Kit's sketchbook and pencils from his brother's ship, and the two women spent the afternoon together. While they nibbled on fruit and cheese, Tara heard all about Kit's adventures in the Midlands of England.

* * *

They dined at Lavalette's Hotel that evening, Nick inviting his brother and sister-in-law to be his guests along with Tara, his first mate and old Nate, who had cleaned up for the evening, appearing the distinguished gentleman with his gray hair neatly combed and wearing a black coat and pantaloons. Nick recalled it was the way Nate always dressed in London whenever Claire Powell was in attendance. Perhaps the old salt harbored a secret affection for Nick's mother. Though ten years Nate's senior, his mother was still a beautiful woman and Nate had never married.

Both Russ and Nate knew Martin quite well. Indeed, they knew the whole Powell family, so it was a time of getting reacquainted and telling stories about Nick and his brothers neither Nick nor

Martin really wanted to have told. But Kit and Tara seemed delighted at the brothers' childhood antics, so Nick accepted it as having a good affect upon the target of his affections.

Despite their night together, Tara still held herself at a distance, and when he escorted her to her room that night, she thanked him for a wonderful evening and went into her room without so much as a kiss. He thought he knew what it was. Tara felt guilty at succumbing to their shared passion and was trying to pretend it never happened.

Well, he would see about that.

* * *

Tara stepped into her room, a single candle casting a soft glow on the four-poster bed. She was glad it was not in this bed she'd so wantonly given herself to Nicholas Powell the night before. Taking the pins from her hair, she remembered how he had run his hands through her hair, scattering the pins. It sent shivers through her as her body relived what had followed.

It had become clear to her during dinner that she would have to steel herself to get through the next weeks as they sailed to Baltimore. The captain had been so solicitous of her and his glances so full of desire she knew it would be up to her to maintain a distance between them. He had not repeated his halfhearted demand that she marry him. Tara assumed the obligatory gentleman's offer, once refused, would not be made again. It was just as well. She did not want to have to summon the strength to reject it. But then, she did not want to be an English broodmare sequestered away from the sea and the ships she loved, which was certain to happen if she married the English captain. How could she reconcile her newfound womanhood and her love of the sea? And what about her family and America? Could she leave the country she loved? As long as she kept her distance from the too-handsome captain, she wouldn't have to answer those questions.

Then Tara recalled what the captain had said when he brought her to her door. If the repairs were complete and the ship provisioned as ordered, they would sail for Baltimore the next day.

She couldn't help wonder what awaited her there.

Chapter 20

The trip north, as far as Nick was concerned, was uneventful. They'd had a bit of bad weather at one point off the Carolinas, but nothing so severe as to damage the ship. And, thank God, there had been no further encounters with pirates.

He and Russ had held their collective breath as they sailed the waters off the coast of Florida, but the Laffite brothers made no appearance. As for Cofresí, Nick hoped the pirate was still in custody answering the questions of the Spanish authorities. Perhaps by now he was even in jail. The thought brought a smile to Nick's face. The pirate had thought to take Tara; Nick would have fought and died before he'd have let the pirate have her.

His bride to be, as he optimistically thought of the American girl, kept her distance as they traveled north up the Atlantic coast. And believing it was what she wished, Nick did his best to keep his hands off her. But it was not easy.

"The tension between the two of ye is like a taut anchor chain in a bad sea," said Nate one day as he stood watching Nick watch Tara as she went about helping his crew with their chores. "The whole lot of 'em," he gestured to the crew, "are watching to see when the tinder will ignite."

"There is little I can do, Nate. The lady has rejected my suit."

"Yer going about it all wrong, lad. A little humility would be better than ordering the lass about."

Nick thought he had been quite humble when he'd made his proposal. Well, it was humble for him. In any case, he was not giving up. If Tara would not come about on her own, perhaps her father could persuade her. But what was he thinking? Her father would hate the idea of her marrying an Englishman, particularly one who'd been a privateer, no matter he'd taken his prizes primarily among the French.

Nick planned to dock his ship where he expected to see his new schooner and then see Tara home. He would speak to her father about courting her, assuming the elder McConnell had recovered whatever ailed him. Perhaps on American soil she would see things as he did. And Martin had given him an idea for a gift for her that would, he was certain, speak to her sailor's heart. It wasn't much of a plan but it was all he could think to do—except to pray.

Yes, he would pray.

* * *

Tara leaned against the rail on the port side of the bow as they entered Baltimore's harbor basin, her heart soaring at the familiar sight of ships sailing through the channel, their white sails set against the green of the surrounding hills. Sighting the white buildings with red roofs emerging from the greenery, she smiled. She was nearly home.

The *Wind Raven* sailed past Fort McHenry, making Tara ever more eager to see her father. Would he be ill? Would he even be alive? She couldn't bear to think otherwise. Anxiety had her biting her lower lip while the ship drew closer to the inner harbor.

She had managed to avoid Nicholas Powell as they sailed north, though each time he was near, her knees grew weak and her resolve threatened to flee. This love, she had come to see, was a physical thing. It nettled her brain and robbed her of appetite. And the ache from the knowledge she must soon part from him, though she believed it to be the right path, would not go away. She hoped in time her love for the brooding English sea captain would fade. Did not time heal all wounds?

Nate strolled to where she was standing and began to talk about the last time he and the captain were in Baltimore. She was only half listening when the first mate approached.

"Are you looking forward to being home, Miss McConnell?" he asked, smiling. He had always been terribly polite to her, and she had come to admire his loyalty to the captain.

Returning his smile, she said, "Yes, Mr. Ainsworth, I am."

"Worried about your father?"

"That, too. It's been nearly two months since I left London."

"Well, you shall know soon enough. I hope all is well."

At the top of the fort a huge American flag rippled in the morning wind, reminding her of three years before, when her countrymen had successfully warded off the British attack. This was her country and she was proud of it.

Soon they would reach the shipbuilding center of Fell's Point. Wondering how far they would be from her home, Tara turned to the first mate. "Where are we making anchor, sir?"

He gave her a winsome smile and then looked into the distance. "The captain wants to dock where he'll be picking up his new schooner, at Stag Shipping. He will see you home immediately after."

"Stag Shipping?" She could hardly believe it. Her family's business was his destination?

"Do you know it, Miss McConnell?"

"Oh, yes. I do," she said proudly. "They built some of the Baltimore clipper ships, you know."

"That is why the captain is here. He has long wanted one of his own and is most anxious to claim it. Ordered the schooner from the London agent nearly nine months ago."

A smile spread across Tara's face. It seemed the captain was sailing her to her very door.

* * *

Nick had just stepped onto the quarterdeck as their destination came into sight. Those crewmembers not aloft furling sail were coiling and stowing lines on deck or standing along the rail by the mooring lines, ready for docking. He joined Russ and Tara at the rail, where they were talking with Nate.

The faint scent of jasmine filled his mind, making him long to hold the woman he wanted. She had confined her golden curls into a proper knot at her nape and was dressed in modest ladies' apparel. He would have her in a gown, in breeches or in nothing at all. But he was determined to have her.

In the distance, Nick saw a row of schooners lined up at the dock. One was under construction and three two-masted schooners looked to have been in service for some time, but the last one, a three-masted schooner, was new. Nick stared at the black-hulled ship. The polished wood of its three raked masts was gleaming in the sun. It was just like his vision the day he'd left London, finally real before his eyes. Though the sails were yet to be unfurled, in his mind's eye, he could see them full of the wind, sailing close hauled. Excitement filled him. It was his ship. It had to be.

"A grand day for our arrival, Captain," Russ said.

"A grand day to claim my new ship. Look," he said, never taking his eyes from the sleek vessel, "there she is."

"Aye, and she comes with a reckonin', I 'spect," murmured Nate as he left them to head toward the helm, where he would take the ship the last distance to the dock. Nick gave him a side-glance, wondering what the old seaman meant by his cryptic remark. But nothing could sour his mood as he gazed longingly at his new schooner. He had loved the *Wind Raven* with an avid devotion, but this new one was special. He intended it to be the only ship he would sail for a very long time.

Russ gave the order to furl sails and Nate guided the ship to its berth at the dock. Nick's gaze shifted to the emerald-green stag painted on the front of the company's main building, the same stag that had been on the confirmation the London agent had sent him of his order for the new schooner. His men scrambled to secure the ship.

Suddenly a door in the Stag Shipping building burst open and three men dashed out to stand abreast at the dock. A greeting party?

"I wonder who they are," Nick thought aloud.

"My brothers," Tara announced with a smile. "It seems we're expected."

"Your brothers?" asked Nick, perplexed. "Your family owns Stag Shipping?"

"Why yes," said Tara, "didn't you know?"

The three tawny-haired men stood together, the tallest with his legs spread and his hands fisted on his hips. To a man, they looked angry and intransigent. No, Nick corrected himself, they looked livid. He couldn't be more delighted. If he could survive this meeting with her brothers, Tara would be forced to take him.

"What could this be?" wondered Russ aloud.

"Judging by their faces," Nick replied, "I'd say it's an answer to a prayer."

As soon as the gangway was down, Nick stepped off the ship and offered his hand to the tallest of the three men. "Captain George McConnell, I presume?"

The oldest McConnell brother scowled and ignored Nick's extended hand. "You are the captain of the *Wind Raven*. Don't you remember me, for I surely remember you from Esmit's Tavern in St. Thomas. I have an excellent memory—even when I've been drinking."

"Ah," said Nick, withdrawing his hand. The pieces of the puzzle suddenly came together. No wonder Tara had looked so familiar when he'd first met her. The drunken American captain he'd encountered in St. Thomas had a better memory than he did. Well, even this could serve his purpose.

"Where is my sister?" George McConnell demanded, obviously the spokesman for the other two brothers flanking him.

Nick turned toward the *Wind Raven*. Tara was just starting down the gangway, a brilliant smile on her face. "George! John! Tom!" she shouted, waving her arm and running the last few steps. She wore no bonnet and wisps of tawny hair blew across her face. To Nick, she had never looked more beautiful. Her brothers reached for her with open arms, each kissing her on the cheek. Nick felt a twinge of jealousy, then reminded himself they were her brothers.

George McConnell gave her a fierce hug and asked, "You are safe? You are well?"

"Yes," she said, breathless, "though the voyage wasn't without its challenges. We were held up with pirates for a time."

Her brothers scowled at Nick.

Russ had followed Tara off the ship and now joined Nick, directing his attention back to the *Wind Raven*. From the rail and the shrouds where they stared at the unfolding drama, the crew watched like anxious parents.

"How did you know I'd be arriving today and on this ship?" Tara inquired of her brothers.

"When you left London without your chaperone, Aunt Cornelia sent a message to Father on the next cargo ship sailing for Baltimore," answered the one she'd called *Tom*. "It arrived before you did."

"How is Father?" Tara asked anxiously.

"Better," said George. "And he wants to see you immediately."

"Oh," she said clutching her throat. "I am so relieved. All right, yes, I want to see him too."

Tara began walking away with her brother John on the path that led up a hill to a large two-story white house overlooking the harbor. After a few steps, she paused and looked back. Wanting to reassure her, Nick said, "I'll see you tomorrow, Tara." Then he turned to her oldest brother. "I'll give you some time to get reacquainted. We can deal with other matters then." As he turned to walk back to his ship, Nick's shoulder was seized in a hard grip that yanked him around.

"You'll not be leaving just yet, Powell," said George McConnell. "I've a few questions that will not keep." Russ stood back and crossed his arms over his chest, saying nothing. Nick looked to his ship, where his crew stood at the rail wearing knowing smiles. They had abandoned their captain to Tara's brothers. A reckoning indeed. Before he could open his mouth to explain, the oldest brother dragged him forward, shouting to his brother Tom to see that Tara's trunk was brought off the ship.

It was time to pay the piper and Nick was only too happy to oblige.

* * *

George shoved Nick into the office and from there into a back room with a desk and two chairs. Nick put up no fight, hoping this might help his cause. Once they were in private, Tara's oldest brother leaned on the desk and turned on Nick with crossed arms. "I have one question for you, Powell. Did you take our sister to your bed?"

"Yes."

The fist slammed into Nick's face, hitting him hard enough to knock him to the floor.

"Damnation! You just had to do it, didn't you? Well, you may be a sorry excuse for a husband but you'll be doing the right thing by our sister—and then we'll kill you."

Nick rose from the floor, rubbing his aching jaw. "I love her, McConnell. I have offered her marriage."

"Damn and you're English to boot." George McConnell huffed and crossed his arms. "And what did Tara say?"

"She refused my offer."

"She'll have no choice. Father will insist, and she will not defy him."

"Good. That was my hope."

George looked at him, puzzled. "You are serious?"

"Yes, I am. I want her for my wife and I'll have no other."

"Father will not be pleased. You're English," he said again, as if that explained it all. Nick supposed it did. "Tara is his pride and joy. He would see her married only to an American. But no matter. The marriage doesn't have to be permanent. I expect she'll make a beautiful widow."

Chapter 21

Tara walked slowly to the upholstered chair where her father appeared to sleep. He looked peaceful, though deep shadows beneath his eyes told her much.

"Father?" she whispered, not wanting to wake him if he was truly resting. John, who had accompanied her, stood just behind her.

Sean McConnell opened his eyes and his face crinkled into a hundred wrinkles as the Irishman she loved smiled. "Tara, sure an' you've come home to me." His large hands swallowed hers as he reached for her.

"Father!" she cried, kneeling at his feet. "You know I would never have left if you hadn't insisted."

He ran his eyes over her gown and her hair, his gaze lingering on her face. "I see you've become the lady I always envisioned. You've a different look about you, Tara me love, more your mother than ever."

She smiled, happy to hear his words. "Are you well, Father?"

"They tell me I am recovering. I feel like I've spent a month at hard labor and find myself napping in the afternoons, but I suppose I'm on the mend."

"What was it?"

From behind her, John said, "Ship's fever."

"Oh, Father!" she cried, aware many seamen had died of typhus.

"Fortunately I didn't take sick until I'd returned from that last voyage. The boys have taken good care of me."

"Well I'm here now and can take care of you too. You'll be fine, I promise."

"That's my girl." He patted her hand.

Rising, she kissed his cheek and said, "I'll let you rest now, but I'll be back."

* * *

She stepped out of her father's study to hear John say in a grim voice, "Tom tells me George wants to see you, Tara."

She nodded. "Where is Captain Powell?"

"He was headed into the office with George. He may be back on his ship by now."

"All right. I'll see George." She expected questions, knowing she had defied her aunt and traveled alone. Bracing herself for a difficult conversation, she entered the main building of Stag Shipping.

George sat behind his desk in the inner office. He was alone. Rising, he said a word to John she didn't hear. When John left, George returned to his seat.

"Sit down, Tara. I will be brief. I know you are probably tired and anxious to see to your things. I've asked Tom to bring your trunk and valise to your room."

She sat in one of the chairs facing his desk, where she had sat countless other times as they'd planned routes and, during the war, talked about the skirmishes at sea. Her oldest brother's face told her he was both serious and disapproving, and for a moment she wondered if he hadn't taken the place of her father in family matters. Perhaps he had.

"Is anything wrong, George?"

"Yes, but the matter will be shortly seen to. And though I have no liking for what must be done, there is no alternative."

"What are you talking about?"

"You know I've no fondness for the English, Tara, but it seems I'm to have one as a brother-in-law."

"What?"

"Tara, had I known Aunt Cornelia arranged for you to sail with Nicholas Powell, captain of the *Wind Raven*, I'd have never allowed it. First, he is English. We've fought a war with them, remember? I shouldn't have to remind you that our brother died in that war. And if I shared with Father all I know of this particular English captain, he would have forbidden you passage on the man's ship. I learned of Powell's attitude toward women from an encounter with him in St. Thomas on that trip you made with me a few years back. I was not surprised to learn he seduced you."

Tara gasped. "He told you that?"

"He didn't volunteer it, no. But knowing him, I asked. At least he was honest. He says he's offered you marriage and that you have refused him. Does he speak the truth?"

"His reasons for marriage were quite unacceptable." Tara rose and walked to the window, her back to her brother. She felt a trap closing around her. Would her brothers really force her to wed Nicholas Powell? The marriage would keep her a prisoner in some grand home in London, and without the love she so wanted. Bile rose in her throat. Though she loved Nicholas Powell, she could not bear such an existence. She wanted a different life.

"Then it seems he's been remiss," George said. "But whether that is the case or not, you will marry him."

She swirled around to face her brother. "I'll not marry a man who doesn't love me!" she yelled across the desk. "And I'll not spend my future days in a drawing room in London! Besides," she continued, feeling the wind leave her sails, "I'd miss all of you."

"Love or no, parlour or no, brothers or no, you will marry him. And if you don't agree, I'll be telling the whole story to Father.

And you know *he* will insist. And then, after the wedding, he will kill the good captain, so you need not worry about London."

George shouted toward the open door, "Bring in Captain Powell!"

* * *

Nick had just entered the outer office when he'd heard Tara shout her insistence that she would not marry a man who did not love her, nor would she be confined to a London parlour. He had to admit his answer to her question when she'd asked if he loved her hadn't been very clear. But she should have realized he loved her, damn it all. If that and her fear of being consigned to the parlours of London were what stood in the way of his suit, he would soon remedy the deficiency.

Tara's brother John, who'd come to fetch him, had also heard Tara's vehement statements, but he just shook his head and escorted Nick into the inner office. Apparently John was the quiet one.

As they entered the office, which smelled of lumber and efficiency, George rose and walked toward him. "You'd better convince her, Powell, and once you do, you will have to convince our father." The tall American left with John, shutting the door behind them. He and Tara were alone for the first time since their night of passion in St. Thomas. He could see she was nervous, twisting her hands at her waist, hesitant to speak.

"Tara, it seems I've done this all wrong." She looked up, a startled expression on her beautiful face. "Oh, I don't mean making love to you. I'd not change that. But I failed to respond as I should have when you asked if I loved you. Lord knows I've thought it many a time, but I'm not a man of sweet words, you know."

Her blue-green eyes fixed on him, a look of wonder on her face as she waited to hear what he would say.

"I love you, Tara. I have for a long time. Perhaps it began that day you climbed the rigging to rescue Billy in those ridiculous breeches of yours. Or it might have been when you talked of your pride in being an American. There were so many times I saw you acting the woman I'd never thought to find. I don't know what finally did it. I do know that I can't—I won't—live without you. You've become a part of me, the best part, I think, and I have no intention of letting you leave me now."

For a moment she just stood there staring open-mouthed. "You mean it? Really? George did not threaten you?"

The look in her aquamarine eyes was so intense he could feel her anxious longing. "Yes, he threatened me," his mouth hitched up in a reluctant grin, "that is, he said he plans to make you a widow after we wed. But I am not a man to bend to a threat. I do mean it, Tara. I love you as I have never loved any woman." Closing the distance between them, he wrapped his hands around her upper arms and smiled down at her. "Marry me or you'll leave me a lost soul."

"And what about our life together if I accept? Will you leave me in London while you sail the world? Expect me to sit in a drawing room all day, embroidering with the ladies of the *ton*?"

He dropped his hands and burst out laughing. "You? Embroider? No, I don't think so. And I've never sought the company of the *ton*. I want a partner in all things, Tara. A woman who will share my love of the sea, who will sail with me." And then thinking of the children they would one day have, he added, "When you must stay home, I promise, so will I." Perhaps, like her brother George, he would one day become involved in the business end of his family's endeavors.

Her eyes lit up and her beautiful lips formed into a smile as she threw her arms around his neck. "Oh, Nick, yes. I'll marry you. Today if you like."

Nick kissed the woman he'd claimed as his own and then stood back. "Yes, I'd like that very much, but aren't you forgetting something?"

"What?"

"Apparently, I must first persuade your father."

"Oh," she said thoughtfully, "that will not be an easy task, I'm afraid."

Together, hand-in-hand, they left the small office to find Tara's brothers waiting for them outside. Nick gazed in the direction of his ship. Several of his crew still stood at the rail, Russ now among them. When they saw him holding Tara's hand, they broke out into smiles and cheers, slapping each other on the back.

"All right, Powell," Tara's brother George said, "I can see you've managed to persuade my sister. Now you must face the real opposition: our father."

Nick and Tara, accompanied by her brothers, walked up the hill to the big white house with the black shutters set amongst the pine trees overlooking the harbor. At the front door, Nick paused and faced Tara. "Are you certain you want to be a part of this? It may not be pleasant."

She returned his gaze with a confident air. "Partners, remember? Of course I want to be with you. I may be able to help."

It was so like Tara to want to be in the midst of the fray and to be offering her help, he did not object, just shrugged his shoulders and walked with her through the door George held open for them. A plump, red-haired woman approached, wearing an apron over her dark blue gown.

"Land sakes, child!" she said to Tara. "You're not even home an hour and already there's trouble. I can feel it." Then facing Nick, she asked, "And who is this?"

"Nicholas," said Tara, "this is Mrs. O'Flaherty, our housekeeper and one of the family." Then addressing the woman, "Maggie, this is Captain Nicholas Powell."

"Her betrothed," Nick added, holding up Tara's hand to show the housekeeper his ring. Tara had never taken it off.

"I see." Then looking at Tara, she said, "I don't suppose yer father knows about this, does he? What could you be thinkin', Miss Tara? The man's English!"

"No, Maggie, Father doesn't yet know. That is why we are here, to ask for his blessing. Can you let Father know my brothers and I want to see him and we have a…visitor with us?"

"Humph," mumbled the housekeeper under her breath as she walked away. "He won't like this none, no sir."

In a moment the housekeeper returned. "He's awake and will see you and your…*visitor*," she said, casting a scowl at Nick.

Nick thought the room they stepped into must be the elder McConnell's study, as books lined the walls and in the center there was a large desk. Two high-backed, well-stuffed chairs were set at an angle to the brick fireplace. In one corner sat a tall mahogany secretary and beneath the window next to it, framed by dark blue curtains drawn back with a sash on each side, was a round pedestal table on which sat a vase of red roses. Souvenirs of a life at sea were scattered about the room, among them nautical charts, a sextant and, over the fireplace, a painting of a schooner cutting through wild seas.

The older man, slumped in one of the chairs with his hands folded on his chest, looked to be an old salt whose leathered face bore the lines of many voyages, though he was paler than Nick would have expected for a ship's captain. His tawny hair was liberally threaded with gray, as was his short, well-trimmed beard. The hair color and his blue eyes, when he opened them, told Nick the man was Tara's father, Sean McConnell.

* * *

As she entered the study with Nick and her brothers, Tara carefully watched her father. He looked tired and her heart reached out to him. "Father, are you well enough to see us?"

"Of course, I'm well enough," he blustered. "Now don't be coddling me. I'm feeling fine as a matter of fact." With that, he rose and stepped forward, seeming the man he'd been before she'd left for London: tall, strong and, at times, forbidding.

"Father, I have someone I'd like you to meet."

"Oh?" her father said and turned his focus on the one man in the room he wouldn't recognize.

"This is Nicholas Powell, captain of the *Wind Raven*," she said. "It was his ship that brought me home from London. It's berthed at our dock now."

"Thank you for bringing my daughter home, Captain Powell."

"It was my privilege to do so," Nick said. Then extending his hand, "I am pleased to meet you, Captain McConnell. I've long admired your schooners."

Tara was glad to see her father accept Nicholas's hand. It was a good sign. "Powell," Sean McConnell said, mulling the name over. "Sounds familiar."

"It might be you saw it on an order for one of your ships. And from the look of the new three-masted schooner docked at your pier, I believe it may be mine."

"Ah yes, now I recall. The one we built for that English firm…Powell and Sons. That'd be you?"

"Yes, I'm one of them, the eldest son."

"Well, she's ready, just needs a name."

"I have an idea for the name, sir. But before I get to that, there is something more important I would like to discuss with you."

"Yes?" The puzzled expression that swept across her father's face unveiled new wrinkles on his forehead.

"Sir, as you know, the voyage from London lasted some time, in fact longer than I'd anticipated, as an errand for the Prince Regent delayed me from leaving the West Indies. During our time at sea, Tara and I became rather...well acquainted, and as a result, I have quite fallen in love with her. I've asked her to become my wife and she's accepted. I am hoping for your blessing and your daughter's hand in marriage."

Tara's father turned to her, a disbelieving look on his face. "Tara, is this true?"

Tara smiled at Nicholas, the English captain she had come to love. "Yes, Father."

"Well, it won't do, missy. It won't do at all. Need I remind you our family has fought two wars with England for America's independence. I'll not have my only daughter marry one of them. No siree!"

Tara had expected this reaction and noticed her brother George nervously entwining his fingers while John stared down at the floor.

"But Father—" Before she could say more, her father held up his palm, cutting her off.

"Would it matter if I told you I'm not entirely English, sir?" asked Nick, seemingly undaunted by her father's reaction to his suit.

"Just what does that mean?" her father demanded, glowering at Nick.

"I'm half French. My mother, Claire Donet, was raised in Paris. Her father was the younger son of a French comte."

"An English captain with a French mother of noble birth," her father seemed to mull the words over in his mind. "Now it's clear! My sister's been at her matchmaking again. Damn me if she hasn't!" Then turning to Tara, "This is all your aunt's doing!"

"Aunt Cornelia?" Tara couldn't imagine what he was talking about.

"She wrote me six months ago, saying she had some friend, a woman of an aristocratic French family married to a wealthy English merchantman. Told me her friend had a son who was a ship's captain." Shoving his index finger into Nick's chest, her father bellowed, "I imagine that'd be you!"

"Possibly," Nick said calmly, his mouth twitching up on one side, "the mater has many friends."

"Your aunt," her father directed his words at Tara, "wanted permission to introduce you to her friend's son. I said *no*. Absolutely not. And now look at what she's done!"

"Aunt Cornelia wanted me to meet Captain Powell?" Tara was bewildered. She'd known she was to take the *Wind Raven* and no other ship, but she thought it was only to assure her safety. She'd had no idea that her aunt was playing matchmaker.

"Why that's—" Tara stammered.

"Treachery!" her father exclaimed. "Ever since she married that baron and moved to London, she's had peculiar ideas. I should have known something like this would happen. If I hadn't been so desperate—"

"But, Father, I love him."

"I'll have none of yer cajoling, missy. You can just manage to love an American, by God. I'll not have my grandchildren thinking they are part of the wretched British!"

Tara glanced at Nicolas and was surprised to see amusement in his eyes. Rubbing his fingers over his chin as if pondering a tough negotiation, he said, "What if I promise you that Tara and I will spend part of each year here—with your grandchildren? And remember, I'm half French."

"That would be your best half," her father insisted. "That would make my grandchildren…"

"Part English, part French and half American. Not a bad blend," offered Nick.

Tara listened to the two men negotiating over her future children and thought it ridiculous. "These children the two of you are bargaining over have yet to be born!"

"Yes, my love," said Nicholas and then whispered into her ear, "but have you considered that one may already have been conceived?" Tara felt her cheeks heat at his words.

"What was that?" her father demanded.

"I was just agreeing with Tara, sir." He shot her brother George a look that appeared to Tara to be a plea for help. It only served to remind Tara he shared in the knowledge of just how well she and the English captain knew each other. It was embarrassing.

"Father," George offered, "perhaps this isn't such a bad idea. Tara does seem to want the man and he can well afford to keep her. Then, too, Aunt Cornelia has been looking after her this last year and remains in London to make certain Tara is well settled. After all, Captain Powell and we are in the same business. You could insist on a partnership—"

"If you'll allow me to interrupt this discussion of me as if I were just another ship, Nicholas and I have already talked about being partners together." She looked at her fiancé, her eyes pleading for his support.

"That's true, sir," Nick assured her father. "Tara and I both love the sea as well as each other. You'll have Powell and Sons as a partner. We can buy your ships and then my family and yours—as well as the grandchildren Tara and I will give you—can sail them."

Tara studied her father. The sudden gleam in his eye told her he was considering the idea.

"Are you certain you'll not change your mind, Tara, me love?" her father asked. "You were none too fond of London, as I recall your letters."

"I wasn't so fond of it," she said. "But that is when I only had Aunt Cornelia and her friends in the *ton* for company. Being with Nick and his family and involved in their shipping firm will be different. I've met one of his brothers and his new wife and I like them very much. Besides, I could not imagine leaving Nicholas." He squeezed her hand. "No, I will not change my mind, Father."

"You are in favor of this marriage?" her father asked his sons.

"Under the circumstances, Father, I am," said George, giving Nick a knowing look.

"I agree," said John.

"Me as well," echoed Tom.

"Well, then, it appears I'm to have a bloody Englishman for a son-in-law." Nick smiled at Tara and she returned his smile. "But, mind you," chided her father, "I expect to see my grandchildren every year. I'm holding you to your promise, Powell."

* * *

The wedding took place the next day in the small Fell's Point Methodist Church. Nick had been amused to learn that the McConnells, like Nick's parents, had a mixed marriage when it came to religion. Nick's father had been a Protestant when he married the Catholic Claire Donet and swept her away to England, where she became a Methodist under the teachings of John Wesley; Tara's father was an Irish Catholic who married a Methodist in Maryland. The result was that both Nick and Tara were Methodists. To Nick's relief, the reverend who married them seemed to have no problem with his being English.

The crew of the *Wind Raven*, wearing their best clothes, was in somber attendance as the vows were said, but the smiles that broke out on their faces following the pronouncement that he and Tara were man and wife told Nick they were pleased with their captain. Congratulations were said all around, with special words from Jake Johansson for Tara, and Peter for his captain. Nate bore the smile of the cat that ate the cream. Finally Nick had done something right in his eyes.

After the wedding, the guests retired to Nick's new, and as yet unnamed, schooner, where the McConnell family and friends and his crew crowded the deck. Even the gray cat had left the *Wind Raven* to join them on the new ship.

"Ah, 'tis a fine day," said Nate to the newlyweds where they stood drinking Champagne and greeting guests on the quarterdeck. "Yer mother and father will be pleased, Nick. Both their oldest sons are now married."

"Sure an' ye had no choice," chimed in McGinnes, who had become fast friends with Tara's father. "Since ye gave yer heart to the *leanan sídhe*," he explained, darting a glance at Tara, "ye be forever hers."

Russ looked at Nick and chuckled. "Perhaps you should name your ship after the Irish fairy," he suggested with a wink.

"I already have a name in mind," said Nick with a wry smile toward his bride. "Don't you know," he said to Tara, as he tightened his arm around her waist and looked into her aquamarine eyes, "the men in my family name their ships after the women they love? My father has the *Claire*, my brother, the *Sea Kitten*, and I...I will have the *Goddess of the Sea*. I'm naming the ship for you, Tara."

Tara beamed her happiness at his choice, her eyes filling with tears. The men standing around them cheered, "Hear! Hear!"

"You and I will sail her together," he reminded her.

His bride leaned in to give him a kiss. The crew cheered again more loudly. Even the McConnells smiled their approval.

"And so we shall, *husband*," Tara whispered into his ear. "And so we shall."

AUTHOR'S NOTE

I chose to set my story on a schooner of the period because I love those ships and the "Baltimore clippers" Nick coveted, which helped America fight the War of 1812, a war that solidified the young country. The Baltimore clipper ships were the fast topsail schooners with narrow hulls and raked masts that enabled the American privateers to outrun the larger English ships. (The huge "clipper ships" we remember today are mostly from the Victorian era.)

I based Tara's family's ships on the *Chasseur*, one of the most successful privateers built in Fell's Point in Baltimore. It had an amazing record of preying on British vessels during the War of 1812. Though schooners were used primarily for the coastal trade, larger ones were known to sail the high seas. Such was Nick's ship, the *Wind Raven*.

Some of you might think it unlikely a woman could serve as a member of the crew, even on her father's and brothers' ships, as Tara did, but that is not the case. In Suzanne Stark's book *Female Tars*, she documents many cases in which women served on ships, assisting a ship's surgeon in patching up wounded men or carrying powder to the guns of naval ships, a job shared with young boys called *powder-monkeys*. One of the earliest cases of a woman seaman was that of Anne Chamberlyne, a scholar's daughter and member of the gentry, who at the age of twenty-three in 1690 declined offers of marriage to don a man's clothing and join her brother's ship to fight the French off Beachy Head. Thus, the fictional Tara McConnell had her real life precedents. And for

Captain Nick Powell, only a courageous woman who loved her independence and the sea as Tara did could be his true love match.

Bel Air, the magnificent home in Bermuda where Nick and Tara stayed, was built in 1816 by the Honourable Francis Albouy, a wealthy merchant and a real historical figure. The house, which still looks out over Hamilton Harbor, does have two guest cottages. And amazingly, long after I'd named my hero Nicholas Powell, I discovered that a ship under the command of a notorious pirate by the name of Powell ran aground on the main island of Bermuda, causing the pirate to be banished by the colonial governor to Ireland Island, where the dockyard stood in 1817, as my characters observed from the Albouys' gallery.

The guests entertained in the Albouys' home that night along with the fictional Nick and Tara were guests were real historical people who lived in Bermuda at the time. I like to think such a dinner might actually have taken place, don't you? If you want the recipe for the Bermuda rum swizzle or Bermuda syllabub, they are on my website (www.reaganwalkerauthor.com).

With the end of the War of 1812 and the Napoleonic wars in 1815, an unprecedented wave of piracy swept the American seaboard and the Caribbean as some of the hundreds of captains who were privateers in the wars became outlaws of the sea, preying upon the growing numbers of merchant vessels. Although some of these pirates, like Jean Laffite, were American, the majority came from farther south and Latin America.

The pirate Roberto Cofresí, "El Pirata Cofresí," was one of them.

Just as I have portrayed him, Cofresí was tall, blond and blue-eyed, being of Austrian extraction, notwithstanding the name his father adopted upon settling in Puerto Rico (then called *Porto Rico*, based upon an error in the Treaty of Paris). And he wore dangling silver and diamond earrings any woman would covet.

In 1817, Cofresí was twenty-six, though he didn't actually become a pirate until the following year, when he began attacking ships sailing under flags other than Royal Spain. Spain looked the other way—at least until 1824, when it gave into pressure from its allies. Cofresí was captured by the Americans and turned over to the Spanish, who executed him in 1825.

While Cofresí sailed a schooner in his early years of pirating, it was not named the *Retribución*. During the time he was a pirate, he had two ships: the *Ana*, named after the woman he later married, Juana Creitoff (who was of Dutch extraction); and what may have been his first ship, a smaller one named *El Mosquito*.

I have tried to be true to all we know of Cofresí. He was a complex character with both noble and brutal sides to his personality. Although Cofresí was famous for his generosity, sharing his booty with the poor, for which the Puerto Ricans admired and protected him, he could also be cruel to his enemies. There were reports he nailed hostages to the deck of *El Mosquito*. And the axe was, indeed, his favorite weapon. Contrasted with this, he was protective of children, often saving young ones taken from prize ships and giving them into the care of Catholic priests along with money for their expenses. Like Tara, he lost his mother at a young age.

There are many legends about why Cofresí turned to piracy, as he was well educated and had older brothers who discouraged his maritime efforts. Some believe it was the evils of the colony under Spanish regime, some say his sister was raped by a group of sailors and others say he was slapped in the face by an English captain. Perhaps it was for all those reasons that Cofresí turned to piracy. I have chosen to include the story of his sister being raped by an English seaman as I can see how that would have led her younger brother to vengeance against the English merchantmen. It would also explain why he was protective toward women, as Cofresí was known to be. And I can see how such a heinous act, followed by a slap to his face when had he tried to seek retribution from the English sailors, could easily lead Cofresí to prey on the ships of England and her allies.

Some biographers have said he was a revolutionary, a patriot and a pioneer of Puerto Rico's independence movement. Perhaps it is so for he flew the flag of the Free Republic of Puerto Rico, not that of Spain. Today there is a monument to Cofresí in Cabo Rojo, his home on the southwest coast of Puerto Rico.

Author Francisco Ortea wrote of Cofresí, "For his boldness and courage, he was worthy of a better occupation and fate." I do agree.

Lastly, I must include a note on sailing times. I have taken liberty with the time for the crossing of the Atlantic and the trip to Bermuda, Puerto Rico and Baltimore. More time might have been required than the few months I've allowed, given the limitations of the schooners of the early 19th century and their time spent in the Caribbean. But for the sake of my story, and Tara's need to be in Baltimore, it could not take longer.

I hope you enjoyed my seafaring, pirate Regency. Watch for the prequel to the **Agents of the Crown Trilogy**, the story of Nick and Martin's parents: Captain Simon Powell, the young English privateer they called "the Golden Eagle," and Claire Donet, the wild daughter of the French pirate, Jean Donet, Nick's namesake, who was indeed the younger son of a French comte. It will be set in late 18th century France, England and aboard Simon's ship, the *Fairwinds*. It's a story of adventure, passion and love, for Simon knows if he is to possess Claire's love, he must find a way *To Tame the Wind*.

ABOUT THE AUTHOR

As a child Regan Walker loved to write, particularly about adventure-loving girls, but by the time she got to college more serious pursuits took priority. One of her professors thought her suited to the profession of law, and Regan realized it would be better to be a hammer than a nail. Years of serving clients in private practice, including a stint in government service, gave her a love of international travel and a feel for the demands of the "Crown" on its subjects. Hence her romance novels often involve a demanding Prince Regent who thinks of his subjects as his private talent pool.

The Agents of the Crown Regency romance trilogy includes the three full-length novels *Racing with the Wind*, *Against the Wind* and *Wind Raven*. Regan has three related shorter works, *The Holly & the Thistle*, *The Shamrock & the Rose*, and *The Twelfth Night Wager*. You can keep up with her through her website, **www.reganwalkerauthor.com**.

Regan lives in San Diego with her golden retriever, whom she says inspires her every day to relax and smell the roses.

A PERILOUS PASSAGE

Ordered by the Prince Regent into the Caribbean, English sea captain and former privateer Jean Nicholas Powell has no time for women aboard the *Wind Raven*, especially not Tara McConnell. The impudent American demanded passage, and so she'll get more than she bargained for: Instead of a direct sail to Baltimore, she'll join his quest to investigate and neutralize the rampaging pirate Roberto Cofresi.

But the hoyden thinks she can crew with his men! And though Nick bans her from the rigging he is captivated watching her lithe, luscious movements on deck. Facing high seas, storms, cutthroats and the endless unknown, he must always protect his ship, his passengers, his crew. But on this voyage, with this woman, there is a greater danger: to his heart.

Boroughs
Publishing Group

Did you enjoy this book? Drop us a line and say so! We love to hear from readers, and so do our authors. To connect, visit www.boroughspublishinggroup.com online, send comments directly to info@boroughspublishinggroup.com, or friend us on Facebook and Twitter. And be sure to check back regularly for contests and new releases in your favorite subgenres of romance!

Are you an aspiring writer? Check out www.boroughspublishinggroup.com/submit and see if we can help you make your dreams come true.

Printed in Poland
by Amazon Fulfillment
Poland Sp. z o.o., Wrocław